THE OLYMPUS PROJECT

TED TAYLER

Vinci Books

vinci-books.com

Published by Vinci Books Ltd in 2026

1

Copyright © Ted Tayler 2014

The author has asserted their moral right to be identified as the author of this work in accordance with the Copyright, Designs and Patents Act 1988. This work is a work of fiction. Names, characters, places and incidents are the product of the author's imagination or are used fictitiously. Any resemblance to actual persons, living or dead, places and incidents is entirely coincidental.
All rights reserved. No part of this publication may be copied, reproduced, distributed, stored in any retrieval system, or transmitted in any form or by any means, including photocopying, recording, or other electronic or mechanical methods, nor used as a source for any form of machine learning including AI datasets, without the prior written permission of the publisher.
The publisher and the author have made every effort to obtain permissions for any third party material used in this book and to comply with copyright law. Any queries in this respect should be brought to the attention of the publisher and any omissions will be corrected in future editions.
A CIP catalogue record for this book is available from the British Library.
Paperback ISBN: 9781036700492

The EU GPSR authorised representative is Logos Europe, 9 rue Nicolas Poussion, 17000 La Rochelle, France
contact@logoseurope.eu

By Ted Tayler

The Phoenix

The Olympus Project
Gold, Silver and Bombs
Nothing Is Ever Forever
In the Lap of the Gods
The Price of Treachery
A New Dawn
Something Wicked Draws Near
Evil Always Finds A Way
Revenge Comes in Many Colours
Three Weeks in September
A Frequent Peal of Bells
Larcombe Manor

The Freeman Files

Fatal Decision
Last Orders
Pressure Point
Deadly Formula
Final Deal
Barking Mad
Creature Discomforts

Silent Terror
Night Train
All Things Bright
Buried Secrets
A Genuine Mistake
Strange Beginnings
Dead Reckoning
A Normal November
Into the Sunlight
Tame the Storm
One True Friend
Whispered Truths
A Morning Murder
Quick to Anger
Red Herring Season
Gathering Clouds
Still Standing

Chapter One

The late evening sunshine bathed everything on the far bank of the river. The man in the water was barely breathing. He hooked his right arm over a lower branch of one of many overgrown bushes and trees scattered along the waterline.

A thinning group of people peered across the water, shading their eyes. The glare of the sunlight blinded them as it disappeared behind the rooftops of the nearby buildings. The group continued to gaze across to the opposite bank. They searched and searched for a glimpse of their quarry but saw nothing. He was too tired to move. The bushes and tethered barges strung along that stretch of water below the Pulteney Weir provided the perfect shelter.

The man rested. Safe, for now, his mind drifted back to the last few hours' events. His plans had gone out of the window when that stupid female copper recognised him and shouted. A bullet shut her up, but an old bag, no doubt her mother, chased after him and lashed out with her handbag. He remembered descending the steps to the towpath in a blind panic, trying to calm his nerves and gather his thoughts.

He thought he could make it back to the Land Rover. Get the hell out of this city. Then he spotted a uniformed policeman running towards him. He had no choice but to turn and sprint back towards the steps. The man remembered running alongside the Weir. He was only a few strides from the spiral steps leading to the street. At least there, he might see a chance of escaping among the city crowds.

He had heard a shout feet away. As he glanced over his shoulder, he spotted his nemesis. That meddling policeman had pursued him the length and breadth of the country. With a warning shout, the policeman was on his heels and launched himself towards him. They both fell headlong over the railings and into the river's murky waters. Both men surfaced, gasping for the air knocked from them by the force of the impact.

At first, the man struck out for the opposite bank, with confidence, despite his lack of experience. The policeman followed. The man soon realised his adversary was a much stronger swimmer and any thoughts of a quick escape were futile. The two men grappled, and while both concentrated on gaining the upper hand, they drew closer and closer to the Weir and its lethal foaming waters. The nature of the water altered around them as they fought, and both men realised the danger they faced. Finally, they disappeared under the surface and got tossed around under the Weir like socks in a washing machine.

The water clutched at the man's legs, dragging him further under the water. He cracked his knees and elbows on the concrete buttresses of the Weir. He punched and kicked at the policeman as they both tried to swim back towards the surface. When they did, the respite was brief. A second to take in an invaluable lungful of air, and then the water snatched them back under the churning waters. They resumed their battle at once, but their struggle took its toll. Their actions grew more and more laboured. Both men soon reached the end of their tethers. Neither man knew which way was up any longer. Battered and winded, each swallowed large quantities of water. The man sensed the policeman release his hold and watched as he drifted away.

The man didn't know if his nemesis had sunk to the riverbed or surfaced and reached safety. The man felt happy he no longer needed to fight and was prepared to resign himself to his fate. He sensed his lungs giving up the ghost as an excruciating pain built within his chest. The man broke through the surface and took a desperate breath. The pain increased. Successive breaths brought little relief, but he willed himself to press forward, away from the direction the policeman had gone.

As he surfaced again for a moment, he realised that he was near the far bank. He drifted in silence behind a barge. The man forced himself, against his instincts, to swim under the near side of the barge's hull, keeping the river wall at his fingertips. When he surfaced once more, he continued to breathe. Each breath was becoming more manageable, but it exhausted him.

With a supreme effort, he got his right arm over a branch and rested; he needed to stay focused because if he slipped under the water again, he understood there was no chance of saving himself.

From his place of sanctuary, he saw people running on the towpath. He heard sirens blaring somewhere nearby. He tried to check his condition. He had suffered cuts to his legs and shoulder, but he didn't appear to have any broken bones. He felt bitterly cold. He was suffering from shock.

There was no time to worry. A helicopter throbbed overhead. As night fell, a searchlight would soon probe the little nooks and crannies trying to find him. If only he could evade capture long enough for them to believe he drowned in the Weir. To assume his body had floated downstream. Maybe he could yet escape this mess.

An hour later, the towpath had emptied. The armed response men had withdrawn; the paramedics and onlookers had disappeared. He looked across to the opposite bank where a distinguished-looking, elderly gentleman stood in the shadows of a bridge talking on his mobile phone. The man looked right at him as if this man knew where he was hiding. Had the man near the bridge called the police? Was this how it ended?

The elderly gentleman smiled to himself. Then he spoke aloud as if talking to someone in a crowded room. Someone who struggled to hear what he said: -

"Hold on for a few minutes more, Mr Bailey. There's a good chap. Our people will be along in a tick to remove you. You'll be safe then and among friends."

Still hidden on the opposite bank, Colin Bailey had been afraid to breathe. He exhaled raggedly and allowed himself the briefest of smiles. Colin didn't know who the well-dressed man was, but he oozed class both in the cut of his suit and the way he spoke. Colin wasn't sure what lay ahead for him, but he convinced himself the police couldn't be involved and friends were always welcome.

Moments later, an inflatable dinghy appeared from downstream and inched its way closer to the bank. Two pairs of powerful arms hoisted Colin Bailey from the icy river. Without a word, the men stripped him of his wet things and helped him don multiple layers of dry, warm clothing. They even supplied a cosy ski hat and thick socks to help with the warming. He struggled to get these on while a man offered him a hot drink poured from a thermos flask.

The other man returned to the wheel and manoeuvred the craft along the river. The dinghy stuck to the far side, hiding from the odd dog walker on the towpath. It carried them further from the city centre. Finally, they moved clear of the dangerous Pulteney Weir, where Colin had escaped a watery grave.

They travelled for a minute, and then the driver deftly turned the wheel, and they darted across the river to the opposite bank. Under the weeping willow trees, only yards from the water's edge, an ambulance waited, its rear doors open, the engine idling.

His two companions grabbed one of Colin's arms and lifted him onto the towpath, where a man dressed in a paramedic's uniform waited. Colin's legs buckled under him as his feet touched dry land for the first time in several hours. The man dressed as a paramedic took a firm hold of him as he stumbled and, surprisingly, swept him up in his arms and carried him into the ambulance. He laid Colin on the stretcher, covered him with a heavy blanket, and closed the doors behind them. With that, the ambulance drove into the night.

In the Royal United Hospital, DCI, Phil Hounsell rested after his ordeal in the water. His wife Erica had visited him earlier. Now she lay tucked up at home with their children. DS Zara Wheeler was enjoying a drink with her two male colleagues in a crowded Bath hostelry. Her beverage was non-alcoholic, but the two young policemen were heading for a hangover.

Colin Bailey wasn't heading for a hangover or an NHS hospital; his ambulance soon drove out of the city towards a

Georgian manor house ten miles away. The only clue to his destination was the unmistakable sound of a cattle grid. He experienced the distinctive rattle when they drove between the stone pillars at the entrance to the property.

Satisfied to be in safe hands, Colin closed his eyes and fell sound asleep before the ambulance negotiated the long arc of the driveway to reach the main house.

Colin sat up in bed. He was suddenly wide awake.

"Where am I?" he wondered. Then yesterday's events came flooding back. He remembered the ride through the countryside in the ambulance and a gradual warmth returning to his body. He must have fallen asleep because he couldn't recall being taken from the ambulance, then into the building and finally reaching this magnificent bedroom.

The bright sun shone outside, and from its height in the sky, he deduced it to be late morning. He had slept for just short of twelve hours. His bedroom had two large sash windows, and the sunlight allowed him to view his surroundings with growing admiration.

The white-painted solid timber bedstead and woollen or flax-filled mattress had been ultra-comfortable. Colin brushed the clean white sheets with the palms of his hands. He gazed around the room and took an inventory, bedside cabinet, check, cheval mirror, check, and a double wardrobe with drawers at the bottom. The sage green walls, intricate ceiling swags, and moulded cornices complemented the idyllic scene perfectly.

"Someone is going to an awful lot of trouble," he thought, "considering they know exactly who and what I am. I wonder if I've missed breakfast."

Colin no longer wore the layers of clothing his rescuers

provided him for the short dinghy trip. So he got out of his far too comfortable bed. As he did so, he discovered he wore a nightshirt, which was not out of place in Georgian times.

Colin tiptoed to the window. Before he could look outside, the door opened behind him, and someone crossed the floor. The elderly gentleman from the towpath came to stand beside him.

"Good morning Mr Bailey. I trust you slept well?" he said.

"Yes, thank you. What is this place? Who are you? And what am I doing here?"

"Time enough for questions, old chap," the old man replied with a chuckle. "What's the rush? The en-suite is through the door to the left of the mirror. Once you've completed your ablutions, you'll find a choice of casual clothes in the wardrobe. Please don't insult me by asking if they'll fit. Instead, I invite you to join us for a light luncheon on the ground floor, and I'll give you the grand tour."

Sensing Colin would soon ask where the meeting was or who he meant by 'us', the elderly gentleman stopped at the bedroom door. With his hand on the door handle, he said, "I appreciate you have questions, Mr Bailey. Sometimes we need to shelve our curiosity and take things on trust. Follow your nose, and the excellent food will bring you to the right door. Of course, if you're wandering around the corridors in an hour, we'll have selected the wrong man to join our enterprise. But, if I were a betting man, I'd say you'll be tucking into a plateful of excellent English fare within twenty minutes."

The bedroom door closed. Colin stood at the window a while longer. Then he checked the second sash window and confirmed that both were locked. There were no signs of a method of releasing them. He should have been at ease in these gracious surroundings as he gazed out at the manicured garden and lawns. Yet he couldn't help thinking he had little choice other than to join this 'enterprise', whatever it might be. To refuse might lead to an unpleasant outcome, and Colin was intelligent enough to let things move along at their own pace for now. Apart from that, he was starving.

It didn't surprise Colin when he found the en-suite bathroom as well-appointed as the rest of his new accommodation. He lingered in the refreshing hot shower for a moment or two longer than usual and speculated on what might lie ahead for him. He imagined he'd discover what he had let himself in for in due course. What he did with that knowledge involved serious thought and meticulous planning.

Colin Bailey had made a career out of doing just that. He towelled himself dry and walked back to the bedroom. He opened drawers and wardrobes to reveal a variety of shirts, tops, and trousers. There were several pairs of shoes and socks and assorted styles of underwear. Colin made his choice, and everything was a perfect fit, as predicted by his host. Minutes later, he stood in front of the cheval mirror and nodded with satisfaction.

"Cool bastard," he exclaimed. Then with a hearty laugh, he assumed the time-honoured position favoured by the inimitable Commander James Bond and said, "the name's Bailey, Colin Bailey."

The corridor and staircase he discovered outside his door didn't disappoint. With each successive step, he descended to the ground floor, admiring paintings of naval battles and personnel. Finally, Colin strode along the pale marble floor towards the nearest door on the lower level. The delicate aromas that enticed him further only heightened his appetite. He entered the room to find the old gentleman, whom he assumed to be his host, talking with three men and a striking-looking woman.

Four faces turned towards him. Finally, the elderly gentleman approached Colin and led Colin back to join the group, taking his arm.

"We can dispense with formal introductions for now. Your reputation precedes you, old chap, so we know who you are and how efficient a killer you have been. That's why you're here. There will be plenty of opportunities to discuss that side of things in due course. For now, you need to know that we share a common goal, and this estate is the centre of our operations. We selected you as the ideal candidate to join The Olympus Project. We will train you to bring a swift end to any direct action we decide is necessary in the cesspit that passes for a civilised world outside this estate."

While the older man talked, servers slipped into the room. They carried the contents of the dishes from the long side table to serve up a sumptuous luncheon for the six potential diners. Colin couldn't help noticing that the servers on duty were men in their late thirties to mid-forties, and each had a military bearing. They moved and conducted themselves in a manner that suggested there wasn't an ordinary seaman, airman, or plain squaddie among them. Colin was sure every one of them had been Marines or even ex-SAS before leaving the services.

Just what nature of outfit was this Olympus Project? An inflatable dinghy on-call at a moment's notice, a fake ambulance to use, and a protection squad that worked in the kitchens. This lot may have former guardsmen mowing the lawns and digging the vegetable patches. Heaven help any burglar who thought this Georgian mansion had a few trinkets worth stealing.

Everything was ready. Colin's dining companions took

their places, and he found his seat at the end of the table opposite his host. The formidable-looking lady sat at the older man's right-hand side, and her three male companions sat on Colin's right.

The remaining chairs that had stood at the elegant table for its eight place settings when Colin first entered the room now stood against the wall. No late arrivals were joining this happy band. The pecking order of this group was pre-ordained.

Colin casually tried to assess the people around him as the servers served their starter dish. By his estimation, the three men to his right could be in their mid to late fifties. The man to his host's left appeared to be a civil servant or a professional. The other two showed every sign of being ex-military. While the waiter attending to him poured a small glass of Cedar Creek Chardonnay, he looked across at the lady and felt his face redden. She gave him a look that, without uttering a word, told him she knew he was sizing up his companions and that she disapproved.

Colin switched his attention to his plate. He felt uncomfortable under the gaze of the lady he was convinced had to be the second-in-command of this outfit. His comfort didn't improve when he saw the warm squash veloute with soft poached egg and pink grapefruit jam. Colin hadn't eaten in ages, and his stomach ached for a full English breakfast. When he had been with his late wife, Sue Owens, in The Gambia, they ate well enough, although they generally preferred simple food. He wasn't a total stranger to fine dining. Heaven knows she and Colin could afford it with the money she'd made selling her home and business.

As soon as he tasted that first mouthful, Colin had to revise his opinion. It tasted fantastic. He forgot his fellow diners and his dream of a big fry-up for the time being and

The Olympus Project

savoured every moment of this first lunch at the manor house. The main course of young Welsh lamb arrived with crushed broccoli, sheep's curd, Provencal figs, and toasted hazelnuts. It was even more delicious. A large glass of Cabernet Sauvignon was more than a welcome companion. Later, the wild honey ice cream proved the ideal dessert for warm summer days. As the stewards cleared away the last few dishes away and served coffee, Colin leaned back in his chair and relaxed. He looked up to find the eyes of his fellow diners, who had remained silent throughout the whole proceedings, turned towards him.

"That was excellent," he said, "I'm looking forward to the grand tour more than ever now. The exercise is essential."

"I shall take my coffee on the patio," said the lady, "I want to enjoy this sunshine while I have a few minutes to spare. There's work to do later. Good afternoon gentlemen. Mr Bailey." With that, she swept out of the room. A waiter placed a coffee pot on a silver tray and added other necessary items for her excursion. When he had finished, he trotted off in her wake. His destination was her sun-kissed and sheltered haven a few steps from the door to the rear of the main building.

"Reminds you of a galleon in full sail, doesn't it, old chap?" said his host with a conspiratorial grin. He looked at the three men on his left-hand side. "No doubt you have things to attend to this afternoon. Don't let us detain you. I propose we six reconvene at 1900 hours. There is much to get through this evening. Mr Bailey will have a better idea of The Olympus Project by then. He'll appreciate how his particular skill set fits into our organisation."

As the others left the room, the elderly gentleman beckoned Colin to bring his coffee to more comfortable seats in front of the large fireplace. "Right you are then," he said, "let's finish our coffees in peace, and then we'll be on our way."

Colin and his host sat silently, savouring their drink and that excellent three-course meal. Colin could sense his eyelids growing heavy. Indeed, the older man had his head on his chest and was dozing peacefully. The period French clock on the mantelpiece struck two o'clock. The elderly gentleman stood up stiffly.

"Time to go, Mr Bailey. Let me take you through the delights of my family home and show you what we've done to update the old place. I'm sure the changes will interest you."

The two men entered the hallway, and the grand tour began.

"Larcombe Manor is a Grade One Listed Manor House lying in a secluded spot eight miles outside Bath. It has been my family's home, without a break, since 1550. Queen Elizabeth the First stayed here for two nights in 1585. I've searched high and low for a written account of her thoughts on the place, but to no avail. So, I can't tell you whether she was enamoured enough to stay an extra day. Nor that she intended to descend upon the place for a week but skedaddled back to London in high dudgeon. The eleven bedrooms, the seven-bathroom house comes with three and a half acres of gardens. We have a formal garden you can see from your bedroom window and a walled kitchen garden to the side. That's where we grow our vegetables and flowers. The reception rooms are full of character and keep many original features from the major extension and overhaul my ancestors carried out in the middle of the nineteenth century."

His host was warming to his task, and Colin strolled alongside him as they moved through the main building. The grandeur of the building was plain to see at every turn. They paused here and there as the older man commented upon the décor, the artwork or the period furniture. Colin had a question.

"If this is your family home, do you have them living with you and the members of The Olympus Project I've met so far?"

His host stopped and emitted a long sigh.

"My wife is in a nursing home nearby. She suffered a breakdown a few years back, old chap, and there's no one else here."

Colin didn't pursue that line of questioning any further. It had raised a painful memory for his host. The next few minutes of the grand tour continued in a far more sombre mood. The older man's mood brightened as they went outside into the gardens. Colin looked across to the patio, but any lingering signs of the ship had gone. She must have returned indoors to work, and the ever-efficient staff tidied up behind her.

The two men walked across the lawn. Colin could only wonder at the immaculate grounds, with trees planted with a precision that protected the house from nosy passers-by in the far-off adjoining fields. Yet, when he looked towards the main building, the magnificent edifice always remained visible as you walked towards the other estate buildings. His reverie was broken by his elderly companion speaking: -

"The orangery, of course, is over there to the right."

"Of course," said Colin under his breath.

"Just here in front of us, to our left, is where the old

stable block stood. When the idea for Olympus took shape, we converted that into staff accommodation. The building you can see one hundred yards further on is the ice-house. Let's wander over and take a look, eh?"

Colin had read about ice-houses. He knew they were in everyday use before the invention of the refrigerator. Most comprised hand-built underground chambers within yards of a water source, and the winter ice and snow were taken inside and packed with insulation. The wealthy owners of manor houses on estates such as this could store perishable foods, chill their drinks, or prepare ice-creams and sorbets. Oh, how the other half lived.

As they approached the door to the building, Colin prepared himself to see a grill covering a brick-lined forty-foot pit. Perhaps he would see the decaying signs of a drain to take away any water. Once they agreed that little remained worth seeing, they could move towards the remaining buildings. From his current vantage point, Colin thought those resembled a terrace of two-up, two-down cottages.

As soon as they stepped through the outer door of the ice-house, Colin gasped.

"That was a shaker Mr Bailey, wasn't it?" chuckled the old man.

After he pressed the call button, Colin heard the lift rise for a few seconds, and then the steel doors opened.

"Shall we?" asked his tour guide.

Colin followed his host into the lift and watched as the older man selected the button for the first of the three levels. A few seconds later, they stopped. When the doors opened, they walked into a room where a computer nerd would have believed Christmas had come early.

"This is our command centre. Operatives in this facility

monitor the movements of our identified criminal targets. They track every possible terrorist threat yet undefined and keep us abreast of any potential global catastrophe. That may be a tsunami, an earthquake, or a volcanic event, everything that has the potential to threaten our social equilibrium. The corridor leads to recreation rooms, a dentist's surgery, and a fully functional operating theatre from this room. We have a few sleep pods at the far end for operatives to use on those occasions when the criminal fraternity keeps us extra busy. Don't confuse this with the old-style Burlington bunker near your neck of the woods at Shaw Park; that's more of an enlarged foxhole. Did you enjoy your wine at lunch today?"

Colin nodded. His host continued -

"We have a constant relative inside temperature in this foxhole, and the insulated hull surrounding it makes this environment ideal for storing our wine. I think we've seen enough here for now. Let's drop to level two, shall we?"

On the next level, they met two armed personnel. The men wore no uniform, just a white t-shirt with Olympus on the left breast, black combat trousers, and boots. Each carried a gun in a holster at the hip. Both had a physique that looked like they used the recreation rooms to good effect. Again, Colin recognised his rescuers from last night. These two had manned the dinghy.

"Good afternoon, men. You've met Mr Bailey. I'm delighted to tell you he is joining our group."

Colin looked at the old gentleman. He couldn't recall getting asked if he wished to join whatever set-up this was, let alone tell anyone he had agreed. The locked windows in his bedroom and the distance between himself and fellow diners led Colin to believe his host was used to giving orders. To say 'No' was inadvisable.

The older man continued, patently aware of Colin's feelings over what he had said to the two guards. "I'm sure he will be in to visit you from time to time. Can I show him what we have available?"

The two men moved aside, and one entered an access code on a pad to the side of the main door. Once inside the room, Colin could see this was the armoury. There were racks of assault rifles, which his host informed him included several varieties of AK and a WASR3. In addition, they had a range of Heckler and Koch rifles that various police and even special forces preferred. The racks contained several items Colin had seen before, mostly in films. He spotted M4 Colt Carbines that had been everywhere in Iraq and Afghanistan when the US forces were in action. The ubiquitous Uzi was among several light machine guns, and the weaponry included far more than rifles. The armoury even stocked hand-held rocket launchers.

Below the racking lay drawers containing handguns and knives; H&K, Browning, Glock, and Sig Sauer models were abundant. The latter's P226 was no surprise since the SAS had favoured this model for years. The elderly gentleman moved from the racks to the drawers with evident pleasure. Now and then, he picked up a gun and spent a moment or two in contemplation. Colin wondered whether he was reliving an occasion when he had used it in action.

"I don't have the key for the other drawers, but they contain our supply of gas canisters, flash bombs, incendiary devices and, of course, hand grenades."

"Of course," replied Colin, allowing himself a brief smile. If you want to wage war on someone or protect your organisation against attack, you may as well have something of everything he thought.

"The rest of this level includes a shooting range, where I

The Olympus Project

expect you to improve your accuracy. You will reach the Olympic standard if possible, although, now you're one of us, you'll never represent your country in competition."

The two men walked along the corridor, which ran along the side of the range. No operatives were honing their skills this afternoon. The door at the end was locked. The older man turned on his heel and encouraged Colin to walk back with him towards the armoury.

"That's the ammunition store; there's something for everything. Once you've seen one magazine, you've seen the lot I find, old chap. Rather boring to stand around inspecting bullets. Much more fun firing them at the enemy, eh?"

With a nod to the two guards, his host led him from the armoury to the lift. A bony hand hovered over the button for the third level.

"Well, we've come this far, so you might as well see the rest," he sighed.

The final level was dark and eerily quiet. A long corridor stretched to the left, and low-wattage security lighting highlighted the pair as they moved past various rooms to their right. The older man pointed a finger. He informed Colin that they were passing the cells and the interrogation rooms. Colin was familiar with a windowless room at the far end of the quiet corridor where a slight odour lingered.

"To add to the information we gather in our command centre, it's necessary, on occasion, to invite people to stay with us for a while. They arrive using the same transport as you, without knowing where they are. We encourage them to answer our questions, and if they give useful data, they leave us unharmed and return to their loved ones."

His guide began the long walk back to the lift. As Colin

hurried to catch up, the older man shook his head and glanced back along the corridor towards the final room.

Wearily he added, "If they get to the far end, then it's not likely they'll see their families again. I'm afraid those visitors' final destination is a plot in the family pet cemetery we have in the woods on the outskirts of the estate."

"I wondered why someone had pinned a small card to the door with 'Hotel California' printed on it," Colin muttered.

Colin and his host rode back up to the surface in silence. The sun still shone when they emerged from the ice-house, and Colin automatically headed towards the final group of buildings, which were the terraced cottages.

"We can give that place a miss. Everything is not as it might appear. We converted the worker's cottages to incorporate a staff canteen, a cinema and a swimming pool."

As he walked back towards the main house, he added, "Of course."

He laughed at his little joke at Colin's expense. Colin drew level and saw that his host was smiling.

"I think you'll fit in well here, Mr Bailey. Let's find a place to rest our weary bones. I'll chase up a pot of tea, and then I'll tell you the history of the Olympus Project."

The woman followed their walk across the lawn to the house from an upstairs window. No doubt the old gentleman knew she was there, but he gave no sign. Finally, Colin spotted her and hung back as they climbed the steps onto the patio. He gave her a friendly wave and a smile. The woman stepped back from the window and disappeared from view.

Chapter Two

Twenty minutes later, the two men sat in one of the elegant drawing-rooms. Their wing chairs faced the enormous windows that gave full access to the sweeping panorama of the Larcombe Manor estate. The sun continued to beat down on the grounds, but it was calm, peaceful, and serene here in this sanctuary. Colin had forgotten the chill he felt as the older man showed him the lengths this organisation would go to.

After they had returned indoors and taken a chance to freshen up, Colin sought and rejoined his host. Erebus summoned a steward. In no time, they had cups of tea, tiny triangular sandwiches and a tray of fancy cakes to refresh them after their long walk.

"I know you are eager to discover the nature of the work The Olympus Project carries out, Mr Bailey. I have tested your patience long enough. My entire career was in the Royal Navy, as I'm sure you deduced. I believe I served my country well. As each successive decade passed, each one quicker than the last, I stood by, unable to help, as my superiors lost their moral courage. I watched them abandon their comrades to political correctness. Governments of whatever colour have continued to shrink the fleet to an unacceptable level. The country is at the mercy of bands of brigands, let alone massive navies. My comrades in the army and air force have suffered the same humiliation. The quality of our armed forces is still among the highest anywhere in the world, Mr Bailey, I have no doubts on that score, but the numbers are far too low. We are vulnerable to attack as a nation in a way we haven't been for five hundred years. The armed services' effectiveness suffers in four corners of the globe. At home, the police and judiciary are falling into the hands of the same weak, hand-wringing milksops. They have stepped away from tackling crime with a big stick and meaningful sentencing. They are now reaping the wind as organised gangs, drug cartels, and people traffickers operate carte blanche the length and breadth of this once great country. I had my reasons for wanting to redress the balance. One man alone could achieve little. Even one with a large family fortune such as mine, I placed an advert in The Times personal column four years ago. It stated: - Help required. Anyone eager to prevent Britain from going to hell in a handcart. Write Box 1815, etcetera. I soon weeded out the time-wasters. I found a handful of people who thought the same and possessed the intelligence, will, and access to added funding to help bring my ideas to fruition. A few of our backers have remained silent partners and do not live here at Larcombe Manor. The four people you met at lunch today are the founder members of Olympus. What do you know of Greek mythology, Mr Bailey?"

"I've heard of the Gods, Zeus, Achilles and um...."

"No matter. There are just six names you need to

remember. While here at Larcombe, we use these names only when we speak of one another. Do you understand?"

Colin nodded.

"It's for our protection, old chap, in case you fall into the hands of a terrorist group or the bumbling fools that pose as our police force while on one of our direct actions. Then you can only reveal your identity, and hours of interrogation or torture are futile. You don't know the names of your masters. So, you have nothing to tell."

"Yet everyone here knows I'm Colin Bailey," Colin blurted out.

The elderly gentleman tapped his forehead. "Think deeper young man. Have you seen the papers or television today?"

Colin shook his head.

"As far as the police and the media are concerned, Colin Bailey and his many aliases perished in the deadly waters of the Pulteney Weir last evening. That body remains undiscovered yet, but no one is looking for you. No one believes you could have survived. Miraculously, you did. From this moment forward, you will be called Phoenix. We will keep you here at the Manor for a few months. You will train in new techniques and hone your existing skills. You will receive treatment in the medical unit to alter your features. It is nothing too drastic, though, as it doesn't take much to fool the authorities on these shores. We will continue to name targets for direct action, and dossiers will be available for you to study. The action planning gives you as much satisfaction as the endgame itself, so the future is bright for you. Don't you agree, Phoenix?"

"It appears so," Colin replied. He realised that this organisation had committed itself to tackling the malaise crippling his country by eliminating the worst criminals.

Instead, his pathetic Street Cleaner idea was elevated to a global scale. What he started years ago with Scott Hall, Leroy Ambrose, and their rotten gangs; then followed up this summer with the evil Neil Cartwright, who had murdered his sweet, innocent daughter Sharron, paled into insignificance.

They had paid the price for their crimes, as had Pete Howlett, the Manchester drug-running affair overlord, and four gang members. Colin had rid the world too of Usman Khan and Mustafa Jobe, just two of the men responsible for the systematic abuse and death of Khalima Darbo. A family friend trafficked the poor Gambian teenager to London for sex. That swine Hounsell had thwarted his progress. In his small way, any others he had identified for elimination continued to abuse children and peddle drugs on estates throughout the country. Heaven knows what else. Colin wished he could start these direct actions his host was so fond of describing.

The old man looked at Colin, "All in good time, dear boy. Be patient."

Colin paused for a second. How did he know what I was thinking? Did I say something out loud without realising it? He gathered his emotions in check and asked: -

"What are you called? What of the others too? What's your story?"

The old man replied, "I'll tell you my story. After dinner, the others will explain their code names and histories. Then you will understand where our motivation for Olympus originated. Finally, you will appreciate what drives us to right wrongs and make criminals pay for their crimes. Our ultimate aim is to remove any threat to the natural order of things."

Colin listened intently, and question after question sprang into his head.

"How do you keep what you're doing here a secret? Surely, people knew your colleagues before they came here. You must be on a naval pension, apart from your state pension. The DVLA, your bank or building society, the list of people who know you must be endless. How did you ever get planning permission for your underground foxhole on a Grade I listed property?"

"Steady on Phoenix. One thing at a time. I'm not getting any younger. I can't cope with this machine-gun questioning. Let me explain. Larcombe Manor lies in secluded spot three-quarters of a mile from a minor road. That minor road carries only a few vehicles. It's a 'No through road.' Just over a mile further on, the road ends in the farmyard of our neighbours, the Davis family, who have lived and worked on Larcombe Farm for three generations. The other families who have lived there have been tenants of this estate since the seventeenth century. We don't bother them as they carry on their dairy farming enterprise, and they don't bother us. As the occasional car or farm vehicle passes our gateway, they can see a sign on the left-hand stone pillar. A plaque signals The Olympus Project's home with a registered charity number. We, five founder members, are the trustees of that charity, and, as you point out, the authorities and many other organisations know *who* we are. We can carry on our business without hindrance. We supply the necessary papers in full to support the illusion that a charitable organisation operates on this site. As a result, we attract no unwanted intrusion, and we can take steps to protect the truth of *what* we are."

"What type of charity is it then?" asked Colin.

"As you are undoubtedly aware, Help for Heroes started

in 2007. They helped offer better facilities for British servicemen and women wounded or injured in the line of duty. This organisation took shape the same year after my advert in The Times. We set up our charity and announced that it would concentrate on service staff whose injuries were far from visible. Our mission statement shows we help service members suffering from Post-Traumatic Stress Disorder or combat stress if you will. This step proved more than useful in camouflaging what we do here. Charity commissioners visit us from time to time. They are not shocked to find men tending to the lawns and gardens or exercising in the swimming pool. They might see men learning new IT skills, playing computer games in the old stable block, or baking cakes in our kitchens. Each is a very therapeutic activity — just the ticket to help them get through the dark days. In time we hope they can return to a position where they can rejoin the hustle and bustle of the modern world beyond the walls of this estate. The general opinion of our efforts has been that we carry out highly commendable work."

The older man chuckled. "We keep them away from the ice-house, of course."

The two men chorused together, "Of course."

"The ambulance driver that brought you here and his companion, who played the role of a paramedic, is our transport section. They have a few vehicles at their disposal. We are in a remote location, and we arranged with the Post Office four years ago to collect the mail for everyone housed on the 'No through road'. After the daily trip into Bath, our driver drops any post into each property for supplies. He acts as a paperboy, too, even on Sundays. It's the least we can do. You arrived in the late evening. We keep the pretence of more PTSD sufferers coming by using the ambulance during daylight hours for our occasional trips into the city. The drivers have to be extra careful on those occasions. We don't want a member of the public hailing them for a real medical emergency. In the past four years, we have attracted no unwanted attention in that regard. The operatives you have encountered are service personnel who have joined us after their armed forces careers. Many left the forces before they wished to go. They were on the scrapheap through these abominable government cuts or court-martialled because they were considered old school by the numbskulls that pass for officers today. They are highly trained and motivated people who need a purpose in life. We gave them that purpose."

The older man rang for a member of staff to collect their tea things. He stood up, walked to the window and stretched, "I'm tired, Phoenix. Let's take a break for a while. I'll go to my room for a nap. I'll see you back here at 1800 hours. My story will be over well before we meet up with the others for dinner. We should have time for me to answer a few questions you may still have. I bid you good afternoon, Phoenix."

With that, the elderly gentleman left the drawing-room. Colin remained seated and reflected on everything he had learned so far. It hadn't even been twenty-four hours since his unscheduled dip in the River Avon, yet so much had changed. If he allowed himself to be dragged along by his host's enthusiasm for his pet project, his life would never be the same. But what options did he have? He had spotted the printed card on the door to the torture chamber. The much-used reference to the song's lyrics that 'you can check out but never leave' sprang to mind. The locked windows in his room and the shadowy presence of staff suggested that he was a virtual prisoner wherever he was on the estate. Colin wondered what the outcome might be if he ploughed his furrow and refused to join the Olympus Project. What if he got back on the road with another band and picked up where he left off with his street cleaning? Although the woods looked like a charming spot, he wasn't in a rush to end up there along with Fido and Smokey.

Colin realised the elderly gentleman was right. Nobody believed he could be alive and had stopped hunting for him. That should have been a relief. Yet Colin was only too aware; it emphasised he was alone once more.

As a child, he had suffered abuse and neglect in equal measure from his parents. As a young man, Scott, Leroy, and their thuggish companions had bullied him. So when he got Karen Smith pregnant and married her, they were little more than children. Although she loved him, he never experienced that same depth of feeling. Sharron, their daughter, had shown him how to love, to experience that feeling of belonging over and above everything else going on around him.

Neil Cartwright had snuffed out Sharron's young life. Then followed the committed relationship he developed in his affair with Sue Owens. She gave Colin the only other period in his life when he didn't feel alone in the world. Colin and Sue married in The Gambia, and he had loved and cared for her until her untimely death.

Everything had come full circle. While Colin was still grieving for Sue, he had resolved to return to the UK to tick a few more names off his list. He had been so busy planning and carrying out those plans that he hadn't found time to consider his loneliness. A few snatched hours with Therese Salter had given him a brief glimpse of a possible future. He might have forged a new life somewhere with her, but she'd be checking the news over the next few days looking for confirmation he had died. It had only been a glimpse of the future. Therese would move on and get on with her life, whether in mainland Europe or wherever she went.

Colin looked across the lawns towards the woods. He had little choice when he had gone over it in his mind. He was invisible once more.

Colin awoke to find the old gentleman standing over him. It was six o'clock; he had fallen asleep in the chair. The older man gave him a brief smile and said -

"It's time for my story Phoenix. Shall we begin?"

Commodore William Horatio Hunt OBE, Royal Navy Retired (code name Erebus)

EREBUS -the primaeval god of darkness and shadow. He was the consort of Nyx (Night), whose dark mists enveloped the world's edges and filled the deep hollows of the earth. Nyx drew these mists across the heavens to bring the night to the world while their daughter Hemera scattered the mists bringing the day.

The older man stood in front of the fireplace and began his story.

"I was born in 1940 here at Larcombe Manor. Male members of my family have served in the Royal Navy for centuries. I had it impressed upon me from a very early age that this was my chosen profession. At no time did I entertain doing anything else. My father took me on a visit to Portsmouth for Navy Day when I was five years old. My enthusiasm for the service and my ambition to do my duty never faltered. I left school and joined up in 1957. I passed out of Britannia Royal Naval College, Dartmouth, and graduated from Plymouth's Royal Naval Engineering College. My sea service included several County-class destroyers, and I sailed on the carrier HMS Eagle. Missions included helping to deter an Iraqi invasion of Kuwait in 1962 and blocking oil supplies to Rhodesia in 1965. We played silly buggers with Iceland and Spain over cod and Gibraltar. I then had the opportunity to move back to these shores. I transferred to Portland and joined the FOST (Flag Officer Sea Training) staff, which had opened there in 1958. FOST was a major success, and the harbour became the world's premier workup and training base. It was a world centre of excellence for basic naval and advanced operational training. Almost every ship in the Royal Navy has participated in training programmes, including simulated warfare exercises. Many ships of NATO countries trained and frequented Portland too. I enjoyed my time there immensely but still longed for another spell at sea. Part of the Falklands task force sailed from Portland in 1982, and I was fortunate enough to be a privileged member of that task force. Several ships and crew were lost. It was not a good time. I saw things in the South Atlantic that I'd have been happy to miss. On our return, I took shore leave. In addition to my rehabilitation, family matters needed attention. I will cover that later. Shortly afterwards, I received the OBE. They described a 'diverse and selfless career' and an 'outstanding commitment to my country'."

"You must have been very proud," said Colin.

"I did my duty Phoenix. No more, no less. They then consigned me to the scrapheap. I just hadn't received the letter from my superiors advising me my career was coming to a premature end. My forthright views on those superiors had harmed my cause. More than a few admirals in naval operations were only interested in promoting their careers. To stay on the right side of Her Majesty's Government was more important than protecting the integrity of the honourable traditions of the Royal Navy. Morale throughout the chain of command had plummeted. Good officers left the service based on hearsay and unsubstantiated evidence. Other senior officers stood by and allowed civilians to say a cultural problem in the Navy needed addressing. They didn't defend the way of life my whole career had helped to shape and to protect. It was diabolical. After generations of our family following the same career and upholding the highest values with pride and dedication, they palmed me off with a gong and a pension. I would not go quietly into the night, Phoenix. I resolved to do whatever I could to redress the balance. If the Navy went down the toilet and I couldn't stop that from happening, my good works must concentrate on other areas. God knows I had plenty from which to choose."

Colin watched as William Horatio Hunt, whom he would only ever know as Erebus, moved from the fireplace to one of the side tables. Erebus took items from a drawer. He came back and took his seat in a chair next to him.

"This is a photograph of my wife, Elizabeth. We were on holiday in this one, in Ibiza in the late Sixties."

"What a beautiful woman," said Colin as he took hold of the photograph It showed a smiling, tanned couple relaxing on a beach.

"She still is to me, old chap," replied his host. "We had been married for a couple of years here. Elizabeth always stayed here at Larcombe Manor while I travelled overseas. My folks were still alive then, and they looked after my wife. I got home on leave as often as I could. Our daughter Helen was born soon after that holiday in the Balearics. Elizabeth struggled with being a mother and with me not being at home to share the burden. I didn't appreciate that at the time. We never had another child. We tried, but for whatever reason, it didn't happen. Elizabeth was adamant; we should keep ourselves to ourselves and not involve the doctors. I suppose she was already struggling with her demons, and I never stopped here at Larcombe often enough or long enough to see the signs. Helen was a smashing young woman. She took after her mother. Helen was twenty-one in this photo taken after graduating from Reading University."

Erebus handed Colin another photograph. The sheer beauty of the girl staring back at him left him breathless.

"I always wonder whether my daughter Sharron might have been clever enough to go to University," said Colin wistfully, "as she was so artistic."

"Helen got a first. She was passionate about ecology and wildlife conservation. We still kept horses here then, and Helen rode every day around the countryside. She would have made a difference in the world. Of that, I'm certain."

Colin looked at the picture he still held.

"What happened to her?"

"Helen worked at various jobs around the country. Footloose and fancy-free, with no deep ties to mention. She moved when the mood took her, working on different projects and building an impressive reputation. The time may well have been coming when she thought of getting married. Who knows? She worked for the local Wildlife Trust in Cheddar Gorge in her last post. She met a young chap called John Maunder, who taught at a school in Bath; they were a good match. I liked the young fellow, at least. One terrible November evening in 2004, Helen came home from work in a happy mood. She looked forward to John taking her into Bath to watch the rugby. Helen wasn't keen on the game, but he was an avid fan. I told her the sooner you leave, the sooner you'll be back. I never saw her alive again. It surprised me when he hadn't returned her by midnight, but I still didn't think anything untoward had happened. John talked to anyone, particularly about rugby, for hours. Then the police arrived at the door. Elizabeth had retired to bed early, so I was alone when they told me the devastating news that Helen and John were both dead. Elizabeth must have heard the doorbell. She had just reached the foot of the stairs when the police told me what had happened. I remember Elizabeth collapsing on the hall floor. Nothing would ever be the same again. When we found out what happened, it was devastating. Helen and John walked along the pavement towards a pub John and several friends used on match nights. A VW Golf hit them from behind, travelling sixty miles an hour in a thirty zone. The driver was a foreign chap, Adam Bosko. He tested three times over the drink-drive limit in a stolen car without a license or insurance. He'd been at odds with the authorities in his home country of Poland since the age of fifteen. Bosko had been in a UK court seven times before in the few years he lived here. He faced dozens of other offences on those occasions. He overstayed his work visa by eleven months and should never have been in the country. I felt sure his record ensured this Bosko received a long sentence. It appalled me when he got just seven years. That was all he got for taking the lives of two people, let alone the other charges of theft and drink driving. It was a shattering blow. We were still reeling from the death of our beloved daughter, and by the time of the sentencing, Elizabeth was depressed. I lost both of them that night. This Bosko's wife and family in Poland got ready to appeal to the European Court of Human Rights. They argued that he should return to serve his sentence as he was due to be deported back to Poland because of the visa situation. His family could visit him in prison more easily. The Home Office caved in, and I later learnt he served only four years before his release. That didn't reflect true justice in my eyes. I couldn't get my head around it then, and I still can't. Adam Bosko got a few years in prison, but Elizabeth and I had to serve a life sentence. Can you understand what motivates me now, Phoenix? Elizabeth's condition has never improved. To live here at Larcombe, with the memories of her only child, became intolerable for her. I got rid of the horses, and the stables stood empty for a while, but this didn't help. Her black moods made me imagine it was always nighttime in my beloved house. I longed for the days when my Helen breezed into the drawing-room with a piece of toast, eagerly relaying a shred of news on whatever project she was undertaking. I couldn't forget how she rode across the grounds on one of her horses or waved as I sat on the patio reading the morning newspaper. Helen had been my Hemera, scattering the dark clouds and bringing blessed sunlight into my life. I arranged for Elizabeth to go into a nursing home. At least she's well cared for there, and I visit her as often as I can, although she hardly knows me, dear boy. While I lived here at the Manor alone for a time, I formulated my plans for Olympus. In due course, I wrote to The Times, and my quest for a return of true justice to our courts began."

Colin looked at Helen's face again in the photograph. He stood up and collected the picture of William and Elizabeth that Erebus was still holding. The older man was somewhere far away. On the high seas, maybe with one of his destroyers or with Elizabeth and Helen in happier times, no doubt. Colin now understood his motivation.

Anyone who lost a wife and daughter cruelly had a right to lash out at those responsible. Sharron's murder proved the final straw for Colin. He lashed out at the thugs who strutted around his town, arrogant, believing they were untouchable and above the law. He showed them they were wrong.

Colin had waited patiently for her killer to leave prison. He was glad, odd though it may seem, that Neil Cartwright served only a decade behind bars. As Erebus remarked, no sentence for Adam Bosko equated to two lives taken with such callous disregard for the law and human life.

Colin returned the two photographs to the drawer in the side table and walked over to where Erebus still sat. Erebus looked at him, and Colin sensed tears were close. Erebus collected himself and stood up, back ramrod straight as ever and took his place in front of the period fireplace. He invited Colin to sit one more and continued -

"Right then, Phoenix, my story is complete. We've a few minutes before the others join us in the dining room for dinner. Do you have any questions?"

Chapter Three

Colin paused for a second; he was on the verge of asking for the considerable sums of money he had in various bank accounts in Switzerland and the Caymans. What happened to that money now he was 'missing and presumed dead'? Colin decided to start from another angle. He didn't want to appear greedy.

It had never been about the money. The money helped get the job done, and one thing Colin needed was his style of clothes. He felt he looked like a tailor's dummy in this smart casual stuff Erebus supplied. He longed to get into the nondescript gear that served him so well in the old days, clothes that didn't make him stand out in a crowd. Clothes that helped him stay invisible.

"What of operatives in the field?" he asked. "You can't merely have been waiting for an opportunity to pick me up to get your direct actions underway."

Erebus nodded.

"Naturally, dear boy, you are far from being our first operative. As you can imagine, the men we have selected so

The Olympus Project

far were ex-forces personnel; we found a whole raft of potential killers and intelligence experts disillusioned with life after leaving their particular branch of the services. Many of us find it difficult to adjust to the humdrum nature of civilian life, particularly when those careers get curtailed by injudicious cuts. Those men arrived here in secret too. The majority of them arrived at night. We reviewed their training and upgraded their skills where required. They have since moved out into their specified theatre, ready to go into action at a moment's notice. They are akin to the sleeper prevalent during the Cold War. You may be familiar with the idea from watching films or TV programmes."

Colin nodded. Erebus continued -

"The agents in the field have jobs and identities; they have blended into everyday life as normal citizens. Most have been able to evade the counter-espionage agencies in their target country. Sadly, we lost people over the last couple of years when their cover was blown or during direct action. As they are in gainful employment, we do not pay them directly. This subterfuge prevents anyone from tracing payments transferred to them from Larcombe Manor. Like you, Phoenix, these agents have code names and infrequently return here for debriefing or extra training. We can pay them more funds in their local currency if they are poised to ramp up the scale of their activities too."

"How do they arrange those visits?" asked Colin. "They cannot phone."

"There is a sophisticated system on level one in the old stable block, Phoenix. They can intercept coded messages from our guys in the field who need to fly back to the UK. As for home-based people, they send a postcard. On the appointed day, they travel by train to Bath Spa station. Transport people will be there to collect them in a minicab.

They can't miss it. It carries a logo of Mount Olympus on the doors, which means it doesn't attract undue attention as it trundles back to the Manor. They could have come here for treatment for combat stress; that might seem natural, given our charity status. While staying at Larcombe, they are referred to by their code name alone. As I explained, the five original members are known only by their mythical persona. We take every care to protect the integrity of the group and the Olympus Project."

"How come I haven't heard a news report on people they've eliminated?" asked Colin.

"Well, if we've prepared the ground properly on level one and identified the target and why he merits direct action, then nobody cares that much in most cases. A plethora of evil exists outside these walls, Phoenix, as you well know. The media have concentrated on the superficial celebrity section of society for the past decade. Imagine if a thug or rotten government official gets killed somewhere in Africa or the Far East. That doesn't get a full-page spread in the daily newspaper in the UK. That is more likely to be occupied by a popular singer having a baby or taking part in a racy video shoot. The latter sells more papers, dear boy. The more vigilant news editors spotted a couple of incidents last year. You may recall a North African army chief being shot dead in February by one of his security guards. An extreme faction in that country claimed to have ordered the death. Based on the recent turmoil in those parts, that was a logical assumption, but one of our guys executed him. In one of the insignificant countries in Central Africa, an Army chief of staff died after a bomb blast at his office in June. Details of vast sums of aid money had emerged in his private bank account. So we took steps to see he never bought any more gold taps for his bathrooms. His fellow countrymen are now using the money remaining in his account to help the people it was intended for when the Department for International Development sent it."

"I lived in Africa until the spring of this year. I can't say I remember seeing or hearing any reports on either of those." Colin remarked. "Of course, I was preoccupied with my late wife and planning every step of my journey this summer."

"That's understandable, Phoenix; your priorities lay elsewhere. Part of the training regime you will undertake here will need to focus on broadening your horizons. We will encourage you to see the bigger picture and enable you to absorb everything that helps Olympus achieve its goals. I expect you've been wondering what's happened to your money?"

Colin couldn't prevent an audible gasp from escaping his lips. How the heck did Erebus keep doing that? *He knows what I'm thinking.*

"That *was* one of my questions," said Colin, "but money isn't a motivator for me. No doubt you know what happened to my money?"

"We will take steps to protect that money," Erebus replied. "The banks in question would receive authentic papers carrying your signature indicating your wishes if you died. There will be a delay as your body is as yet undiscovered."

"What do you mean… 'as yet'?" Colin asked.

"Fear not, old chap, as you are worth far more to Olympus alive. We need to get you legally declared dead, but there's no tremendous rush to do this. We may hold off until any remains discovered are so decomposed that the authorities will find it tricky to attribute them to a particular person. We may use the clothes you wore at the time and the odd personal items to clinch matters. Last night's scenario gave enough circumstantial evidence to lead a reasonable person to believe Colin Bailey died in Pulteney Weir on the balance of probabilities. We could use that to get a court order directing the registrar to issue a death certificate. Then the foreign banks could be persuaded to action your last requests as outlined in our cobbled-together documentation. Leave it to us, dear boy. It will be authentic enough to serve its purpose, as we have the best people at our disposal here. If the worst comes to the worst, then we'll have to sit and wait for the prescribed time the current law uses."

"How long is that?" asked Colin.

"Seven years," replied Erebus.

"Terrific," muttered Colin.

"I thought money wasn't a motivator, Phoenix? Don't worry. When you go into the field in the UK, a good result will receive its just reward. Let's call it a performance bonus. Different from a banker's bonus, as you will have worked for it."

"Of course," said Colin with a smile.

"Goodness, just look at the time," said Erebus. "We had better scoot to our quarters to freshen up and change; the others will soon be in the dining room for pre-dinner drinks. No doubt you're hungry, Phoenix?"

"Hungry for food *and* information," answered Colin.

"Let them enjoy their meal first, old chap. I'm sure my colleagues will be more friendly this evening. You caught them unawares when you arrived last night. You have been on our radar for a while. They voted in favour of your selection, but we couldn't have foreseen the fortuitous nature by which you landed on our doorstep."

The two men exited the drawing-room and walked

along the corridor towards the staircase. As they reached the foot of the stairs, the formidable-looking female suddenly appeared on a direct course to collide with Colin. He executed a neat sidestep to avoid disaster. Even so, the contact between them was enough for him to raise his hands to cushion the impact. One hand found a naked shoulder. She looked stunning in an olive dress which fitted where it touched, her high heels bringing her face to face with Colin.

He stared into her grey eyes, and her intoxicating perfume reminded him how long it had been since his brief time with Therese Slater. Thoughts of that affair vanished as he sensed the look she was giving him was more fiery than friendly. Colin knew he should move his other hand soon. It had successfully prevented her from crashing into him and ending in a heap on the floor. In doing so, it was now resting on her left breast.

"Good to see you two are getting on," quipped Erebus as he ascended the stairs. "Come on, Phoenix. First, you'd better have a cold shower, and then you can choose one of the suits we've got for you. Athena, Phoenix, I'll see you two in ten minutes."

Athena moved away from Colin. With one of her trademark glares he knew so well, she swept across the corridor and into the dining room. Colin could hear voices. The Three Amigos were in attendance. He had no mythical tags for the three men, but he felt they belonged together, so the Amigos or the Stooges sufficed for now.

Athena, on the other hand, Colin smiled at his unintentional joke; Athena was another matter altogether. Despite her iron-clad exterior and those piercing grey eyes, Colin couldn't help but admire her incredible beauty when they had been so close.

In his room, Colin showered, turning the temperature lower as he soaked away the stresses and strains of the past twenty-four hours. Being aroused was not an unpleasant reaction to the firmness and proportion of the female form he had just handled by accident, but it needed to stop. The lines of his suit could be spoilt.

Colin checked his wardrobe. After the grand afternoon tour, several new items had been added to his collection since he left his room. He resolved to ask Erebus whether they had a tailor on-site. To have provided three suits in varying colours, as 'made to measure' as made no difference. Colin looked at his reflection in the cheval mirror. The rugged-looking guy of forty-three summers impressed him.

"Amazing what a good suit can do," he thought. "I resemble a male model, worse still, as if butter wouldn't melt. I need to dirty up a tad with a pair of jeans, a Judas Priest t-shirt, and a clapped-out leather jacket. I need to get back to the guy who has nineteen kills to his name. Nineteen and counting. This Larcombe Manor style of life will make me soft."

As he descended the stairs towards the dining room, Erebus waited for him in the hallway.

"Very presentable, Phoenix. Well done. A word to the wise. Athena experienced a torrid time of it before she came to us. She'll tell you what she can tonight. But she's buried much of her ordeal deeper inside, and she's vulnerable, despite her outer shell. I'd hate to see her hurt, my dear boy, understood?"

"Perfectly, Erebus," Colin replied.

Colin accompanied his host and leader into the dining room. The other four senior Olympus members fell silent. Colin would not be privy to everything discussed when they spent time together. Either that or Erebus expected a respectful silence when he entered or demanded it.

"Good evening," Erebus began, "let us both get a drink, and we'll join you. Let us make time for proper introductions before we enjoy our dinner."

The steward who brought the afternoon tea and cakes became their barman. There was nothing as vulgar as a bar in the room. A silver tray on a side table held an array of soft drinks and glasses. As soon as they returned to the others with their chosen drinks, Erebus began the introductions.

"May I introduce our newest operative to you? His code name is Phoenix."

He moved to sit next to Athena, between her and the three men.

"Phoenix, may I introduce Thanatos, Alastor, and Minos."

Each man stepped forward and shook Colin by the hand; he was surprised by the warmth of their welcome, expressed by Thanatos -

"Welcome. We're glad you could join us. People of your calibre are thin on the ground, Phoenix. I'm sure the Olympus Project will profit from having you as a member."

Erebus took Athena by the elbow and persuaded her to step forward. "You two have bumped into one another. For a more formal introduction, Phoenix, may I introduce Athena."

Colin took the hand she grudgingly extended and lowered his head. Without breaking eye contact, he lifted her hand to his lips and kissed it. Athena glared at him, but with Erebus watching their every move, she looked away and headed off to take her place at the dining table. Before she took her seat, she looked back and said -

"I expect you are unaware of this, Phoenix," she said, stressing his code name as if it tasted of something nasty or inferior. "A gentleman waits for a lady to offer her hand with the knuckles towards him. Such a move shows her willingness to receive a kiss."

"I'm no gentleman," replied Colin, "I can only apologise. Your colleagues gave me such a warm welcome I assumed I was among friends. The training I am scheduled to receive while staying at Larcombe Manor will include matters of etiquette, I imagine? Will you be my teacher, I wonder?"

Athena scowled at him and shook her linen napkin vigorously as if she wielded a bullfighter's cape. Colin smiled to himself. He knew he was getting to her. It might be interesting to find out whether the ice-maiden melted. He spotted Erebus at the opposite end of the table. The older man was frowning as he switched his attention from Athena to him and back again.

"I think we should forget this nonsense and enjoy our dinner. We have lots of ground to cover later."

A drinks steward had slipped out to summon the dining room staff, and they soon brought in the first course. The steward returned to the role of the sommelier, and the meal progressed, akin to the luncheon earlier, with superb food accompanied by a sympathetically selected wine. The conversation was sparse on either side of the table, and Colin allowed the various courses to tickle his taste buds.

They had Var salmon from the Faroe Islands as a starter with Avocado and Grapefruit Sabayon. Colin wondered where the salmon paste in his sandwiches at Shaw Park Mines came from because they were never this good.

The Three Amigos chatted to Colin as they waited for the main course. They asked how his grand tour had gone and what he thought of the ingenious conversion of the ice-house. The frosty sidelong glances still came from the lady on the opposite side of the table from his new friends. Those glances reminded Colin of the ice-house in the days before its remodelling.

The six people tucked in with relish when the Bresse Duck with beetroot, cabbage, and verjus arrived. It was magical, and the Pinot Noir that the steward poured proved a more than an acceptable companion. As he finished his third glass, Colin rested for a while. He was mellow.

Dessert was light on the palate. They enjoyed a slice of champagne cheesecake with elderflowers and raspberries. Erebus informed him they came from the walled garden, as did the beetroot and cabbage for the main course.

"My compliments to the gardener," said Colin, "in that case."

Athena stifled a laugh.

Had that been the first crack in her armour, Colin wondered? Erebus ordered coffees and brandies for the drawing-room and suggested they move along the corridor for the night's main event. It was time for the stories behind the other founder members of Olympus and how they came by their chosen code names.

"Are we sitting comfortably?" asked Erebus five minutes later, "then let us begin."

Annabelle Grace Fox, Cambridge, Random House, MI5 (code name Athena)

ATHENA – the goddess of intelligence, skill, peace, and warfare. Goddess of battle strategy, handicrafts, and wisdom. According to most traditions, she was born from Zeus's head, fully formed and armoured.

Poets describe her as 'grey-eyed or having exceptionally bright, keen eyes. Her symbol is the olive tree.

Athena rose from her chair and stood beside Erebus.

"I was born in London in 1974. My parents owned a place near Vincent Gardens in Belgravia. I spent my school days at boarding schools in Surrey and Berkshire. I studied Classics at Clare College, Cambridge, leaving in 1995 with a first-class honours degree. Until I went to Cambridge University, I'd never met real people. Suppose I saw any when home for the holidays, my parents' friends were upper class, privileged and wealthy, as are my mother and father. None of them had much to say to a small child or a teenage girl. Even at University, there existed a divide between them and us. Students from schools such as my own were well represented, and we stayed within our social circle; we joined the right clubs and societies, and so forth. I heard an accent different from my own that marked that person as among the 'them' tribe. Out of mild curiosity, a few of us mingled with fellow undergraduates from the North, the West of England, and even overseas students. We frequented various Cambridge pubs or went back to someone's room. We spent hours talking, reading and absorbing new ideas on politics and society. In those three years, my eyes opened. I could never return to the closeted world my parents wanted for me. When I finished my degree, I joined the publisher Random House as a Publicity Assistant. I wrote press releases, prepared press kits, and mailed publicity materials for several months. I was involved in coordinating author tours and book signings. I wanted to break free from my closeted existence because it stifled me. My ambitions were to move up the ladder, but the truth of the matter was I felt lost. Everything I learned in my first eighteen years had been disturbed by what I found at Cambridge University. Yes, 'disturbed' best describes it."

Athena paused to remember the quote she needed.

"I still clung to the values Robert Kennedy alluded to when he wrote: *'Let us dedicate ourselves to what the Greeks wrote so many years ago: to tame the savageness of man and make gentle the life of this world.'* At University, I came to appreciate another world that existed out there. It was one where the savageness of man was omnipotent and unreachable. Evil, poverty, injustice, and more horrors besides existed with no one to fight the corner of the people who lived under that oppression every day of their lives. I wanted to help change that, but as an ingénue of twenty-one vacuous years, I didn't know how to take that first step. I continued to live in Belgravia. One Friday evening after work, a friend and I visited a crowded local pub. It was better than drinking a bottle of wine in her flat. She spotted a school chum across the room and threaded her way through the scrum of people for a chat. I sat alone at our table. A casually dressed woman in her late thirties stopped as she passed. She dropped a card in my lap and said I should ring this number if I wanted a more challenging job. That proved the turning point, although I didn't realise it at the time. I put her card in my handbag and forgot it. My friend returned with her pal in tow, plus a trio of young chaps. The rest of the night involved several drinking games. Later a struggle in a taxi resulted in a young man receiving a knee in the groin for his troubles. A week passed before I used that bag again. As I hunted through it for my mobile phone, I saw the card and remembered that evening in the pub. I'd had another obnoxious author to work with that week. Feeling fed up once I'd found my wretched phone, I rang the number on the card. They invited me to a meeting in an unmarked building in central London. When I arrived, I sat across a desk from a young man who informed me he was an intelligence officer. I took the first step towards my life as a spy. After that exploratory conversation, the intelligence world enveloped me. It was akin to being returned to the womb, insulated from the outside world. Yet my everyday working life at Random House carried on in the same humdrum manner; until the intelligence committee completed my vetting process. That process seemed interminable. They have to be sure they have targeted the right people. I understood that. I couldn't tell anyone what I might be doing. My family, friends, and work colleagues were gradually at arm's length. As soon as I signed the Official Secrets Act, it became less and less possible to keep the same familiar degree of contact with them. My wish to make a difference attracted them. They told me I would be protecting the country and helping to save lives. Although the secrecy part is huge, little glamour or financial reward comes with the territory. Later on, I received a home visit. My parents were abroad in Cannes. The personal questions they exposed me to for the next hour would have turned my poor parents' hair white overnight. They interrogated me over every single personal relationship. No stone was left unturned. That sense of being cut off from the real world became all-consuming at the outset. When I left Random House and my first posting came through, I walked from home to my new office and started as an Intelligence Analyst. In due course, I became an MI5 officer, coordinating various counter-terrorist operations. The team needed to work as a cohesive unit. I only socialised with other officers and developed several close friendships as it became impossible to have a life in my old world. We talked the same 'in-house' language, and if anyone overheard snatches of our conversations, they would have been hard-pressed to work out what we discussed. Most of the operations we tackled were fast-paced, and officers worked around the clock on those occasions. If things go well and we nip a terrorist threat in the bud, you crash into bed bushed. You find no mention of it on the news or in the papers when you get up later. You're so proud of your efforts, of the damage to property and loss of life you prevented. Yet nobody knows it ever happened, and you can't share your contributions with anyone. Those were the times of greatest isolation. The service didn't always get it right. If we missed something, such as the tiniest piece of information, that might have avoided a bomb exploding and prevented people from dying. That's when frustration and anger creep in and, above everything, *guilt*. 2005 saw us inundated with recruits, training sessions, and new initiatives. The terrorist threat on the streets of the UK had risen. The government's reply was to pile more work on us. MI5 became stretched to breaking point. I joined a team investigating the threat of a terrorist attack in 2004. Two suicide bombers who carried out the July London bombings had appeared on the fringes of that inquiry. Surveillance photos of them existed, but we had not identified them or followed up in detail, as they appeared to be petty criminals not involved in attack planning. We had no reason to believe *they* would do what they did. We finished up the 2004 investigations with arrests of the main protagonists and switched our attention to another item on our ever-growing list. Hindsight is a great thing. Every day I wonder how my life might have turned out if we'd put those two bit-part players under the microscope. Over Christmas, I attended several parties with friends and colleagues from the service at the end of that year. I drank too much and slipped on an icy pavement as we left the seventh bar. One of my friends helped me get to the closest Emergency Department, where a young doctor attended to me. He judged my ankle sprained, and I'd be suffering from a hangover in the morning. As he held my ankle gently and looked into my eyes, I sensed something I'd never experienced."

"Cold hands?" Colin asked with a mischievous grin.

Athena glared at him and continued.

"Despite my job's problems and the unsocial hours he worked, I had to see him again. We started dating in the New Year and got engaged in June. I can't tell you his name for security reasons, but I loved him. On the morning of the seventh of July, he rang me minutes after I got out of bed. I stayed at his flat overnight. He had transferred to Great Ormond Street Hospital to specialise in paediatric conditions only a fortnight before and had just finished a crazy day-night shift. I had to be at Thames House, and he needed to crash on the bed I had just left. We tried to work out whether we could snatch an hour together later in the day or have to wait until the weekend. I was in a rush to get in the shower, get dressed, and then dash to King's Cross for my ten-minute tube journey to work. He was too tired to think straight, and we ended our last phone conversation without deciding a thing. Nothing prepared me for the next few hours as I travelled to work with hundreds of other people going about our normal routine. I remember a sudden heat coming from further along the train. The blast must have knocked me out for a minute. When I recovered my senses, I was groggy, and the first thing I noticed was the silence. How long that lasted, I don't know. It was eerie, and then around me, I heard people crying, screaming, terrible screaming. I tried to stay calm and work out what had happened. Did we hit something on the track? Had we suffered a derailment? From either end of the carriage, the groans and screams continued. Then the driver spoke, and people quietened to listen. He managed to edge the train forward. Those of us who were walking wounded got out of our carriage. We edged our way in semi-darkness to Russell Square station."

The memories were still raw, and Athena struggled to continue.

"Then we emerged above ground, in the station foyer. Every one of us was in shock; our clothes blackened. People comforted us and gave us bottled water. A woman looked at my left leg and left arm, peppered with glass fragments and covered in blood. I hadn't realised. I never noticed the pain. They ferried us to UCL hospital, and, in time, I was treated. My cuts were cleaned of glass, and I received several stitches. Around me, they dealt with people with far worse injuries. I felt guilty at having gotten off so lightly. During the waiting periods, I rang my partner to tell him I was safe, but my calls kept going to voicemail. I assumed he was fast asleep in bed and didn't know there had been an accident. Then, early in the afternoon, people around me referred to it as a terrorist bomb, not a collision or derailment. They said the Metropolitan Police Commissioner confirmed it as 'a coordinated attack'. I tried to find out what that meant. How many bombs had there been? When they released me from the hospital, I took a taxi home to my parent's house. None of the buses was running. I wondered how long they had stopped and how my boyfriend managed to get back to the flat. I rang him again, and someone answered. It was a nurse at the Royal London. I asked her why she had my boyfriend's phone."

Athena couldn't continue. Erebus put a comforting arm around her shoulder.

"I don't know whether you have followed the story of the bombings over the years, Phoenix, but everything was not as reported in the media. Confusion remains around the bombers' identity, how many actual casualties there were, and so forth. More conspiracy theories surrounded this event than every other catastrophic event in living memory. A long shift at GOSH had shattered Athena's partner. Confusion reigned over the earlier bombings, and transport across the city had been disrupted. Why he boarded the bus he did, we'll never know. He died at the Royal London from the injuries he received. His name never appeared on the official list of casualties. Athena's employers deemed it embarrassing if a victim was in a relationship with a security services officer. Doubly so, if the press uncovered that she worked on a covert investigation only twelve months earlier where they could have intercepted two of the suicide bombers."

Athena was still clearly emotional, but she recovered sufficiently to finish her story. Erebus stayed on her shoulder to give her moral support.

"I couldn't carry on in my job. I took time off to recover physically and grieve for my late fiancée, but going back to Thames House wasn't on the cards. I suffered from PTSD. The nightmares I still suffer from six years on are horrible and dreadful. During my waking hours, the sound of a siren makes my spine shiver. From my perspective, I saw that the public was fed an awful lot of misinformation about the attacks. The advert in The Times gave me a purpose in life, a cause I believed was worth the fight. Until then, I drifted alone, reading reports on inquests, inquiries, and conspiracy theories. Nothing made sense, and the numbers never tallied. The timelines became jumbled, and I couldn't untangle them. In the end, the only conclusion I drew was that there had been a degree of cover-up. HMG *needed* an atrocity to sell the anti-terrorist legislation it had formulated, and it got it, one way or another."

Athena returned to her chair and sat unsteadily. Colin wanted to go to her, to reassure her, but he knew that would not be appropriate. She was vulnerable, as Erebus suggested, but she didn't want pity. After hearing Erebus and Athena tell their stories, he recognised the formidable number of grievances these two alone brought to the Olympus group. No wonder the scope of the project was so wide-ranging.

Colin looked to see which man would next tell his story.

Chapter Four

Christopher John Rathbone MM, former SAS Sergeant (code name Thanatos)

Thanatos - the demon personification of death; often referred to but rarely seen in person.

With a fresh glass of brandy, Thanatos remained seated and began his story.

"I was born in 1958 and joined the regular army at sixteen. Ten years later, as an SAS sergeant, I worked with FRU (Force Research Unit), an undercover security op. I conducted covert intelligence and military operations alongside other soldiers and double agents. My superiors encouraged me to infiltrate the UDA. In 1987 after three years of participating in various armed robberies and other criminal activities to gain their trust, they finally accepted me as one of them. Over the next five years, I provided details of suspected IRA members to the UDA. My army paymasters supplied details. On occasions, I carried out assassinations myself when directed to by the British Army. Every day was a nightmare. I risked being killed by the IRA in one of several reprisal attacks or uncovered as a British agent by the UDA. Throughout the Troubles, the British government colluded with paramilitary organisations. People such as me worked on the inside of those organisations. Little security existed during that period. In the spring of 1992, they withdrew me. My handlers became concerned about my mental state. Later, they posted me to Bosnia for Operation Joint Endeavour. A pig of a job. Yet oddly, I didn't feel as threatened there as in Ireland. Then at Christmas 2004, after I served my country for thirty years, they dispensed with my services. Extracting me from my undercover role in the UDA exposed me as a mole. I received several death threats in the post. I demanded the MoD give me a new identity and relocate me if necessary. They promised protection and support when I agreed to act as an agent. Without that support, I was sure to be assassinated. I discovered that I wasn't alone. The majority of us had no protection. The authorities have never officially acknowledged the existence of FRU and have taken steps to prevent reports of sensitive and classified information surrounding the network."

Thanatos looked at his glass and knocked back the contents, and then he leant back in his chair; his tale was at an end.

Colin couldn't imagine what living a double life for so long must have done to him. He wondered how many demons still lurked in the poor devil's mind.

Michael James Purvis, Major, Blues and Royals Retired
(code name Alastor)

Alastor – was the avenger of evil deeds: specifically for familial blood-

shed. The Greek tragic writers use his name to name any deity or demon who avenges wrongs committed by men.

"I was born in 1954 in Aldershot. My father served in the British Army, and I joined as an officer after University in 1975. I was stationed in Detmold at the Lothian Barracks with the 4th Armoured Division. I did two tours of Northern Ireland. In Londonderry in 1977 and Belfast in 1979, both well before Thanatos came over for his stint. The MoD had finally woken up and acknowledged this was a guerrilla war. They established special counter-terrorism training and a covert role for us soldiers. We slowly got a handle on things. We had lost the best part of fifty soldiers since the Troubles began, and the Provisionals still had two hundred gunmen and several dozen godfathers. One thing was clear, though. The pictures on the wanted posters in the operations rooms were of younger and younger kids. They looked as hard as nails. A look of hatred and ill-will emanated from those faces. During our four-month tour, we scarcely saw the light of day inside the barracks. We may as well have been on a submarine. The threat of mortar bombs flattening our quarters was ever-present. We lived in bandit country but maintained professionalism, discipline, and excellent morale. It was inspiring to a young officer. I married in 1982 and moved into married quarters with Jennifer at Detmold. The Eighties and Nineties were happy times for us there. I soldiered on, and we looked forward to me getting out of the Army and moving back to England. I thought teaching might be a job I'd enjoy. Jenny came home to stay with her parents for a while. We looked at houses near their place in Yorkshire. We'd never managed to have children. The two of us were enough, if you know what I mean. Things kicked off in the Middle East, and everything went pear-shaped. The Iraq business escalated, and we transferred out there in May 2004. My regiment formed part of the First Mechanised Brigade. Jenny flew back to Yorkshire from time to time. It helped her to cope with my being away. There were plenty of wives in Germany to get together, but she hated the hordes of screaming kids around her ankles when she visited them. On September the twenty-third, I got the call. Jenny was dead. Her parents had gone out for the evening. According to her mother, Jenny went to bed with a book as she felt under the weather. The police told me she was stabbed several times in the chest. The intruder thought the house would be empty, having seen the car pull off the driveway. When she heard someone moving around inside the house, Jenny must have gotten up and confronted them. There were signs of a prolonged struggle inside the house. They never caught whoever lashed out with a knife and took my wonderful wife from me. Just a burglary that went wrong as far as the police were concerned. The intruder was left empty-handed. If he stole something and tried to sell it for quick cash to buy drugs, then the police said they might have found him. The investigation stalled within weeks. I tried to throw myself into my work, but I found it difficult to think of a reason to get out of bed in the morning. I kept asking the police what was happening to Jenny's case. It got to the point where they appeared to be on the verge of charging me with wasting police time. I left the Army at the end of 2006 and looked into the possibility of teaching, although my heart was no longer in it. Six months later, I saw the advert in The Times and instinctively knew this was what I needed. It was a way to strike back at the criminals and get this country back on the right track."

Erebus thanked Alastor for his contribution and invited

the final member to take the floor. Colin watched as the only non-military man stood beside Erebus by the fireplace.

Sir Julian Langford QC, RGS Guildford, Churchill
Cambridge (BA) and Worcester
(BCL), Lincoln's Inn, High Court of Justice (code name Minos)

Minos – the judge of the dead in the Underworld

"I am fifty-six years old and retired four years ago, having spent a lifetime in the legal profession. Claudia and I had three children; twin girls and a boy. Our daughters are both married with children of their own. Five years ago, our son Harry committed suicide. He was nineteen. Harry was a first-class student who excelled in physics, chemistry, and mathematics. Harry was on a gap year before going to Cardiff University. He played a range of sports and enjoyed a wide circle of friends. We couldn't understand why he might want to take his own life. Claudia found him in bed at our home in Maidstone late one morning. Harry always rose early and had places to go, people to see, and you know how teenagers are. She shouted for me to come upstairs, and we tried to resuscitate him. We called for an ambulance, but they pronounced Harry dead at the hospital. The post-mortem and toxicology tests indicated high levels of a particular drug in his system. There were signs he had been drinking alcohol too, plus they found traces of cocaine. It was too much to take. We knew he enjoyed a drink when he socialised, but we had no clue he used cocaine. As for what killed him, it was incomprehensible. When the police examined his computer, they discovered Harry had visited online forums and researched how to end his life. He trawled the internet to find a site where he ordered supplies of the same drug used for lethal injections in the States. The police traced the invoice to a Chinese firm. They sent the drug in liquid form to Harry without checking why he wanted it on earth. The coroner had no other course but to return a verdict of suicide. We assume Harry suffered a crisis of confidence and inexplicable fear of the future. Obviously, it was something he couldn't share with us, his parents, or his many friends. What a tragic waste. Over the decades, as a judge, I have seen a steady increase in the number of criminals. I've endured a steady decline in the justice the law courts have dispensed. My life now is centred on those that manufacture and peddle drugs. I aim to see that they face the correct level of justice."

The room fell silent as Minos finished the final story of the night. Colin wasn't the only one feeling the effects of a long day.

"Well, Phoenix," said Erebus, "there you have it. Those are our stories and our code names. As far as possible, they fit our circumstances. The Olympus Project exists to give us closure, in modern parlance, and to redress the balance for the justice system's shortcomings."

"It offered a chance to take revenge, too?" suggested Colin.

"But who could blame us if it did, dear boy?" asked the old man, looking frailer than Colin had seen in his short time at Larcombe.

"You joined us to carry out those direct actions for which you are most suited. You've shown over the years you are equally capable of planning and exacting revenge," said Athena sharply.

"That's true, Athena," admitted Colin. "I didn't mean to criticise. You must realise I'm struggling to take in everything I've seen and heard today. While in The Gambia, I convinced myself I was the only person capable of doing what was needed. That is to clean up the country's streets. To see the scale of what Olympus can achieve and the tools you have available to support it is mind-blowing."

"We have to be careful, Phoenix." cautioned Erebus. "Our targets must be selected with care and dispatched without drawing attention to the true nature of Olympus. Our direct actions must be apportioned, across the country, worldwide, and with different methods. A cluster of bombings or shootings in one country might encourage a bright spark to connect the dots. We must avoid that whenever possible."

"That makes sense," said Colin, "but it will take much longer that way."

"A few of us have more time than others, old boy." the old man said.

With that, he wished them goodnight and went to his room.

"Erebus wishes to leave a legacy, both in the essence of what the Olympus Project stands for and in financial terms," said Athena. "He'll ensure his wife is cared for if he goes before her. This estate and the vast fortune his family left him will pass on to those of us who stay here at Larcombe. The charity cover will continue as a protective shield for our operations. Thanatos and Alastor will recruit from their old professions to add to our agents. We will replace our losses when they occur. Minos will flag any issues that need redressing in cases that don't result in the right verdicts in the criminal courts."

"I imagine you will take over from Erebus when the time comes?" asked Colin.

"Erebus and I have talked. Yes, that's the plan," replied

Athena. "Why? Is that a problem for you, Phoenix, being controlled by a woman?"

Colin smiled. He thought back to happy times during his affair with Sue Owens in her old house a few miles from here in Larcombe and Africa as husband and wife. He resisted the temptation for a risqué reply; he sensed Athena watching him.

"Not in the slightest," he said, "I've worked for a female boss before, as you will know from your research into my background. I enjoyed it so much I married her."

Colin stood up and made his way to the door. He was unable to resist one last quip.

"I reckon it's time for bed. Goodnight gentlemen. Sweet dreams, Athena. I look forward to seeing you in the morning."

Colin left the four in their chairs and closed the door behind him. He went to his bedroom, undressed and got into bed. He fell asleep in no time and slept the sleep of the just.

The following day heralded a cool summer's day with light winds. The clouds drifted across the sun and provided a pleasant atmosphere for taking exercise. Colin was very pleased. A staff member burst into his room at six o'clock and informed him it was time to 'rise and shine'.

Colin showered and donned shorts and trainers. His training regime had begun. As the morning progressed, he was relieved that whoever put together his exercise routines at least considered that he was in his early forties. Most of the former SAS personnel at Larcombe endured far worse when they applied to join the elite force. They had been in their mid to late twenties and were abler to carry out the rigours of the selection process.

He ran for as long as possible. He lifted weights until his

arms felt as if they were on fire. Then, after a stern talking-to from his instructor, Colin had to grow a pair and get into the pool. His instructor ordered him to swim as many lengths as he could physically manage. When Colin finally gave up, he was exhausted. As he pulled himself from the pool, he was sick. After his near-death experience in the river, the fear of the water, not the physical exertions, caused his stomach to react with such violence.

"Well done, Phoenix," said his instructor, "it'll be easier tomorrow,"

"Tomorrow?" asked Colin.

"Same time, same place, and same routine until the boss says you're fit enough for duty," came the reply.

"Of course." thought Colin. He was glad to get that finished. He headed back to the main house to get breakfast. The others had eaten earlier. He was alone.

A steward rustled up a healthy plateful of something designed to be good for him and asked Colin if he wished to eat on the patio. Colin sat outside in the fresh air, trying to get the feeling back in the muscles of his arms and legs. He wasn't sure if he had the strength to cut things up this morning after his workout. When the meal appeared on the table in front of him, it was just as well the steward hadn't prepared sausage, bacon, and the works. Colin made do with spooning something tasting of cardboard soaked in milk into his mouth instead and a slice of toast. He might have complained if he had the energy.

Colin rested in the warm sunlight, mulling over what he had learned last night. It wasn't difficult to understand the motivation behind Erebus and his creation of the Olympus Project. First, a lifetime's service in the Royal Navy was cut short after the horrors of the only real war he'd fought.

Then, years later, his only child was mowed down by a drunk driver who received a laughably short sentence.

Erebus deserved to be looking forward to a happy retirement, taken on his terms. He had foreseen happy years with his family around him, with several grandchildren running across the lawn. Now, he faced it alone with his wife in a nursing home, broken by tragedy.

Thanatos had served his country with distinction. He did a dirty job that many others shunned. He lived cheek and jowl alongside the people who killed his fellow soldiers, blowing up innocent civilians in their own country and mainland Britain. What was his reward? Then his masters abandoned him to his fate, to live in hiding with no protection — the constant fear of a knock on the door from a gunman sent to execute him. The government didn't even acknowledge his unit's work and the many lives it would have saved. Any wonder he was bitter?

Alastor left the Army after many years of serving his country at home and abroad. His wife was killed by a young layabout stealing to feed his habit. A man the police never caught. Police who were so used to a crime driven by the desperate need for a fix that they had given up the fight.

Colin knew from experience this was typical of a country paralysed by drugs. The people who peddled them laughed at the police and the courts' ineffectiveness in tackling the problem. He remembered telling his first wife, Karen, he had his solution. He wondered whether he might find an ally in Alastor or maybe Minos that helped create direct actions that made a real impact.

The judge no doubt sat through dozens of criminal cases where drugs were the principal element. His son Harry killed himself with a drug sold on the internet with no control over the age or mental state of the person buying.

Also, Minos sat and watched as the CPS and the police screwed up cases over the years, forcing him to dismiss them. He had spent years being obliged to follow sentencing guidelines handed to him by a judiciary that was ever more liberal and limp-wristed. Colin could appreciate how Minos might enjoy poring over court transcripts to identify criminals who got off scot-free or only received a pathetic custodial sentence. Then he highlighted them to Erebus and Athena for further action.

As to Athena herself, Colin thought back over each occasion they crossed swords yesterday. Why was she so 'prickly' with him? Why did he find it necessary to wind her up as soon as he had a chance? Could it be because she was so stunning? Before he arrived at Larcombe Manor, he never rubbed shoulders with someone from her class. She was a 'rich bitch' in the areas where he lived as a child. He didn't see many of those girls on the Greenwood and Westbourne estates.

In the few months since he returned to these shores, there had only been that night spent scratching an itch with his landlady in Aberdeen. It was an episode to forget. The only other woman he connected with had been Therese Slater. The lusty barmaid from Manchester was more his style, with a great body that she knew how to use. Colin wished he still had his mobile. For the life of him, he was unable to remember her number.

Colin's daydream was rudely interrupted. A guy from the armoury arrived at the double in his now-familiar white t-shirt, black combat trousers, and boots.

"Morning, Phoenix," he called out, running on the spot

at the bottom of the steps. "Off we go then; we're ready for your next training session. Follow me."

"Where are we off to?" gasped Colin as he trailed along in his wake.

"You sound unfit, Phoenix," the man shouted over his shoulder. "In a week or two, you'll be able to have a normal conversation after a six-mile run."

"Six bleeding miles?" cried Colin. "That's a bus ride, not a bloody run."

"Try to get your breathing under control, Phoenix. Your shooting will never be accurate if your chest is heaving. We're putting you through your paces for the rest of the morning: target practice, stripping apart and cleaning your weapon, then reassembling the item, followed by more practice. Everything you'll need in the field when you receive an assignment."

"Good. That will make a change from that running, lifting, and swimming."

"I'm glad you think so, Phoenix. The only difference tomorrow after breakfast will be the choice of a weapon. When we've exhausted the weapons specified you will need, we'll go back to the top and start over again. No rest for the wicked, or practice makes perfect. Take your pick."

Colin groaned. Erebus hadn't warned him his training regime would be so extensive. Despite the discomfort he knew awaited him, he looked forward to a spell in the medical centre.

The next three months soon passed. Colin grew fitter and more energetic, and his shooting with several handguns was now deemed 'excellent' by his instructors. Several other techniques were drilled into him by staff engaged in other activities in the ice-house complex. He learned how to play a different character, something new to him. Colin's trainer stressed that the aim was to do the job and get out. With no one knowing that it had happened. Colin was used to being invisible and not drawing attention to himself, so a few training elements came as second nature.

Learning advanced computer skills and picking up foreign languages was another story altogether. So many years had passed since Year 11 when Colin achieved an A grade or higher in every one of the eleven subjects he took.

Colin spent many hours in the company of Rusty Scott, an SAS veteran, in the first intake of the Special Reconnaissance Regiment in 2005. The regiment showed him the door in 2009 after a fight with a superior officer. Rusty taught Colin to drive like a lunatic. He showed Colin how to fight with concealable weapons, the art of breaking and entering and, most frightening for Colin, how to use explosives. Colin learned the procedures required for overseas operations. He mastered the art of assuming a fake identity. Rusty taught him how to survive alone, armed and in plain clothes. Olympus could never provide overt help. The organisation must be protected. If something went tits up, they would abandon him if they couldn't pick him up without the foreign security services being alerted.

Rusty didn't waste time training Colin in techniques to withstand interrogation. Instead, he shrugged and told him, "If you get caught, Phoenix, tell them what you know. We'll change our codes, so whatever you tell them won't do them any good. In many countries, they'll kill you either way, so, at least, if you talk, you won't lose any fingers."

Throughout his training, he saw nothing of Erebus and the others. After completing his first session in the ice-house, he transferred to the crews' quarters in the stable block. All his clothes and other items arrived from the bedroom he occupied on his first few nights. The routine was relentless:

exercise, skills training, canteen, skills training, canteen, and sleep, blessed sleep.

After completing his stint, he transferred to the medical centre. Erebus left instructions requiring only a minor facial reconstruction, which was done and dusted in a fortnight. Colin hadn't had an eye test for a few years, and after an examination, he found he needed glasses. Blue contact lenses changed his appearance dramatically, and a pair of clear glass spectacles to wear in the field helped mask his true identity.

Colin hardly recognised the face in the mirror when he got ready to return to the main house to meet with Erebus. As he walked across the lawn, he wondered if his first direct action was just around the corner. If so, happy days.

Chapter Five

Colin made his way into the main building. He looked around for any sign of Athena or the Three Stooges. The building was quiet. As he drew closer to the dining room, he heard several people talking. He had been awake for an hour. He grabbed a quick snack in the canteen before walking across the lawn in time for his appointment with Erebus.

Colin knew better than to barge in to see if Erebus was ready to start. Far better to stay in the corridor and wait for the boss to emerge. Then he could listen for any titbits of news to pass back to his colleagues in the stable block—unless the people in the dining room were discussing him, in which case he would keep quiet.

As he strained to pick up the conversation, Colin heard footsteps nearing the door; it was Erebus.

"Ah, there you are, old chap," said the old man, "let's go to the orangery for an oasis of calm. We can order a pot of coffee later if that suits you?"

"That's great, sir," replied Colin.

The two men walked the rest of the way in companionable silence. Inside the orangery, the décor was as tasteful and understated as the rest of the house. Erebus looked around the room in admiration—as if he hadn't been there for a while and remembered how wonderful it was.

"Opinion is divided among us, Phoenix," said Erebus as he finally decided where to sit. Colin sat next to him and wished he had overheard who was for him and against him.

"That wasn't my intention Erebus," said Colin.

"Let me say right away, Phoenix, that your performance over the past three months has been exemplary. As far as your physical and mental fitness are concerned, you have applied yourself to every task thrown at you with commendable effort. You are, without a doubt, ready to carry out a direct action effective from today."

"Thank you, sir," said Colin, "it was hard work, but I've never been fitter, and I feel thirty-three rather than forty-three. So why do I sense misgivings among the others?"

"It's my fault, I'm afraid, old chap. I remember a few unfinished business items on your summer tour. I proposed we let you loose on a target you researched earlier — a quick job to get you back into the swing of things. Athena disagreed; she thought I indulged you. However, the lads shared my opinion. We want to get you into the field and back doing what you excel in."

"What's the final decision?"

"A green light Phoenix. Refresh your background on DCI Richard Armitage (SOCA London) as soon as we conclude this meeting. You now have a laptop in your quarters. I've arranged for our IT people to pass you their files on Armitage. The police have the material you gathered before you joined us. We lost that edge when they found your Land Rover in the car park across the road from the

Pavilion, but that's tough. There have been no signs of the police focusing on your non-appearance in the river. It's too soon to assume it's a closed book, but we believe you can carry on in the field with caution on balance. Remember Phoenix; you must complete your task without leaving clues for the authorities as to your identity."

"Nor my links with Olympus," said Colin, "yes, Erebus, the instructors drilled that into me often enough over the past twelve weeks. I understand."

Erebus took his mobile phone from his suit jacket pocket and rang for their refreshments. Five minutes later, they sat enjoying delicious cups of hot coffee while they chatted over the details of the Armitage case. Colin recounted everything he learned while planning for the hit while on tour with Maiden's Hair. Erebus listened carefully. He marvelled at the level of detail that Phoenix amassed and how much he remembered despite the three months gap since he had access to his files. If Athena had been listening to this conversation, perhaps her misgivings might have been allayed—unless she had reservations over another aspect of Phoenix's nature. He needed to keep an eye on these two. The older man wasn't blind to the sparks that flew whenever these two came into contact with one another. Erebus might be old, but not *that* old.

Richard Armitage served with Sussex Police for sixteen years and worked at their headquarters in Lewes. In April 2007, he joined the Serious Organised Crime Agency in London. He worked with teams targeting drug gangs across London and the southeast. A thankless task, but one which the public expected to be carried out diligently and by officers who acted with honesty and integrity. These were men and women who never compromised or abused their position.

The Olympus Project

During his time in London, Armitage rose to the rank of DCI, and on the face of it, he was a model policeman. In 2010, the forty-five-year-old officer shook down drug dealers for cash and guns, planting narcotics on them and then arresting them. He also had falsified police reports. The charges he faced included conspiracy, official misconduct, and theft.

Four witnesses testified in court that Armitage robbed people, planted drugs and violated his oath of office. However, the defence barrister argued his client's arrests were legitimate. His career was devoted to getting drugs and guns off the streets. One of his accusers had been a former colleague dismissed from the force in 2008 for corruption and received a custodial sentence. The others were career criminals escorted to the court from prisons across the country.

It was their human nature to lie, the barrister said. He told the jury they should reject their evidence as unreliable. The defence barrister told the court that Armitage's former colleague only agreed to testify against DCI Armitage in exchange for a reduction in his sentence. The jury listened to the men lined up to accuse the DCI. They heard those witnesses discredited and listened to the perfect record of Richard Armitage over two decades and found him not guilty.

DCI Armitage declined an offer to return to duty with SOCA and took up a post in his old stamping ground on the south coast. His current position was as a Superintendent in Corporate Development.

Erebus looked up when he realised Colin had reached the end of his account.

"What opinion did you form of his case Phoenix?" he asked.

"Guilty as hell," replied Colin.

"I agree. If you take advantage of the most recent data for Armitage, you will discover he has large sums of money salted away in bank accounts his superiors have no idea existed. He appears to be seeing out the next few years in a cushy 'non-job until he takes his pension at fifty. After that, I expect he'll retire to Spain or Portugal and play lots of golf. That is his main preoccupation from what our surveillance has uncovered."

"I'll look at the new data and plan when and how to dispose of Mr Armitage. The sooner, the better. Thanks for the coffee Erebus, and the green light."

"The 'how' is up to you, Phoenix; the when is preferably within a week," said Erebus as Colin stood up and prepared to leave the orangery.

Colin grinned. "The clock is ticking, tick-tock."

With a spring in his step, Colin strode across the lawn towards the stable block. Once inside his quarters, he checked out his laptop. Sure enough, more files populated his inbox, forwarded by Giles, one of the IT guys who tutored him in the dark arts of computers.

Colin couldn't help recalling those first tentative keystrokes back at Shaw Park Mines and how long it took him to figure out how to send an e-mail. A long time ago now. He became more proficient in Africa and had time to spare and a thirst for knowledge. Knowledge was paramount. The more he discovered about the people he hunted, the easier it became to dispose of them.

Colin spent the rest of the day studying the files. He had various CCTV photos of DCI Richard Armitage in London and Lewes. Colin was confident in recognising him when the time came. Colin reviewed the information he had gleaned about the policeman's early career and his fall from grace on the mean streets of London.

It gratified him to see that Olympus staff only found the same incriminating evidence he detailed earlier this year during his meticulous planning stage. He hadn't missed much except for items added over the past three months while running, shooting, and undergoing the operations.

A detailed analysis of the bank accounts that Giles and his friends had traced showed that Richard Armitage had around half a million stashed away. His two-bedroom, end-of-terrace house in Chapel Hill in Lewes was worth just four hundred thousand. It stood as close to the golf course as he could get without having a caravan behind the nineteenth hole.

"What *is* the fascination?" thought Colin.

Colin knew Armitage was married until 2009, but his wife disappeared with a personal trainer half her age while Richard feathered his nest in London. She might have stayed if she'd known how much he added to his pension pot.

"Women are fickle souls," he said loudly, but nobody heard him.

The family home, a detached four-bedroom property on the outskirts of Lewes, had gone. Mrs Armitage snaffled her share of the sale proceeds and moved to Margate, where her new beau Carlos wanted to open a fitness studio. The kids moved out long since to live in towns across the South East of England. Most of their generation didn't get the family thing and rarely visited their parents. Colin could understand not going to see Mum. Nobody wanted to go to Margate out of choice.

Time passed in a flash when you were having fun. Colin was back in harness, doing what he did best — planning the method to remove a bad apple from the barrel in minute detail. One rotten apple can ruin the whole crop, as we know. Unfortunately, the police service had several such poisonous articles in their midst. In his guise as 'The Phoenix', Colin wanted to help them clean up their act. An improvement was long overdue, and Colin could find only scant evidence they could do the job for themselves.

He glanced at his watch. At midnight, food must wait. Sleep was the next thing on the list. Tomorrow was another day, and he needed to check his itinerary with Erebus. If he got the green light, he could get equipped with the necessary items for the trip. Then the transport section could be contacted to run him into the city. He saved his work on the laptop, closed every file, and crashed on his bunk. Sweet dreams.

Colin had been awake since six o'clock. He had showered, got dressed, and then trotted to the canteen for a hearty breakfast. As Colin read through his proposed programme for direct action against DCI Armitage, he satisfied himself everything was in order. Then he contacted the main house and asked for Erebus. It was now the appointed hour for their meeting, and he sat with his boss in the orangery.

"It's good to see you have grasped the urgency of the situation, Phoenix," enthused Erebus, "this looks waterproof. When do you leave?"

"I need to pick up a few clothes and the right weapon from the armoury," said Colin, "plus, I need a lift to the station early tomorrow morning. When I finish the job, do I contact the transport section for a minicab ride back here?"

"On this occasion, old chap, please do," said Erebus. "We'll debrief the mission once you get back. We can take account of any wrinkles in the planning process that need ironing out. Once we're happy that you can work in the field without revealing your true identity, you can deploy to London or one of the major provincial cities for other assignments. Lengthy stays back at Larcombe Manor will be less frequent the more successful you are. Naturally, if there were to be any fallout from a mission that left you exposed in the field, we'd spirit you back here for safekeeping."

Colin's meeting with the older man soon ended. Erebus returned to the main house, and Colin made his way to the ice-house and the armoury.

"Morning, guys." he said to the two who had been with him when they played 'Three Men in a Boat' in July. He now knew they were Sgt. Pete Thommo Thomas and Sgt. Barry Bazza Longdon. Both men were ex-SAS.

"What do you recommend for this scenario?" Colin asked them.

He unfolded his sheets of paper. Among them was a diagram of the 'kill zone' and a list of his proposed clothing. In addition, there was a complete itinerary of his journey to and from Larcombe Manor.

"How about a Russian PSS," said Thommo.

"What's that when it's at home?" asked Colin.

"A simple double-action pistol, Phoenix," replied Thommo. "Their special forces used them on covert ops when they needed a completely silent option. It's lightweight, weighing in less than a bag of sugar when loaded, and has serious stopping power."

"Looking at this spec," his mate Bazza added, "you'll be up close and personal. If you need to make a hit, this thing will do the business up to twenty-five, maybe fifty metres at a push."

"How does it work?" asked Colin holding the pistol Thommo fetched from one of his well-stocked drawers.

"When you fire, the piston delivers enough oomph to get the cartridge out of the barrel, then seals the cartridge neck. There's no noise, smoke or blast with this baby."

"Impressive. Does it kick back much?" asked Colin.

"A little," smiled Bazza, "why don't you try it for half an hour on the range? I'll sort ammunition out for you; blanks for now and the real thing for when you leave us."

"Great idea," said Colin. "This feels good. Let's practice."

Forty minutes later, Colin left the armourers with his weapon of choice, thoroughly cleaned and with a six-round detachable box.

Erebus had sorted his financials. When he dropped by his quarters to lock the weapon away, he found a money clip on his laptop. He had more than enough for a day trip to Lewes. Erebus left a note scribbled on a sheet from Colin's notepad.

'Bon voyage. Receipts are traceable. Always use cash. Good hunting.'

The next stop was the clothing store. This was a misnomer, as, in reality, the crew members had a wide range of clothing available in a large trunk in the stable block. His trainer, Rusty, used to call it the dressing-up box. Operators saw what was available, found the right size, signed it out from the store, wore it, cleaned it and threw it back in the box on their return.

Colin had a good rummage around and found what he needed. It was a reversible zip-up windcheater. It was baggy enough to allow him to conceal his PSS and gave him the choice of wearing it in navy blue or maroon. He had a pair of jeans and a pair of sturdy walking shoes in his quarters. He grabbed a red bobble hat and a white baseball cap from the box and stuffed them into the jacket pockets. Phoenix was good to go.

Colin climbed out of bed with the first buzz of his alarm. He showered but didn't shave. Instead, he took his underwear, socks, jeans, and shirt from the neatly ironed pile by his laptop on the table and put them on. Colin looked in the mirror. It looked okay.

He ate a full English breakfast at the canteen and returned to his quarters. He put on the navy blue jacket, slipped the PSS pistol and ammunition into the left inside pocket, and zipped it closed. Colin checked the way the jacket looked. He tried with his hands in the side pockets and then in his jeans. Only a genius would guess he carried a gun.

Colin spotted the IT whiz kid, Giles, on his way in to start work.

"Where can I grab a rucksack, mate?" he called.

"Best bet is Rusty. He's got a stock of most things. It'll cost you, though."

"Yeah, yeah," said Colin, "I can hear him; remember the six P's, Phoenix."

"Piss poor planning, etcetera. Where is Rusty?"

"Most likely to be in the pool doing hundreds of lengths."

Colin didn't want his hands or pockets full of odds and ends. He needed the bag to carry a few necessary items and free his hands. He ran across to the pool. Sure enough, Rusty was swimming length after length; the guy was a fitness freak. Colin looked around him. A couple of other keen beggars were in the pool. Nobody took much notice of him. He spotted a rucksack on a chair at the end of the pool. He tipped the contents onto the chair and made to leave.

"Phoenix," shouted Rusty, as he touched the wall at the far end and paused, "that'll be a tenner, pal. There'd better not be any kit missing when I get out, either."

Colin waved a tenner from his money clip. He called out. "Done that, Rusty. I hope I haven't made you lose count of the number of lengths you've done."

"Bastard." cursed Rusty, "I've got to start over now."

Colin shook his head. Why couldn't people work out that you only need to get fit? It wasn't compulsory to get fit enough to drop out. Back inside his quarters, he threw his two pieces of headwear, a travel shaver, a pair of binoculars, and an Ordnance Survey map of East Sussex into the rucksack. He checked his wristwatch. It was just after seven-fifteen.

The minicab with the Mount Olympus logo waited outside the stable block with its engine running. He got in and nodded to the 'paramedic' he vaguely recognised from that first night.

The cab arrived at Bath Spa station in good time for Colin to catch the seven forty-three train to London Paddington. Nobody gave him a second look at the platform or the train. He dozed for a while with his head on his chest. Colin wanted to shield his face from any passengers wandering along the aisle who might glance at their fellow travellers.

The train pulled into the station at a quarter past nine. Colin made his way along the concourse towards the stairs leading to the Tube. A Circle Line ticket deposited him at London Victoria in under twenty minutes. Colin checked the timetable for the next train to Lewes; he had less than thirty minutes to kill. He told himself *not* to make such puerile jokes, but sometimes they slipped out.

With a newspaper and a cup of scalding hot coffee, he

sat on a bench waiting while he went over the planned itinerary in his head. He needn't have bothered; he had gone over and over it so often that there was no chance he'd forget a single step. The old clock above him ticked around inexorably, and the station announcer broke into Colin's reverie with news of the imminent boarding of his last train ride this morning. Finally, just before half-past eleven, Colin walked along the platform at Lewes station and made for the exit.

Colin turned right on Lansdown Place and made for Eastgate Street.

He enjoyed the walk even though the sun wasn't much in evidence this morning. The skies were filling with clouds, and Colin felt the threat of rain in the air. However, nothing would dampen his spirits. There were two particular reasons for this. First, he was back doing something at which he excelled, and when Colin glanced at the OS map on the train coming from Victoria, he spotted a familiar name.

Was this an omen? He was now crossing the River Ouse using the Phoenix Causeway. How cool was that? It would be even cooler if it represented his mythological namesake. Colin discovered later that it referred to an old forge in the town. A little more prosaic, but even so, he was happy to accept it as an omen.

He continued his stroll; there was no rush. He continued via Malling Street and Chapel Hill, passing the Lewes Golf Club entrance and arriving at his destination just before noon. He looked back towards the town. Colin could see the property at Chapel Hill, where DCI Richard Armitage lived. He lived a bachelor's existence and worked at his cushy number in Corporate Development. This post gave him ample opportunity to take time off to wander over the road and play a round of golf. Unfortunately, he told his superiors he was 'networking' enough for them to look the other way.

Colin knew Richard Armitage finished work early. He drove the three minutes from the Police HQ in Church Lane via Brooks Road and pulled up to his parking spot near his home. This guy had the work, home, leisure equation off to a fine art. Colin remembered the haggard, careworn faces of the commuters on the train to Paddington. Those poor buggers spent at least three hours every working day just travelling, let alone the stresses of whatever job they did.

Meanwhile, on the south coast, a criminal had his job, home, and main leisure activity on his doorstep. If you forgave how he amassed the fortune that he squirrelled away from his dirty dealings, then the way he managed to come up smelling of roses every time would still mark him as a target.

Colin heard the bolts go back in the door behind him. His destination had been The Snowdrop Inn, which opened at noon, according to their website. Colin followed the other early arrivals to the bar. While they ordered a meal and a drink, Colin took in his surroundings. The pub didn't get its name from the herbaceous plant he assumed might pop up in various spots around the Larcombe estate in the spring. He discovered that the inn stood on the site of a fatal avalanche. When it was his turn to order something, Colin decided to take it to the beer gardens. That way, he could keep a weather eye on the nearby hillside and glance towards Chapel Hill to wait for Richard Armitage.

He was pleased to see umbrellas still available on several tables if the clouds brought a more persistent shower. The threat remained, but the October sun was still warm, and with his jacket fastened to keep the pistol hidden, he felt comfortable enough. The food arrived and proved to be excellent pub fare. It was not up to the cordon bleu experience of his first day at Larcombe, but the fresh fish and local vegetables were just the tickets.

Colin left the Snowdrop Inn after a quick trip to the gents and a friendly wave at the staff at the island bar. He threaded his way through tables with a growing number of the lunchtime crowd now seated, drinking and eating in pleasant surroundings. It was a pity he was unlikely to be around these parts after the afternoon's intended action; it had been a friendly place to spend an hour.

When he got outside, he waited while a line of traffic meandered past, nose to tail, on its weary way towards the town centre. He checked his wristwatch; it was fast approaching a quarter past one.

"There you are," whispered Colin. The policeman had found a kind motorist. Fed up with travelling in crocodile file any longer, they had stopped to let him cross the line of traffic. He pulled into his parking spot. Richard Armitage jumped out of his Mercedes sports car and trotted to his front door.

The traffic moved even slower as the crocodile took a while to get back up to crawling speed. Colin waved at a grey-haired old lady driver and darted in front of her car. He took advantage of the long gap between vehicles coming up the hill from town. Soon he reached the Golf Club. Colin retrieved his bobble hat from the rucksack and the binoculars. He hitched the backpack over a shoulder and set off along the path that ran alongside the course.

The footpath veered off towards New Road. After a short hike, Colin threaded his way through bushes and trees until he reached the approach to the eleventh green. There were several couples and foursomes out on the course.

Seeing someone wearing sturdy walking boots, a weatherproof jacket, and a bobble hat raised no suspicions, especially if someone was spotted scanning the skies with binoculars later in the afternoon. Birdwatchers got everywhere, didn't they?

Colin kept his distance from the golfers. He moved fifty yards towards or away from the spot if a ball landed nearby. If anyone asked them later if they saw anyone, they might have said they saw a man in a blue jacket, a red bobble hat, jeans, and boots. They may have thought he wore glasses. They might even have said he had designer stubble if their eyesight was exceptional. Of course, any description would be vague. Height, weight, and age were tricky to gauge at the distances Colin kept between him and the object ball.

Richard Armitage was a creature of habit. Colin imagined him preparing a light lunch, showering, and changing into something suitable for eighteen holes with one of his cronies. An Olympus operative had played here a handful of times over the summer and checked out the start time that the 'crafty copper' adopted. The two o'clock slot was pencilled in for Armitage every Wednesday.

Most people ensured they got off the course well before dusk in early October. Unless delayed by a group of hackers who didn't know one end of a club from another, Armitage and his playing partner should reach the eleventh hole by four o'clock. Colin prepared to wait. Patience was the key.

Colin used the protective screen offered by the trees and shrubs to remove his pistol from his jacket's inside pocket. Colin loaded it and replaced it. As he watched another two golfers play their approach shots to the green through the foliage, he stifled a yawn. He stretched his body and looked at his wristwatch. His target would be on his way.

The undulating nature of the course high on the

downs meant it was as tricky for Colin to pick out Armitage with his binoculars as for golfers using the fairways and greens to see him hidden away in the undergrowth. The footpath lay a short distance to his right and behind him, and Colin kept a constant lookout. He wanted to see if any ramblers were on the course to witness affairs. But the clouds had gathered. So far from the clubhouse, it wasn't a case of if it would rain, but when.

The drizzle started at a quarter past three, and it got steadily harder and harder. The breeze had picked up earlier. As two married couples made their way up the eleventh fairway, Colin saw they had donned their wet weather gear. They kept their umbrellas pulled close to shelter themselves. He could have run naked across the green without either of them noticing.

Hardy annuals these golfers, Colin thought. Gentlemen, too, he realised as he watched them take care of drying their clubs. They were solicitous in keeping their partner covered with their umbrella until the last few moments before they played their shot. So courteous, it reminded Colin of Sir Walter Raleigh.

"Get on with it. You're holding up play. The last thing I need is people backed up on the tee because of slow play," muttered Colin. What was he doing? He found himself passing comments on a game he had little knowledge of and cared about even less. Colin shook his head — the stuff you must read up on if you want to do a proper job.

He needn't have worried. The course wasn't too busy further back towards the clubhouse. The threat of rain had put off a few who considered turning up on the off-chance of getting a game. Instead, they left their clubs in the car's boot and walked over the road to get a drink at The Snowdrop Inn. A pint or two was a much better way to pass an afternoon.

Richard Armitage was with one of his regular playing partners, a solicitor from Lewes named Peregrine Watts-Williams. Today was no different from any other occasion they played together. They played a money game at a fiver per hole. Perry was a rank amateur whose handicap was that he couldn't play golf. Unsurprisingly, the crafty copper was forty quid up as he put the pin back in the hole at the tenth.

"Unlucky, Perry. It's not your day today, is it?" said Armitage without a hint of irony.

"Eight holes left, Richard," said Perry. "The comeback starts here."

The wind and rain were unrelenting as the pair made their way over to the eleventh tee. Five minutes earlier, Colin had walked back towards the point on the hole where the right-hand dogleg came into play to view their first shots through his binoculars.

Planning is everything. The operative who visited the Lewes course had provided a blow-by-blow description of the shot that these two were prone to play, given their ability level. Armitage had a better-than-even chance of finding the middle of the fairway. Poor old Perry zig-zagged his way up the fairways as he negotiated the three hundred-odd yards.

Colin watched the pantomime unfold as Richard Armitage, and Perry Watts-Williams shuffled onto the tee. There were umbrellas, golf trolleys, towels, and technicolour wet weather clothing everywhere. Colin ran back through the trees and awaited the first shot. He had a small window of opportunity where he could dart out and do what he planned, hidden from the view of the players.

Armitage drove first, and as he watched it sail away, he made a mental note to work on correcting a slight tendency to slice his tee shot. Maybe he was relaxing because he found it more comfortable than usual to pick up sixty or seventy quid from the old fart next to him. The ball landed four or five yards from the thick rough, and Colin congratulated himself on picking the perfect place to hide. He walked over to the ball, picked it up, and dropped it amongst the denser vegetation.

Perry smashed his drive towards the left-hand side of the fairway twenty yards further than his opponent. It was the best shot he had played that afternoon. Colin groaned and ran after it. He picked it up and lobbed it into the rough — just the job. The two men were now far enough apart for what he had in mind. They would be unable to see each other play their second shots.

Colin listened for the two golfers to arrive. There they both were. Bang in the middle of the fairway, ever hopeful. They walked up the couple hundred yards together and then parted company to search for their ball.

"Can't see either of them, Perry," called Richard Armitage. "I could have sworn I was on the fairway, even though I admit I tweaked it a touch."

"I smoked mine, Richard. This game is not over yet. I'm hunting my ball way up on the left."

"You wish," replied the policeman. Perry laughed. The two set off up the fairway.

Colin slipped the pistol from his jacket and waited. Richard Armitage parked his trolley and hunted for his ball in the grass at the edge of the fairway. When he looked further into the trees, he saw where Colin had placed it. The crafty copper tiptoed towards it, a little puzzled, wondering how it ended up this far to the right.

He knew Perry couldn't see him from the other side of the fairway. So he picked it up, found a decent lie, and placed it on the ground. Colin watched him from his hiding place.

"I've got mine," shouted Perry. "It's in the rough, but at least I've got a clear shot. Any luck with yours?"

"Just found it in the light stuff, Perry," Richard called back. "My turn, I believe?"

He selected his club, and after a few flashy waggles, he hit the ball. It sailed away into a stiff Lewes breeze. He was engrossed in his shot. He hoped Perry didn't see him pick up his ball. Armitage didn't realise until too late that someone had emerged from the trees and now stood right behind him.

"Cheating bastard," whispered Colin and squeezed the trigger.

DCI Richard Armitage pitched forward onto the fairway, dead before he hit the ground. The PSS pistol lived up to its reputation: - silent and deadly. Perry was twenty yards ahead. With few people left on the course and nobody on the footpath away in the distance, no one was any the wiser.

Perry had seen the ball flying straight as an arrow towards the green and cursed.

"Lucky sod. I prayed Richard might not have a shot," he muttered. Perry was unaware that he had. It was just not the shot he expected.

The corpulent solicitor tried his best and hacked the ball from the rough. He shuffled after it with a melancholy air, dragging his trolley behind him.

"Still my turn Richard," he called out to his playing partner. "You carry on, and I'll see you on the green in a tick."

There was no reply.

Colin had not been idle in the minutes since he murdered the corrupt police officer. He reversed his jacket, stuffed the bobble hat in the rucksack, and removed items from inside. Colin strode back to the footpath, wearing a maroon top and a white baseball cap. When he put enough distance between himself and Richard Armitage's body, he took the shaver from his pocket and removed the designer stubble. When he was clean-shaven, he took off his glasses and put both the shaver and the glasses in the rucksack to complete his transformation. There were no eyewitnesses in the vicinity. People may have remembered a walker in town this morning. Maybe they would recall a customer in The Snowdrop Inn or a bird watcher on the footpath by the golf course. The man strolling away from the crime scene late in the afternoon resembled none of them.

Meanwhile, Perry had played his third shot, and his ball landed on the front of the green. Perry huffed and puffed along the course, looking for his partner. Had he slipped off behind a gorse bush for a pee? Perry was curious to discover what shot Richard had left. Did he still have a chance of salvaging a miracle half?

Perry kept looking over his shoulder, expecting to see the policeman striding up to join him. Instead, there was no sign of Richard's ball on the green. Fingers crossed, he had flown over the green and landed in a heap of trouble at the back.

"Come on, Richard," he called out.

"Where the bloody hell has he got to?" he said.

There was no sign of the ball at the back of the green. Perry felt a chill run down his back. He walked over to the pin. Shit. The ball nestled up against the stick an inch below the lip of the hole. DCI Richard Armitage never knew it, but he holed his second shot at the eleventh. The eagle had landed.

"I don't believe it!" shouted Perry Watts-Williams. "That's another fiver I owe you."

Still fuming at his playing partner's slice of luck, he returned to the fairway. Perry found Richard Armitage face-first in the grass by his trolley. There was blood on the collar and shoulders of his wet weather jacket. No shouting or shaking would do any good. He wouldn't be getting up again.

Perry looked around, but there wasn't anyone in sight. How on earth had this happened? What should he do? A golf ball landed ten yards away. He ran out into the middle of the fairway as another ball skipped by him and ran towards the left-hand rough. Perry stood still and waved his arms frantically. What a terrible thing to have happened. As he saw club members striding towards him, he had one consolation. Realisation dawned. He could keep his money in his pocket. Richard Armitage wasn't collecting from him on this occasion.

The two golfers realised something was wrong and ran towards the by-now distraught Perry. The shock of finding his dead colleague had made him incoherent. He imagined that he, too, might be in danger, stuck out here at one of the furthest points on the course. When the emergency services arrived and the murder scene preserved, Colin Bailey sat on a train heading for London Victoria. He was coolness personified and satisfied with a job well done.

Chapter Six

Erebus had watched the minicab disappear up the driveway as it carried Phoenix to the station. The Armitage action was the first he had sanctioned to be carried out by someone not ex-military. His reputation was on the line; Phoenix must not fail him. Erebus had turned away from the window and prepared for the morning's meeting; there was nothing more to do. He had put his trust in the man they had plucked from the river, and he would know whether that trust was misplaced in less than twelve hours.

The Olympus head was now in the drawing-room where he, Athena, Thanatos, Alastor, and Minos met to discuss the status of the operations they were running. Also, there were new targets to consider for direct action. The most important item on today's agenda was the emergence of a possible terrorist threat to the London Olympics, which were less than ten months away.

The five leading members of the Olympus group discussed the ongoing operations. Seven agents in various European and African countries were each declared 'code red.' Their target was now due for removal. To further disguise things, the group selected specific days and times for the tasks on top of the lengthy steps taken by the agents themselves.

They took account of significant events in the countries involved; religious holidays, strikes by public servants, and even a celebrity wedding. Any extra item that could add to the list of newsworthy articles on the day selected was pertinent. No stone was left unturned in the search for a good day to bury news of the sudden death of a gangster or politician in whichever part of the world it occurred. Everything hinged on diverting attention away from anyone linking these deaths to Olympus.

The next series of items covered potential new targets. They postponed several until the surveillance staff in the ice-house had gathered further data. Other straightforward assignments were passed to agents in the right areas. Erebus paid particular attention to one background story from Scotland. It sounded as if it might be tailor-made for Phoenix.

A sixteen-year-old girl from Dunfermline expressed her disgust with the lenient sentence handed to a policeman who assaulted her and her sister. As a result, the forty-eight-year-old constable received a one-year's community order.

In March 2009, the girl walked home after a study session at a school friend's house. The constable had been on duty when he stopped his patrol car fifty yards ahead of her under a streetlight. He opened the passenger door when she got alongside the car and told her to get in. He gave her a lift home and told her to be careful when walking alone on the streets late at night. "You never know who's around," he told her and said he'd keep an eye out for her so she didn't come to any harm.

The Olympus Project

The following month she went into town with her twenty-year-old sister's workmates. The other three girls had half bottles of vodka in their handbags. Although they bought just tonic waters in the bars they visited, by chucking out time, the girls got hammered. The youngster was drunk for the first time in her life.

When she came onto the pavement from the last pub they'd been in, she staggered and grabbed a street sign to stop herself from falling. Then she was violently sick. A police car switched on its headlights across the street, and then the vehicle approached. The girl's sister was comforting her with a protective arm around her shoulder. Her two workmates had long gone, making their way up the street on unsteady legs, looking for a kebab shop that might still be open.

Once the police car driver got out and walked around to the young girl, she realised it was the same constable who had driven her home last month. He suggested that both girls get into the back of the car, and he drove off towards the estate where they lived. He said he was deciding whether to charge the younger sister for being drunk and disorderly. As for the older sister, he said she would be in worse trouble for supplying alcohol to someone underage.

When they were a hundred yards from their front door, he stopped the car in a quiet spot, away from any street-lights. He told the younger sister to get off home. He said she was lucky. This time he'd forget her drunkenness and the throwing up in the street.

The constable told her sister to get in the front seat with him. The youngster left the two talking and ran inside the house, where she spent time in the bathroom being ill. She found her sister's bedroom door shut when she crept along the landing to her room. She wanted to know if he had charged her or given her a rollicking, but it had to wait until the morning. She had fallen into bed and slept until lunchtime.

After seeing her sister in the afternoon, she learned the awful truth. The officer had suggested there was a way to avoid either sister going to court. He leaned over, fondled her sister's breasts, and placed her hand on his groin. When she asked him what he meant, he unzipped his fly and exposed himself. He said he would forget any thoughts of the charges in return for oral sex.

Her sister was so drunk she did what he asked. When it was over, she tried to get out of the car, but the constable grabbed her arm and said she hadn't done enough to persuade him to drop the case. He wanted the younger sister to meet him at the same place, at the same time next week. Her sister had agreed to get out of the car and escape from him.

The two sisters argued. First, the younger sister couldn't believe her sister had agreed to do what the policeman had asked. Second, the older sister didn't want to go to court to face a charge of buying alcohol for her sixteen-year-old sister. Nor did she want her workmates dragged into the whole business. She persuaded the young girl to meet up with the policeman. The young girl left her home the next week and walked to where the car was parked last Friday night. She waited for the police car to arrive.

When it pulled up to the pavement and switched off its lights, she got in and asked what he wanted from her. The policeman told her to take her sweater off and sit next to him in her bra. He didn't try to touch her, but he touched himself and became aroused. He asked her to pleasure him with her hand. The young girl told him she had never done it before and was frightened. The policeman laughed and gripped her wrist. He had thrust her hand into his crotch and encouraged her to get on with it.

It was over soon after, and he told her she could go home. He said he would keep an eye out for her and her sister and always be available if they ever wanted a lift home. When she had run into her house crying, her sister rushed downstairs and told her parents what had been happening. They made a formal complaint. Two years passed before the case got to court. After the long delay, he pleaded guilty as soon as the court usher read the charges.

PC Donald MacDonald was single and lived at home with his invalid father. He had been in the force for twenty-seven years. The girl had complained that the sentence was only half the time she and her sister had had to cope with what happened to them. "I think he got off lightly," she said. "He kept us hanging around for two years, then he pleaded guilty."

The judge referred to MacDonald's actions as 'sleazy, if not pathetic'. He used his position to make inappropriate sexual advances to young women. Given his family circumstances and the nature of the offences, the judge decided a custodial sentence would be disproportionate. He stressed that a community order was not a soft option. The officer should address his behaviour and correct it so that the young girls of Dunfermline walk the streets safely at night.

"What do you think of this one, Minos?" Erebus asked the former judge.

"The punishment doesn't fit the crime," replied Minos.

"Any recommendations?" the old man inquired, looking around the table.

"Castration?" said Athena.

"Were these two sisters his only victims?" asked Thanatos.

Erebus looked at the supporting documents that arrived with the story.

"Several colleagues flagged their suspicions about MacDonald in the past without acting on them. It wouldn't surprise me if he became a serial offender. We'll get our people to step up the search for more victims. I believe we'll uncover more evidence to support a more permanent solution for the Dunfermline problem."

"Who do you have in mind?" asked Athena.

"If today's sortie is a success, this might be an assignment for Phoenix."

Athena did not look happy, and Erebus asked her to explain her obvious displeasure.

"Are you sure he can remain objective? He lost his only daughter to an attacker that preferred young girls. We should wait until he returns from this first mission before we commit ourselves."

Erebus nodded.

"As you wish. If only I could persuade you to trust Phoenix. He pays such attention to detail. He'll cope with whatever we throw his way through systematic planning and efficient execution. Of that, I have no doubts."

"We'll see," replied Athena. "Let's move on to the next item on the agenda. I fear it may keep us occupied for a while."

"In that case, I suggest we break for an early lunch," said Erebus.

The meeting resumed in the drawing-room. Erebus looked up towards Thanatos.

"Over to you, old chap. Let's understand the construction of this terrorist cell."

Thanatos stood before a white screen that had been brought into the room during lunch. Erebus was not in favour of visual aids or modern technology invading the beautiful rooms in his family home. On this occasion, though, it was a vital tool to help understand the complex nature of the enemy they were facing.

"Al-Qaeda's cell structure differs from the typical Western style because of cultural differences. Their minimal core leadership group is a ring network with each leader heading their particular hierarchy. The ring networks overlap; they are links in a chain. Trust and personal relationships are paramount, with far more family and in-group linkages than in the more bureaucratic Western model. Such complexity makes these in-groups hard to infiltrate. We have operatives working on compromising selected fringe members of rings operating in the UK, but progress is slow."

Thanatos drew circles on the whiteboard and linked them with arrows.

"The core group is a ring, superimposed on an inner hub and spoke structure of ideological authority. Each core member formed another hub and spoke system. The spokes lead to subcells that support the infrastructure and, sometimes, operational groups. In this way, an operational cell can become autonomous of the core."

"So they keep positive control from the core, but specific roles can operate without reference back to them for every action they take," commented Erebus.

"True," said Thanatos, "but they can be more random and unpredictable too, which makes them far more dangerous."

"Do we have names for any of the participants in the chain that concern us most?" asked Alastor.

"We're getting names, the different camps they trained at, the hierarchy and evidence of in-fighting. Certain factions want to move far quicker on operations than the core. We might have occasion to use this weakness in the future. So far, we have avoided opting for a 'catch and release' programme. None of the cell members associated with this chain has been picked off the streets and brought here for Level Three interrogation. We don't want to create distrust by the central core of any individuals lower on the ladder. We may increase our intelligence, but at what cost?"

The group continued to analyse the infrastructure of the cells for the rest of the afternoon. In time, the whiteboard contained names, dotted lines, solid lines, and question marks. After a short break for their evening meal, they shut themselves away again.

The full extent of the country's threat in 2012 and beyond became evident. The Larcombe Manor surveillance section highlighted twenty terrorist investigations that the national security sources were investigating. The Olympus Project's in-house ability to track and monitor internet and phone traffic was equal to any other system in the world. There was nothing they couldn't scrutinise.

When you added agents in the field who were intelligence-gathering experts, Erebus and his colleagues had everything they required to mount a counterterrorism strike.

Erebus hadn't told Colin Bailey everything on his grand tour. The Olympus group monitored the secret services. If they ordered a direct action, they didn't bump into any of their people and risk exposing the true nature of the Larcombe operation. At this stage, they were building a picture of the terrorist cell and monitoring its activities. If an attack on the streets of London was imminent, they needed to be ready.

Because of her involvement with the 7/7 bombings in London, Athena was keen to play her part. However, she preferred to smash the cell before giving the green light to strike targets in the city. Likewise, Erebus chose to take a cautious approach.

"If we are correct in our interpretation of the data we've gathered, it's foolish to assume we could remove the threat in one attack, Athena. There are a series of interlocking cells. As Thanatos described it to us on the board, and, in this case, these cells are sure to overlap. We could not guarantee the disruption of the entire cell."

Thanatos continued with his analysis.

"We recruited a mole from within the Muslim community to infiltrate the alleged plot. Progress is slow. Our man on the inside has to act with extreme caution. Two of the members of his link in the chain are brothers; another is their uncle. The three men have been backwards and forwards to Pakistan this summer. Calls to Britain and internet communications have been under surveillance. Our informant is supplying us with details of their movements in the capital now they are back in the country."

Athena stood up and stretched. It had been a long day with no sign of it ending.

"If we have twenty initiatives under scrutiny by MI5 and ourselves, how can we even be sure of the right one to give our total focus?"

Minos was unconvinced they could select a target that crippled the cell's capacity to carry out an attack.

"There are too many players, Erebus. We might need to remove fifty terrorists to disable the cell. That's a nonstarter. The Olympus Project has to continue for many years to come. Our work is too important to sacrifice resources on one piece of the jigsaw."

"We could take out the suicide squad on the streets,"

suggested Alastor. "That might only mean removing three or four bombers."

"It still leaves us exposed," said Minos, "and we have other targets which need our attention. I vote that even if it means we risk a tragedy in the capital, we leave the matter to our nation's security services."

"God help us," said Athena.

"What other targets are you alluding to, Minos?" asked Erebus.

"The country's high-security prison population is twenty per cent Muslim. Over the last decade, many have been Afro-Caribbean and white Caucasian converts. The most radical prisoners have become adept at targeting vulnerable prisoners and offering them protection and support through religion. They have plenty of time in which to do this. So we find many prisoners who are members of organised gangs outside gaol convert to Islam. When they leave prison, they spread the message. The risk is the recruitment of more and more criminal gangs by groups such as Al-Qaeda. The challenge of prison extremism will not go away."

"We can't send an operative to a high-security prison to kill the more prominent jihadists; that's a suicide mission at worst. That agent would be charged with murder and banged up for the rest of his life," said Erebus.

The room fell silent for a while, and then Athena spoke.

"Could we persuade the authorities to transfer prisoners to limit the influence of these extremists?"

"It needs our communications people to cover their tracks completely," said Thanatos. "Any such instructions must never track back to Larcombe. We could arrange an accident if several big hitters left in a van and moved to another establishment."

"The accident needs to be catastrophic. The occupants have to die. Driver, warders and prisoners," said Athena. "We can't ambush the van and shoot the extremists. That exposes us to too many questions."

Erebus spoke. "Prepare a plan, Thanatos. The collateral damage is unavoidable. We have to think of the greater good. This situation concerning the mole, or the removal of our prison population extremists, remains unresolved. We need to revisit those matters on another occasion. Can we get more intelligence in these areas, Thanatos? See to it, please. If that means getting more people on the inside, so be it. If we need to invite one of their numbers to spend time with us at Larcombe, then we should organise that as soon as possible."

Alastor asked, "Are we intending a 'catch and release' visit?"

"One-way ticket only," replied Erebus.

Colin had returned to the West Country. He had sent a text message to the transport section as the train pulled out of Swindon, designed to confuse anyone monitoring mobile phone traffic.

'Fireboy home in fifteen. See you soon.'

Colin walked out of the station and straight into the passenger seat of the Olympus minicab.

"Good trip?" the driver asked.

"For me, yes," replied Colin.

The driver chuckled and eased the cab into the slow-moving line of cars. It was a mild autumn evening, and the trees were shedding their leaves in larger and larger numbers. Colin watched the changing scene as they drove out of the city into the countryside. His training over the past three months had made him forget how time had passed. Today had been a breeze. He was back doing what he did best. Colin wondered what Erebus and the others would make of his performance. Perhaps he might receive a gold star?

The minicab negotiated the leaf-strewn driveway and pulled up beside the stable block. Colin assumed any performance review would be on hold until the morning. He thanked the driver for the lift and wished him goodnight. When he got into his quarters, he unpacked his rucksack and changed his clothes.

Colin stood holding the pistol and thinking back over the past twelve hours. Would he find someone at work in the armoury? Should the gun and spare ammunition go back underground tonight? He glanced at his desk and spotted another 'post-it' note on his laptop.

The note had come from Erebus again. 'Pop in when you get back, Phoenix, as we're working late.'

Colin stashed the gun and ammo in his locker. He walked to the main house, where he found Erebus and the others in the drawing-room. They were relaxing with coffee and sandwiches. Thanatos waved a lazy hand towards the supper spread on the side table and told him to get something for himself.

Colin hadn't realised he was so hungry. A long time had passed since lunch at the Snowdrop Inn, and he had travelled back to Bath without delay once he'd finished the job. The luxury of idling away an hour in the restaurant car or the station buffets at Victoria or Paddington had been tempting but too risky.

He was burying his teeth into a salmon and cucumber sandwich when Erebus spoke.

"Everything went according to plan then, Phoenix?" he said, sipping his coffee.

Colin was poised to reply when Erebus continued: -

"Your plan worked to perfection. DCI Richard Armitage was discovered by his playing partner on the Lewes golf course late this afternoon. He had been shot at close range. The Sussex police have no eyewitnesses. They have few leads to follow. A senior officer trotted out the usual stuff: - our thoughts are with the family. He added that Richard was a valued friend and colleague. The truth is they were glad to see the back of him—one less rotten apple in the barrel. The police investigation is centring on his earlier court case. While working with SOCA, criminals he came into contact with were annoyed when he wriggled his way out of the charges brought against him. The drug gangs have long arms. Any gang whose members had narcotics planted on them or got involved in any of his other money-making activities may have ordered a hit. Our people in the ice-house are contributing to the misinformation. We don't want the local police getting imaginative and thinking outside the box."

"Why am I not surprised you're so well informed?" said Colin.

"Needs must, dear boy," said Erebus.

"Should I return the gun and spare ammo to the armoury tonight?" asked Colin.

"Yes," said Thanatos. "We have someone on duty twenty-four seven. We have strict rules for items of that sort being above ground for longer than necessary. They might be difficult to explain if the charity commissioners dropped in for an unannounced spot check tomorrow morning."

"I'll finish my sandwich and get back to my quarters

then," said Colin. "I've secured them in my locker for the time being. I didn't know how long I'd be tied up here."

Athena allowed herself a brief smile.

"Did you imagine you might be tied up then?"

"A man can dream," replied Colin and made to leave.

"Hang on, Phoenix," called Erebus. "We have another direct action for you."

"When do I leave this time?" Colin asked. "In the morning? No rest for the wicked, I suppose."

"I didn't realise we agreed to Phoenix being the right man for the Dunfermline problem," whispered Athena. Erebus laid a hand on her arm.

"I believe he is the right person, without question. We still have the intelligence to gather in that regard. The direct action won't receive confirmation until we have everything we need to hand. In the meantime, Phoenix needs a change from a policeman, don't you think?"

Erebus invited Colin to retake his seat.

"Sir Godfrey Penrose is a former Parliamentary Under-Secretary of State for Defence Personnel, Welfare, and Veterans. He stood down at the last election after a long career in politics. His father was a Brigadier and, after Oxford University, worked in the City and dabbled in corporate finance and management consultancy. He never followed his father into the regular army but spent several years in the Territorial Army. The Tories saw him as a safe pair of hands. After contesting a safe seat in the Home Counties, he became a solid backbencher for the first few years. He held minor posts in Education and Transport before ending up with Defence. We believe many of our former colleagues got a raw deal on his watch. Have you heard of the Armed Forces Covenant, Phoenix?"

"Can't say I have," Colin answered.

"In simple terms, Her Majesty's Government has agreed to enshrine in law its duty of care to its serving service personnel. It has agreed to sustain and reward them for the rest of their lives. The House of Lords is playing silly beggars with it, but everything should be signed off well before Christmas. Our veterans should be better protected than they have been hitherto. We have carried out a thorough investigation of Penrose and found black marks against his name. Apart from the veterans who suffered deprivation and a distinct lack of 'sustenance and reward' before their deaths, there were rumours of incidents while he served with the TA, during their so-called Annual Camps. These are an intense period of learning for any reservist, whatever their rank or level of experience. The more junior members focus on necessary skills such as first aid, map reading, and weapon handling. Several eighteen-year-old boys and girls found themselves up close and personal with the future MP in tents scattered across the Brecon Beacons and Dartmoor. The rumours, as confirmed, described how these youngsters woke up in the night to find Penrose lying next to them. He touched them intimately; the assaults included penetration of both sexes. The victims were frightened and confused; for many, it was their first sexual experience. Penrose told them it formed part of their training. He convinced them they needed to cope with adversities. If they cried out or struggled when they found themselves in action, they could give away their position to the enemy, endangering the lives of their comrades. The victims are still living with what happened. They continue to blame themselves despite the passage of time. We sent agents posing as documentary filmmakers to interview these men and women, who are now in their thirties and forties. The agents recorded their evidence with their faces, never appearing in shot and disguising their voices — a move which persuaded them to tell us everything. We paid them for their cooperation but warned them we couldn't guarantee the programme was ever featured on their TV screens. The victims found the courage to tell someone about the abuse they suffered from a man who acted as their protector and carer; it was a gross breach of trust. A couple may have come forward in the future to get the justice they deserve. We will not wait for that to happen. We will see Sir Godfrey Penrose receives the proper punishment for his heinous acts."

"Can I have a dossier on this Penrose character?" asked Colin.

"It will be with you first thing tomorrow morning, Phoenix. Pay a quick visit to the armoury tonight, and then get a well-earned rest. Goodnight."

"Goodnight, Sir," Colin replied and then said his goodnights to the others, reserving an extra slight nod towards Athena and left the drawing-room.

Colin rose bright and early the next day. When the dossier arrived, he was ready and waiting to start on his new assignment. Colin reviewed the information Erebus gave him last evening and paid closer attention to the most recent data that the surveillance section had gathered. Since he retired from politics, Sir Godfrey had taken several non-executive posts on the boards of prestigious companies in the City.

"He's not short of a few bob, is he," exclaimed Colin.

He scanned the list and found a one-bedroom flat in Egerton Gardens, Knightsbridge, valued just short of two million. Sir Godfrey used it when in town on business. The family home was a converted barn near Stowmarket, Suffolk, which weighed in at a cool one million, and he owned a modest two-bedroom cottage in Princeton. The cottage was very much a rural property, and buying on this part of Dartmoor requires a particular love of moorland and foul weather. The raw beauty of the last wilderness in England took some beating. Colin noted that the property could be reached in less than half an hour by car from Plymouth across the moor via Yelverton. A little light switched on in Colin's head, and he started on his plan.

It appeared Sir Godfrey owned several luxury cars to take his pick from when running around London. He owned two top marques Range Rovers into the bargain to use in the country. Sir Godfrey married Penelope Bradley in 1977; they had no children. She was the only daughter of a wealthy wine merchant. These days she appeared to spend most of her time in Suffolk, drinking her way through her late father's cellar, plus the odd bottle or two from Waitrose. Colin determined how often the couple spent time in each other's company. It looked to be eighty days per year at most. Less if they didn't see eye to eye.

The rest of the day Colin spent in planning mode. First, he made a list of the items he needed when travelling further west to have a few final words with Sir Godfrey Penrose. Next, Colin asked the surveillance section to determine if the Dartmoor cottage was a regular weekend retreat for the happy couple, which Colin doubted, or whether Sir Godfrey had a male or female companion that shared his rural bolt hole. Or did he buy the cottage to escape London's mad world to recapture his younger days camping out on the moorlands?

Colin was right about one thing. No evidence existed that Penelope Penrose ever visited the property. Her married name reminded Colin of a programme Sharron liked as a little girl, but he couldn't bring the title to mind.

Godfrey might have had company in his London pad, but again, no evidence suggested the cottage was a love nest. As far as the surveillance section had found out, Sir Godfrey let the train take the strain on Thursday or Friday afternoon and travelled back late on Monday. "The joys of a non-executive post," thought Colin. "Grafting three days a week for a small fortune, plus share options. Nice work if you can get it."

The problem would be the frequency of Sir Godfrey's visits. They appeared to be random. Colin checked the local press for events that might attract the former politician. He was sure a car boot sale in Yelverton wouldn't appeal, and he couldn't imagine him having signed on for the local darts team. No, the event needed to be more refined.

He thought he might have to change his plans. To stake out the pad in London, with the associated problems of getting rid of a body in Knightsbridge, had to be a nightmare. More by luck than judgement, he stumbled across the answer. Various courses and expeditions took place across Dartmoor throughout the year. These were trips where young people faced a range of adversities trying to complete elements of an Outward Bound scheme or a Duke of Edinburgh award. At seventy years of age, Sir Godfrey was too old for the rough and tumble of his earlier TA days, but he remained a voyeur at least. He got his kicks watching youngsters scrambling around the moors in all winds and weathers. In time, Colin hoped to discover whether Sir Godfrey had more to hide.

Colin couldn't see what persuaded these kids to do outdoor activities. Every Easter, the media covered the plight of those poor lads or lasses that got lost on the Ten Tors challenge. They ended up suffering from hypothermia while everyone else ate their Easter eggs. Why nobody thought only a bloody idiot would be willing to go out in a wilderness to walk fifty-five miles was beyond him. Then they had the cheek to expect the emergency services to risk their necks rescuing them when things went wrong, as they often did.

These days you've got a job to get the emergency services to come out for sane people, let alone nutters. Colin had a view on that. He remembered telling his first wife Karen that people who went potholing and got stuck were idiots too. She 'oohed' and 'aahed' at the TV when they surfaced safe and sound after an anxious wait or wiped tears from her chubby cheeks when they winched a body bag to the surface. But she never grasped Colin's logic that the money wasted on these adrenalin junkies would have provided more support for her when she gave birth to Sharron. Karen might not have suffered her postpartum haemorrhage if an older doctor had been on call. Maybe she would have been able to have more kids.

Colin told himself he must stop thinking back. Those dysfunctional family days were behind him, though they might have been. He must concentrate on the here and now. He checked the activities on the moors scheduled over the next few weeks. The surveillance reports indicated Sir Godfrey was a creature of habit. There was nothing on the books for this weekend. He anticipated the old buffer would drive up to Stowmarket to endure a frosty reception from Penelope.

Sir Godfrey would have a few warm thoughts to keep him going to help get him through to Monday morning when he escaped back to Egerton Gardens. Several hundred youngsters would be on the moors the following weekend, and Colin would put good money on Godfrey being on that train west.

Chapter Seven

Colin worked through the evening, putting the finishing touches on the itinerary of his proposed assignment. Once he completed it, he saved it on his laptop and crashed out on his bunk without bothering to undress.

He slept fitfully through the night, dreaming of Karen and Sharron for the first time in a long time. He had suppressed those painful memories so well. But, reading how Sir Godfrey Penrose had taken advantage of those innocent children caused those emotional times in his life to come tumbling back.

Colin dragged himself from bed at six o'clock and made straight for the pool. He stripped off, showered, and put on a pair of trunks. Colin dived into the water and swam until he couldn't raise his arms or kick his legs. Then he clambered out of the pool and sat on the edge with his feet dangling in the water. Tears were close, but not that close. Gradually, he fought against the feelings that sought to overwhelm him and regained control. Colin Bailey, the stone-cold killer, was back.

He looked up when he heard someone else enter the building.

"Good morning, Phoenix," said Athena.

Colin watched as she stepped out of her tracksuit bottoms and peeled off her sweatshirt top to reveal her one-piece grey swimsuit. She looked incredible.

"Do you come here often?" he managed. His tongue seemed to have stuck to the roof of his mouth.

"Is that the best you can do?" Athena mocked and slipped into the pool. She set off with long smooth rhythmical strokes and tumble-turned at the end of the lane. Her appearance looked so graceful that Colin sat and stared at her for a few minutes, mesmerised. He knew he should get up and dry himself before he got a chill. He wanted to stay a while longer to get his breath back. Well, that was his excuse.

Eventually, he tore himself away from seeing her long powerful back and the grey costume that made her look more fish than human. Although Colin was under no illusions when she had removed her outer clothes: - Athena was all woman. He dried himself and dressed in a hurry. First, Colin needed to return to his quarters and get into clean, warm clothes. Then he had to get to work to take his mind off Athena.

Colin had visited the canteen and had breakfast, wondering if Athena had come here to get something to eat. She wasn't about to sit with the hired help. What was he thinking? It didn't stop him from looking up every time the door opened. He took his time over his second cup of coffee to no avail. As he strolled back to his quarters, he remembered he needed to contact Erebus and set up a meeting to go through his proposal for direct action against

Penrose. As he walked through the door, he saw yet another 'post-it' note on his laptop.

"I'll teach Erebus how to use a mobile phone or e-mail," he thought and picked up the note. But, surprise, surprise, it wasn't from Erebus.

'I dropped by, but you were out. A,' it read. A sad-faced emoticon lay under the A.

Colin smiled to himself. The ice maiden had a softer side. What a shame he had to put one hundred per cent of his energies into his new assignment. Erebus summoned him to the orangery to meet him at two o'clock. One of the transport guys delivered the message. Colin asked what was going on this morning. Erebus and the others had been in a heavy-duty meeting. The only thing the guy knew for sure was that Athena needed to go to London. Also, the government had just escalated the terrorist threat on the streets of the UK from 'moderate' to 'severe'.

When the two men met in the orangery, Erebus seemed distant. Colin ran through his proposed itinerary, knowing damn well that he was only half-listening. When he finished, Colin waited for a response.

"Are you happy that you've covered every eventuality, Phoenix?" asked Erebus.

"Yes," replied Colin, "but.."

Erebus interrupted him. "Then, I'm happy. It's cleared for direct action. We have bigger fish to catch."

With that, Erebus levered himself up and out of his chair and left. Colin watched him go. He thought he'd aged since last night. Something serious had happened.

Colin spent the rest of the day ordering supplies. Not food and drink, but clothing and equipment for next weekend's trip to Dartmoor. This assignment didn't warrant a weapon, Colin had decided. He had a far more ingenious exit strategy for Sir Godfrey in mind.

The next seven days passed slowly. Colin spent time in the gym and the pool, but his sessions never coincided with Athena's. He didn't know whether that was a good thing or not. Finally, Colin spent a few hours in the shooting range to sharpen his skills. New data came to him from the surveillance section on Donald MacDonald, and he did several minutes' preliminary work on his plans for that gentleman.

As for the people in the 'big house,' they were conspicuous by their absence. Whatever threat this terrorist cell promised, it occupied many hours of their time and resources. Colin had received a green light for the Dartmoor job, and they left him to get on with it. When he went to bed the following Thursday evening, he was cool, calm and ready to do just that.

Colin awoke early. He showered, dressed and collected together the items of the kit he had ordered. For this trip, Colin picked up his rucksack. Rusty had given him hell when he returned his after the Lewes assignment.

"I've had that since Kuwait, mate," he snarled. Colin hadn't the nerve to ask to borrow it again.

Colin jogged to the canteen for breakfast; he saw Athena striding away from the swimming pool entrance as he entered. He turned back to speak to her, toying with the idea of asking her to join him. Although he convinced himself she spotted him, Athena turned her head and walked away. She looked to have things on her mind.

After eating his full English breakfast alone, Colin returned to his quarters. He double-checked the contents of his rucksack and satisfied himself that it contained everything he needed. He looked at his wristwatch, still only half-past seven. Transport wasn't due for another hour. He searched his laptop to see what he could discover about the threat levels of 'moderate' and 'severe'. He wanted to learn why moving to a higher level had become necessary. Then he might be able to participate in the Olympus Project's more significant assignments. Now he felt like an odd job man, getting rid of minor irritations. The preservation of the nation's safety was restricted to agents several steps further up the ladder than he appeared. He wondered when he would find his way off the bottom.

Colin's search gave him food for thought. He hadn't realised a step existed between 'moderate' and 'severe'.

"Blimey, it must have been something big to jump past 'substantial' and straight to severe," he exclaimed. "Thank goodness it hasn't reached the 'critical' stage yet."

He learned the situation had moved from 'possible but not likely' to 'highly likely' in a heartbeat. The intelligence surrounding these people must have flagged up a suicide bomb plot. Either that or something of the same magnitude had moved forward far quicker than expected. People might think with the Games opening next July, factions planning to make the world sit up and take notice were still months from following through on their plans. Instead, events could escalate into a significant problem in weeks, if not days. No wonder it had Erebus and the others so preoccupied.

Before he knew it, the clock had ticked around to half-past eight. The minicab waited outside the old stable block. He collected his gear and jumped in beside his driver.

"Here we go again then, Phoenix."

"Same old, same old. A few days of fresh country air. What could be nicer?" Phoenix replied.

Colin got out of the cab when they pulled up outside

Bath Spa station, bought his ticket, and waited for the Plymouth train. Once on board, he knew a three-hour trip via Temple Meads in Bristol lay ahead. Colin bought a newspaper to give him something to do and help ward off fellow passengers who had the urge to engage him in conversation. He managed that with ease, as his carriage was only half full.

When he arrived, the number of platforms at the station gave him a big surprise. He always thought Devon and Cornwall contained quaint, picturesque villages with roses around the door. Colin hadn't expected a city. At least he was relieved when he got outside the station that a five-minute walk took him to the town centre.

Colin found a pub that looked as if it served a good pint and a pie. He stayed there an hour, discovering that it was far better than that. Colin was in no rush to go outside. It was a miserable, wet and windy day. It was typical for an autumn day in that part of the world. Colin had checked the weather forecast and knew he could expect this throughout the weekend, and overnight temperatures would drop to freezing.

Once you considered everything, conditions were perfect.

At just after half-past two, Colin set out towards Plympton. He then headed for the southwest corner of the national park and Shaugh Prior village. He wanted to get half of the journey to Princeton done tonight. Signposts highlighted the walking route most of the way. When it got too dark to use his map and compass, his torch would help him stay on the right track.

The weather helped keep most dog walkers home, and the minor roads contained little traffic. However, if a vehicle headed towards him, Colin ducked under the shelter of the roadside trees when he spotted their headlights.

At last, he arrived at the tiny village and went into the fields behind the old church. Colin found a sheltered spot and erected his one-person tent. The training sessions he had endured with Rusty and his colleagues were now paying dividends. The former SAS men had schooled him in living rough for long periods. If necessary, Colin could have waited until next weekend for Sir Godfrey to arrive. He knew how to hole up in the woods with nobody knowing he was there, except for the small animals he would need to kill to sustain himself.

Colin was happy knowing he would meet up with his target tomorrow. He had brought enough tinned grub and a spirit burner and stand to cook up a meal tonight and in the morning. A few bars of chocolate would keep hunger at bay while he waited for the opportunity to dispense with Sir Godfrey during the day tomorrow.

He survived both cooking with alcohol and a night in the tent. It was not without a disturbed sleep, though, as a fox paid a brief visit to the newcomer to the neighbourhood.

Before dawn broke in the morning, he packed away his kit. He tidied the ground where he had pitched his tent. Then he set off to walk the eight miles to Princeton. Colin stuck to the tracks and minor roads at the start, as there wasn't much chance of any early traffic. He set out across the country as he got closer to the village.

Colin took a pair of field glasses from his rucksack and scanned the surrounding scene. North Hessary Tor lay to his left. The prison was straight in front of him. He hurried on with his search; he didn't want to overthink that place.

He made out the small cluster of buildings that included Sir Godfrey's weekend retreat to his right.

He crossed the rough terrain towards the village. As he peered through the glasses again, he spotted the Range Rover outside the cottage. There was no sign of anyone being up yet. He rechecked his wristwatch. It was half-past nine, so it seemed Sir Godfrey was having a lie-in.

Colin spotted movement outside the cottage. He recognised his target. He wore a familiar brand waxed jacket, faded red cord trousers, and a flat cap. Sir Godfrey threw a large blanket and a holdall into the back of the vehicle and carefully placed a sizeable wicker hamper in the passenger seat. With a glance left and right to see if his near neighbours were watching him, he jumped into the driver's seat and sped away.

Colin watched as the Range Rover headed towards Tor Royal Lane, and he set off on foot in the same direction. Colin's map showed that moorland surrounded the village. Several footpaths across the moor passed through the village, including one leading west to Sampford Spiney and one leading south to Nun's Cross and Erme Head.

Tor Royal Lane appeared to lead from the village to a disused tin mine two miles southeast. If Penrose headed there, it would take Colin thirty minutes at least to catch up with him. He tried not to think what the old sod might get up to while he trudged across the moor. Colin looked again at his map and scanned the surrounding fields for signs of life. Right across the moorlands, he saw splashes of colour.

"Anoraks," he whispered, not being derogatory. They *were* anoraks, highly coloured ones, with boys and girls aged fourteen to nineteen inside them. They were walking from the National Park Visitor Centre. An activity hub based where an old hotel once stood.

"What is he doing?" thought Colin. A look at the map showed that the Fox Tor Mires were further on from the tin mine. He had read somewhere this sometimes boggy region was the basis of the Grimpen Mire in that story about Sherlock Holmes. A load of tosh, though, according to the picture they had put in the book he read. That showed a herd of sheep grazing slap bang in the middle of it without a care. So there wasn't much chance of the Mires swallowing up Sir Godfrey.

The distance between the walker and the Range Rover closed. Colin spotted the open rear door. He worked out Sir Godfrey's intentions as he continued his steady yomp across the wet moorland.

"The crafty bastard is posing as a volunteer. In an hour, the first bunch of kids will arrive near the Mires, and they still have around an hour's walking, probably longer because they'll be exhausted. That hamper has lots of food and hot drinks; I'll bet. The blanket in the back will be there to give them a comfortable, dry place to rest up for a while if they're struggling. Sir Godfrey will be the perfect host for groups of two or three as they stumble across his unscheduled pit stop. The ones in danger are the poor souls detached from the group who soldier on alone. The first sign of a blister or a touch of cramp, and he'll have them in the back of the Range Rover. Penrose could take them somewhere they don't want to go. What did he have in that holdall he threw in the back with the blanket? Shit. It doesn't bear thinking about."

With the weather closing in, Colin got as near as he dared. There wasn't much cover out there. At least the kit he selected on the advice of Rusty gave him as much camouflage as possible. He baulked at wearing the hat that looked like a clump of earth. That might be fine in the movies, but walking along the side of a B-road, he would stick out like a sore thumb.

Colin was prone now as he watched the scene unfold through his glasses. Here they come. Penrose sat on the tailgate of the Range Rover holding a thermos flask up high in his left hand. Three kids stop to chat. Others walk past. Good for you, keep going, he thought. The pattern continued. Colin had four squares of his chocolate to keep him going. It was freezing and wet, but he knew he had to keep watching and waiting. The anoraks thinned out, and the gaps between them got longer and longer. It won't be long now.

Three or four minutes after a group of boys had set off again towards the Visitor Centre, warmed with a cup of coffee or tea, a single red anorak appeared across the bleak stretch of moorland. Colin saw a girl of about fifteen, blonde hair plastered to her head with the rain. She was limping.

Sir Godfrey hurried towards her. He swept her off her feet with one arm around her shoulders and the other under her legs. Colin watched as Penrose lowered the girl onto the blanket by the Range Rover. She was too tired to sense danger. At first, Colin thought Sir Godfrey would drive off straight away, but he leant into the back and started touching the young girl.

Colin looked in both directions. There were no anoraks in sight. His only chance was to get up and start running. His field glasses bounced on his chest, and the rucksack hit his back with every step. He soon covered the distance between his hiding place and the Range Rover. The girl lay on her back with her anorak on the ground beneath her. Sir Godfrey was talking to her in a soothing tone: -

"Jessica," he said, "I'm just going to loosen your clothing. I'm worried your core body temperature is low. You may be suffering from exposure. I recommend we get you warmed up with a brisk massage."

Sir Godfrey jumped when he heard Colin scrambling on the wet grass and loose stones. He found it difficult to stop once he reached the vehicle.

"What the hell?" Godfrey began, but Colin held him by the front of his coat. It was no contest. The younger man overpowered him in seconds. Colin would have liked to brain him there and then. There were enough small rocks on hand to do the job. The man's red face beneath him and the heavy breathing he heard when he leant over the defenceless girl was evidence enough for Colin. There was no first aid coming her way. Sir Godfrey planned to rape her.

Colin bundled Penrose into the passenger seat of the Range Rover. Twisting his arms above his head, Colin handcuffed him to the headrest. He wasn't going anywhere. Sir Godfrey cursed and swore, telling Colin what would happen to him when his friend, the Lord Lieutenant, heard of this outrage. Colin had heard enough. He grabbed a roll of duct tape from the rucksack, and once he tore off a strip and wrapped it around the predator's mouth, silence reigned.

In the back of the vehicle, Jessica was confused and semi-conscious. Colin realised she didn't have a clue what had happened. He found a flask in the hamper with plenty of tea to spare. He poured her a cup and added three lumps of sugar. Penrose came well prepared. Colin eased Jessica out of the Range Rover and gathered up the blanket. He wrapped it around her shoulders and encouraged her to finish the warm drink.

Colin looked across the moorland behind the vehicle

and spotted more dots of colour two hundred yards away. He left Jessica the flask and food. He pointed towards the approaching youngsters.

"Your mates will be along in a minute," he said. "They'll get you back to the Visitor Centre."

"Where are you going?" she asked. "What happened to the other man?"

"He had a nasty turn," said Colin, "so I'm rushing him off to get medical attention."

"Okay," the young girl said. "I hope he's OK. He was so keen to help. I felt faint and so cold. I must have gone for a minute or two." Jessica nodded at the cup she cradled in both hands. She smiled up at him and said, "Thanks for this."

Colin squeezed her shoulder; he didn't tell her what a lucky escape she'd had. He fished a pair of gloves out of his pocket. After Colin slipped them on, he closed the rear door and climbed into the driver's seat of the Range Rover. He found the keys in Sir Godfrey's jacket. Penrose started writhing around, trying to get free. Colin thumped him hard in the stomach and told him to stop wasting his time.

Once they got underway, he started to re-evaluate his plans. He was doing things off-the-cuff today, and that wasn't the norm. The map showed the disused tin mine on the route the walkers may be taking. To hide there was out of the question, so Colin drove towards Tor Royal Lane. He had about two hours' daylight left. Sir Godfrey was a frequent visitor to Princeton. The Range Rover was unlikely to attract much attention parked outside his own house, but it was too risky to take him back there just yet.

The surveillance team hadn't found evidence of Sir Godfrey forming many social contacts in the region, apart from the Lord Lieutenant and possibly a few other notables.

They were the acquaintances a creep like Penrose was prone to attach himself. Colin doubted if the ordinary man in the street would blink if the Range Rover parked up somewhere off the beaten track in the countryside. There were a few unnamed roads and trails within a five-minute drive towards Two Bridges. Colin headed off to find a suitable hiding place until it got dark. He needed a quiet spot that gave him a chance to put the finishing touches on his new plan for Sir Godfrey.

The rain continued to fall. The dark clouds heralding the night almost touched the roof of the farm buildings in the distance. Colin sat huddled up in the driver's seat while Sir Godfrey Penrose huffed and puffed next to him. Time to move.

Colin took the minor road back through Princeton's scattered communities and edged the Range Rover into its parking place outside the cottage. He killed the lights as he approached. He wanted to keep his arrival a secret from a neighbour poking a nose through a window in a nearby property — the last thing they did before drawing the curtains and preparing for a long autumn evening.

Colin looked at the keyring in the ignition and found half a dozen other keys on the chain. It was his lucky day. He got out, flicked through the options, picked one and opened the front door. As he returned to the passenger door, he stared hard at Sir Godfrey; a pair of beady frightened eyes stared back.

"We're going inside now, Penrose. So don't cause me any grief."

Colin grabbed the holdall from the back of the vehicle and then released his prisoner from the headrest. He bundled him through the front door of the cottage. With a glance to check no one had seen them, he closed the door behind them.

"Right, let's get you sorted," he said. Sir Godfrey was uncomfortable due to the length of time and how Phoenix had handcuffed him. Parts of him were numb; others had life coming back to them. One piece needed emptying. Overall, he wasn't a happy bunny. Colin showed him no sympathy.

He dragged Sir Godfrey upstairs into a bedroom and shoved him onto the bed. Colin retrieved the handcuffs from his coat pocket, and his prisoner found himself firmly secured.

"This place must look as if it's shut up tight for the night," said Colin. "So you'll lie there while I'm working.

Sir Godfrey mumbled something, but the duct tape made it incomprehensible. Colin didn't listen as he drew curtains, switched on a light or two and wondered what was on the TV. Colin channel-hopped for two minutes, but nothing took his fancy. He spotted a CD player and a collection of classical albums. After a few minutes, Colin found a copy of Vivaldi's 'Four Seasons' among them and started it playing. It wasn't Iron Maiden or Judas Priest, but it would do.

Colin wandered around the cottage, peering into drawers and cupboards. He had no specific reason for this search; he was just nosy. Colin didn't expect to discover anything to further incriminate Sir Godfrey here in Devon. The surveillance boys hadn't found evidence on his phones or computers to suggest he was into pornography via a digital medium. Penrose was a 'hands-on' person, pure and simple, but with little emphasis on the pure.

When he got fed up with mooching around the cottage,

he opened the holdall he had left in the hallway when they entered the cottage. Inside was a camera, several lengths of rope, a phial of something or other, and a cloth. He unearthed a packet of condoms and a packet of wet wipes. Colin stopped rummaging; he had seen enough. Sir Godfrey had intended to take his time with this victim. Chloroform or something similar had been in the phial he planned to use to knock out Jessica. Sir Godfrey needed her out long enough to find a remote spot. Somewhere he could do what he liked with her and then take pictures of the poor girl.

Colin returned to the bedroom and looked in on Sir Godfrey. He had wet himself. Colin shook his head and tutted.

"Oh, dear," he said. "I suppose I'd better get on with it; there's no sense keeping you waiting any longer. You have abused young people since your early days in the Territorial Army. Young Jessica, today was fortunate that I stopped you from adding another victim to the list. We may never know how many others you abused between the TA and today. It might amuse you to learn we uncovered your secret by accident. When you worked for Defence Personnel, Welfare and Veterans, you didn't defend the moral obligation this country owes its service personnel when they finish active duty. You left veterans to struggle, mentally and financially, on your watch while you lived in luxury. My superiors felt the proper punishment was required. To have the best evidence available, they dug deeper. As soon as they discovered the truth, they took statements from the men and women you molested. My superiors agreed it was impossible to settle your account. Closing it was the only option."

As Colin spoke, Sir Godfrey's eyes grew wider and wider as he realised just how much this man knew. Who were his superiors? What statements were these? Account closed? These thoughts crowded into his head as he grasped the seriousness of his situation. He crawled away from Colin until he hugged the headboard. It was a vain attempt to escape from the devil standing at the foot of his bed.

"We're taking a trip," said Colin.

He left Sir Godfrey and walked downstairs to the lounge. He emptied his rucksack onto the carpet and replaced the items. Colin checked those items he needed close to hand lay at the top. Then, Colin resumed his search of the cottage to see things lying around that belonged to Penrose. When the police inevitably found his body, the fewer unexplained items, the better.

In the spare bedroom, he found what he wanted. Sir Godfrey didn't entertain overnight guests, it appeared. The bed lay unmade, piled up with clutter. The floor space held several unopened cardboard boxes that looked untouched since moving here. Colin collected a tent, a groundsheet, a lamp, a propane cooking stove, matches, paper plates, and plastic cutlery. When he returned to the kitchen, he found cans, a tin opener, and a mug. He put a few teaspoons of coffee granules into a ziplock bag and ripped a trash bag off a roll he found in a cupboard.

Colin reviewed what he had gathered. He thought it enough to convince people that Sir Godfrey only intended to spend one night in the great outdoors and expected to be home by the following evening. Moreover, it fitted with the usual itinerary that saw him scuttling back to London on the train on Monday in time for his first board meeting on Tuesday.

As he passed the bathroom on his way to add his haul to his rucksack, he put his head around the door. Perfect. Penrose brought a wash bag from London for his face flannel, soap, toothbrush, toothpaste, razor, and shaving gel. Just a couple more things to find, and he would have everything he needed.

Colin located the drinks cabinet and selected a bottle of a ten-year-old malt. The fridge had an almost empty container of milk. He emptied the last few dregs, rinsed it out, and then filled it with drinking water from the tap. Once he had loaded everything into the Range Rover, they could get going.

Colin turned off the downstairs lights. His first job was to move the rucksack, the equipment, and the holdall into the Range Rover. The holdall now held other odds and ends, such as bottled water, whiskey, and a wash bag to reduce the items he needed to carry. There was no movement within a few hundred yards on either side of the cottage.

Colin returned upstairs, released Sir Godfrey, and led him downstairs. With a quick check before he stepped out of the doorway, he pushed the predator into the cold night air. Once Colin tethered him to the headrest again, he returned indoors. He tidied the bedclothes upstairs, switched off the lights, and turned off the CD player. Just as he made to leave, he remembered to return the CD to its case and replace it on the pile where he had found it.

The door closed behind him. Neither man was going to return to the cottage, so Colin double-checked it was securely locked. Then, in the darkness, Colin drove away from the cottage. When he got far away from the group of houses, he switched on his headlights and headed towards Tor Royal Lane. Fifteen minutes later, Colin turned off the lane onto one of the many unnamed roads on the moors and drove alongside Crazy Well Pool. He left Sir Godfrey in the Range Rover and carried the equipment into the field. It was only a two-minute walk.

Colin got the lamp going, erected the tent and stacked the provisions at the rear, covering the lot with the groundsheet. He got the whisky bottle out of the holdall and placed it on the ground by the tent flap, stowing the trash bag underneath it ready for later — time to invite Sir Godfrey to join him.

Penrose stumbled and nearly fell several times as Colin dragged him across the rough ground. He whimpered, with no idea what was in store for him. Colin thought this was how his victims felt over the years. Now it was his turn. Colin shivered. It was not because of his thoughts but because the temperature had dropped.

Colin removed the handcuffs and put them in his pocket for the time being. He ordered Sir Godfrey to remove his clothing. Colin thumped him hard in his flabby stomach when the older man shook his head and mumbled something behind the duct tape. Penrose crumpled and collapsed to his knees.

"Do it," said Colin. "You're going for a swim."

He kept a close watch as his prisoner undressed. In the rucksack, Colin had stashed a coiled length of rope and a flashlight at the top. He removed these two items, and when Sir Godfrey was naked, he tied the rope tightly around his wrists. With the flashlight clipped onto his jacket, leaving his hands free, Colin led Sir Godfrey across the grass to Crazy Well Pool and pushed him into the water. Then he walked along the poolside dragging him through the water. His captive found it impossible to alter his predicament with his arms tied and stretched out in front of him. He was dragged through the freezing water for what must have seemed hours but was only minutes.

Colin knew what was happening to Penrose. His physical condition was weak, his skin blue and puffy *before* he entered the water. He showed symptoms of cold shock, breathing rapidly through the nose, and inhaling water every time his head ducked under the surface. His blood pressure increased, and the massive strain on his heart would finish him. The time had come for the next stage of the plan.

Colin turned around and started back towards where he had pitched the tent. Sir Godfrey floundered in the shallow waters at the edge and struggled to stand. He crawled through the grass behind Colin; Godfrey's legs refused to work. His body was shutting down. Colin unscrewed the top of the whisky bottle.

"Fancy a drink?" asked Colin.

Penrose lay in a heap two yards in front of him. He wasn't going anywhere. He trembled violently. Colin gathered his captive's clothes and stuffed them into the trash bag. He put the container on the groundsheet with the rest of the things at the back of the tent. He dragged Sir Godfrey into the tent. It was a tight squeeze for a one-person tent, but Colin didn't plan on staying the night. After ripping the duct tape from his captive's face, he returned for the whisky bottle and poured the spirits into his throat, past his chattering teeth. Time and again, Sir Godfrey gagged, and Colin waited until he could continue to pour each time. When the bottle was empty, he laid it on the ground by Penrose. He removed the rope and, leaving the tent flap open to the elements, backed out of the tent and gathered up his things.

He looked inside the tent and saw that Sir Godfrey no longer shivered. His core temperature was dropping fast. The shock of the water, the alcohol, and the prospect of spending the night naked added to one thing. Penelope Penrose would spend her weekends in Stowmarket alone in the years to come.

Colin waited until midnight. Inside the tent, nothing stirred. He left the lamp lit. It might survive until tomorrow, but it didn't matter if it didn't. The Range Rover was parked up by the side of the road and securely locked. The keys now sat in Sir Godfrey's jacket pocket. The rest of his clothes were in the trash bag. Colin lifted his rucksack onto his back and set off cross-country towards Shaugh Prior. He had to travel eight miles at night due south. Colin thought he might get his tent pitched and sleep for a couple of hours. There was no chance of a lie-in. He had to make that return leg from Shaugh Prior to Plymouth early in the morning. No rest for the wicked.

It was noon, and Colin travelled to Bath Spa, looking forward to a hot shower, a decent meal and a few hours of sleep this afternoon. Instead, he skimmed through the newspaper he bought on the platform while he waited for his train. There were pages of coverage on potential strikes by terrorists on mainland UK; airports and government buildings were taking extra security precautions. Across the pond, Wall Street was due to be occupied by people protesting about the financial crisis. Colin knew Sir Godfrey Penrose was unlikely to feature in the press. Far too early for that.

Colin had trudged on through the night, finding his way at last to Shaugh Prior. His timing was accurate; he settled for his nap well before four o'clock. Colin awoke by seven and packed everything away. It was freezing, and his fingers were slower to respond to what he asked of them than usual. Nevertheless, Colin soon got warm as he walked and jogged back towards Plymouth. He got to the station not long after half-past ten. Fifteen minutes later, he stowed away his rucksack and found a seat on a train that carried him back to the Roman city by two o'clock at the latest.

There was little change from the previous night in the countryside near Crazy Well Pool. The lamp expired just before dawn. It was as light as it would get today, with the thick cloud and drizzle that hung over the moorland. No vehicles were on the unnamed road this morning, nor were any hikers or anoraked youngsters on organised walks.

Chapter Eight

Colin had phoned ahead for transport and fallen asleep in the minicab on the trip back to Larcombe Manor. The driver elbowed him awake as they drew up outside the stable block.

"There you go, Phoenix," he said. "I should sleep for a few hours, mate. Nobody in the big house will bother you today. The balloon's ready to go up, and everyone's involved in meetings."

"Thanks," said Colin. He dropped his rucksack inside the door of his quarters and crashed out on his bed. It was nine o'clock before he awoke, and he headed to the canteen for a meal. Several other people were around, and the general chit-chat concerned where and when this inevitable strike would hit. Colin gathered that London was the odds-on favourite, not that anyone kept a book.

By ten o'clock, Colin was ready to get back to his bed. The exercise in the West Country had exhausted him. He unpacked the rucksack and sorted the things he had taken with him, ready to drop them back to the store's staff in the morning. And so, to bed, as someone said.

In Milton Keynes, three young men rested. They had been awake since five o'clock. It was essential to have a morning routine. Prayers, supplications, and reading from the Quran came before a hearty, healthy breakfast. They were well-trained. Eighteen months ago, they travelled to Pakistan, studying alongside Al Qaeda and making homemade explosives. Each member recorded martyrdom videos during their stay to be released after their deaths.

Arshad, Irfan, and Karim were born in Britain. They were the chosen ones. They had volunteered to strap on an explosive rucksack and detonate it in a crowded place.

Everything was ready; all they had to do now was wait for the text message that identified their target.

The streets surrounding the maisonette contained other little boxes with smart new cars on the forecourt. Their occupants went about their business without knowing the plans Arshad, Irfan, and Karim discussed just a few yards away.

Many miles away, Erebus chaired another Olympus meeting at Larcombe. Athena sat on his right-hand side, head forward, contemplating the tabletop. Thanatos, Alastor, and Minos sat on Erebus's left and waited anxiously for their leader to tell them the latest information from the surveillance section.

Colin Bailey swam length after length in the pool alongside Rusty. Neither man was aware of the other. Both knew Larcombe Manor was as quiet as it had ever been. Everyone on site held their breath as they waited for news.

Was it possible for the surveillance section to track the whereabouts of the cell before the secret services? Could one or the other find the bombers and capture them before they left their hiding place and set out for their target? Or did another scene of devastation and misery lie in store, as there had been in July 2005?

Erebus studied the information in front of him. He pursed his lips and thought for a moment. Then he spoke.

"We have traced internet traffic between Pakistan and the UK that may prove useful. Various messages were passed to addresses in Birmingham and Leicester. If we combine this with mobile phone traffic between Birmingham, Leicester, and Milton Keynes over the past twenty days, we may have found several links in the chain. We might have the most vital link, which is the one that leads to the bombers themselves. On the other hand, they may not have included the hit squad in the messaging loop yet. We may only get one chance to catch that message giving them the go-ahead."

"Do we have people on the streets watching these addresses?" asked Athena.

"We do," Erebus replied, "and we are alone. The security services haven't traced these links yet. So, we won't be treading on anyone's toes. We can't go into the three properties we have identified with guns blazing without revealing our hand. We must try to take out the bomber or bombers and leave sufficient evidence at the property that a trained monkey could trace it back to the hubs."

Thanatos leant forward in his chair.

"How much do we know about the property in Milton Keynes?" he asked.

"I think that's the one to concentrate on for now," said Erebus. "It's more likely that the other two cities have the more senior cell members, and that's why the direct traffic is arriving there. The property in question is a two-bedroomed maisonette owned by a shop owner in the centre of town, and he rents out this place to college students."

"How many students occupy this maisonette at present?" Alastor asked. "Have we identified them yet?

"The stakeout team has seen four or five different people entering and leaving the house; they were around twenty years of age," answered Erebus. "We don't have a complete history of them."

"We should step up our efforts to confirm the Milton Keynes house as the bomber's bolt hole," said Athena. "Then we should move in and dispose of them before they can do any damage."

"Agreed," said Erebus. "In the meantime, we will put the surveillance section on red alert. Any message between the known suspects might be the instruction to start the mission. Our man on the inside may be in danger. We haven't heard from him for a while. If we miss them getting a green light, we'll be chasing shadows and risk being too late to stop them. If there's nothing else, I need to get Phoenix to come over to the house to debrief his Devon assignment. I have complete confidence it passed off without a hitch, but there has been no news yet on the demise of any prominent former politician."

As the others stood up and prepared to leave, Erebus called Athena back to him.

"Are you travelling up to London this week?"

"My parents are back from the South of France on Wednesday. My father has concerns about my mother's health. I want to be with them after they return from her Harley Street appointment on Thursday."

"That's understandable, my dear; go with my blessing."

Colin received a call at five to eleven. Erebus wanted to meet him in the orangery on the hour. Colin trotted to the building and found Erebus sitting in a chair, deep in thought. Colin sat beside him and waited for Erebus to speak.

"A successful trip, Phoenix?"

"Without a doubt," replied Colin.

"Good. What do we need to do next?"

"The body will be discovered in time. Marks found on the body at the post-mortem will show his wrists were secured before he died. He will also have bruises on the midriff and other bumps and scratches received while in the water. I left damaging material that I discovered in a holdall for the police to follow up on, and there should be enough clues for them to uncover his murky history."

"We can help with that. I'll make sure the police receive a tip-off from a concerned member of the public that Sir Godfrey interfered with young people. There's a big enough witch-hunt for crimes of that nature committed decades ago, as we know. They can't afford to leave it off the list. A preference for rough sex might explain the bruising; a word in the right ear will handle that. Well done, Phoenix. Onwards and upwards."

"Scotland?" asked Colin.

"Correct," said Erebus, "but not before the weekend. I have another task for you between now and then. Athena is travelling to London to spend time with her family. I want you to run surveillance on her while she's in Belgravia. For God's sake, don't let her know we're watching her. I'm concerned for her. The imminent terrorist attack is too close to home for her, having lost her partner the way she did. I fear she may try to exact revenge. The Olympus Project can't allow her to endanger our secret organisation with a vigilante attack on any cell members she identifies. As my designated successor, we must do everything to avoid losing her.

"I understand," said Colin, wondering what clothing he needed to wear in Belgravia. He wasn't sure he had the right stuff hanging in his wardrobe.

"A dossier on Donald MacDonald to look through will be available when you return to your quarters. Everything you will need is in there. I'll also get you more cash to cover your expenses while in London. I'd give you the name of a good tailor, but we haven't got time for something 'made to measure'. Just try not to stick out like a sore thumb, won't you, old chap? The details of Athena's trip will be with you later today."

Erebus signalled the meeting had ended by getting up and walking out. Colin returned to his quarters. Sure enough, the promised dossier had arrived. Colin lay on his bed and read through it.

He glossed over the preliminary stuff of which he was already aware. The surveillance team and an agent on the spot had added a few interesting items in the past week. Donald MacDonald's internet connection mysteriously failed, and he contacted his service provider. An Olympus agent arrived and sorted the 'problem' within half an hour. While at the property, he downloaded a copy of everything on the crafty copper's computer. He noted that the invalid father no longer lived on the premises.

Larcombe had evaluated several possible scenarios to explain the engineer's arrival from the genuine internet provider, but sometimes you get lucky. The policeman suddenly left the house for an hour or two after the bogus repair guy left. The genuine engineer arrived and found nobody in; he left a card. When Donald returned, he threw it in the bin, thinking a second van must have turned up by mistake. The policeman was none the wiser.

The computer 'techie' who conducted a forensic analysis of the policeman's hard drive found around fifteen hundred images of girls, plus one hundred hours of video footage. Ninety-five per cent of the photos depicted girls under fourteen. Over four hundred images fell into Category A, the most severe category. The analysis also showed elements of the video footage had been watched the evening before being retrieved.

Colin knew that if this evidence found its way into the hands of the Fife Constabulary, Donald MacDonald might only be banged up for months and made to sign the Register. However, that would never be enough to stop him from re-offending. Direct action was essential to save any younger women in Dunfermline targeted by this pervert. So he formulated the best exit strategy for his next target.

It only took Colin an hour to put the details into his laptop. He printed off the itinerary to pass to Erebus for approval and sent an equipment list to the stores for collection on Friday. This babysitting duty in Belgravia with Athena would be over by Thursday night. Erebus wanted her back in the fold at Larcombe by then.

Colin lay on his bed thinking of Athena and keeping a close watch on her for a few days.

"It's a dirty job," he thought, "but someone has to do it."

His thoughts drifted to the morning when they swam in the pool together.

"This isn't doing me any favours," he muttered. "I'd better get off this bed and either take a cold shower or maybe go to the pool and cool off for an hour."

Colin spent the next few hours exercising; first, in the

gym, then in the pool. He ate a light lunch and returned to his quarters. The promised cash had arrived, and his e-mail inbox included a positive response from the stores. Everything he needed would be ready on Friday. Sketchy details of Athena's trip were also there. He might need to be adaptable. It would be okay if she stuck close to her parents most of the time. If she went off-piste, he might have a problem.

Colin delivered the proposed itinerary for the Dunfermline job to Erebus in the main building.

"Ingenious, dear boy," he chuckled. "That shouldn't raise too many suspicions. Well done. Good hunting at the weekend. It's a long trip, so if you get home late from London, you can sleep on the train on Friday morning."

Colin was leaving when Erebus added: -

"Try to remember what this London job is about, won't you, Phoenix? The bright lights of London and the beautiful people it attracts can be beguiling. You must be on your guard throughout; there must be no, shall we say, distractions?"

"No problem," said Colin. "I'll be on my best behaviour."

He had barely made it through the door and was closing it behind him when he heard Erebus say,

"Ah, but will she, dear boy? Will she?"

Meanwhile, in deepest Devon, it was Tuesday afternoon. The lousy weather of the weekend had cleared, and a worker from a nearby farm passed the Range Rover for the fourth time. Alarm bells rang, and not just in a literal sense.

Later that afternoon, the local newspaper carried a brief statement in its website's 'Latest' column.

'The naked body of a man, believed to be in his seventies, was discovered in a tent near Crazy Well Pool, Princeton, earlier this afternoon. Clothing and other camping equipment had been laid at the rear of the tent. Police are not seeking anyone else in connection with this incident. Police have informed his next-of-kin. More news in our next update.'

A copy of the extract arrived from the surveillance section. Colin asked them to pass the information on to Erebus and ensure the boss saw future updates. He explained that he would be absent for the next seventy-two hours. Maybe Erebus needn't feed the police any misinformation on Sir Godfrey. Better safe than sorry; the subsequent updates might differ if the police can't find plausible answers to their questions.

Colin trawled through his wardrobe and found a few things that fitted the bill. With no luck, he asked the others in the stable block to see if they had items to spare. He discovered that the 'dressing up' box wasn't much use for this job either. Most agents had to blend in with the lowlifes of the world, not rub shoulders with the high rollers.

Phoenix settled for a minimal choice from his shirts and trousers but selected various jackets and coats. He might as well be comfortable and warm on takeout, at least. He wanted to get to London and find a place to stay tonight. To avoid bumping into Athena on the train up to town in the morning. Colin was aware he needed a suitable hotel. Erebus might baulk at paying three hundred quid for two nights, bed-and-breakfast.

Colin Bailey had his comfort zone. He could rough it in a bandwagon or sleep in a field if required. But with the chance to spend time in the 'smoke', Colin needed to stay true to his roots, even if someone else paid for it. He didn't need five-star accommodation. He'd be just as happy to find the closest budget-price hotel to Athena's parent's gaff and use that as his base.

The train arrived at Paddington Station just before a quarter to six that evening. A ten-minute trip took him to Kensington Road, where he found the perfect spot. He soon settled into his forty-nine pounds a night room and felt at home. Well, maybe not at home, but not out of place; that was a start.

The next couple of hours Colin spent on a survey of the Belgravia home and the surrounding district. He didn't stand around in one place too long in case the local neighbourhood watch reported a dishevelled person in the vicinity. A short trip to Harley Street familiarised him with where Athena's mother had to visit for her appointment. He made copious notes on tube and bus timetables, then identified shortcuts that might be helpful. At ten o'clock, he found a pub and drank a beer; then, he found himself drawn towards the Pizza Express. He was powerless to resist. It seemed just the thing to help a man have a good night's sleep—exercise, beer, and a pizza. He slept well and dreamt not of Athena but of a cuddly comedian from Dudley, West Midlands.

Athena endured the commuter-packed journey from Bath to Paddington. She was swept along by the crush of people leaving the platforms, making their way into the dark corners of the earth. She hated this mode of transport; she much preferred the car. Her preference was for something with a throaty growl under the bonnet; open-topped would be even better.

These days, the problem was that London had become a nightmare for a car driver travelling in from the sticks. Congestion zones, bus lanes, and nowhere to park that didn't cost a fortune made this frustratingly tricky. The train and tube had become a necessary evil made more horrid because of her experiences six years ago.

Athena cut herself off from the world, the horns and sirens with white noise through her headphones. Nobody ever looked up or talked to anyone nearby on the underground these days. She prayed she didn't run into a face from her past. This trip was a quick dash to her parents' house. She wanted to wait for them to get home and then give her Mum moral support tomorrow when she faced that worrying appointment with the specialist. As soon as they learned what they were dealing with, she could decide on a plan of action with her father and return to Larcombe Manor.

The next stop was Sloane Square. She had opted for this, as it was handy for her family home. Plus, she could pick up a few things at the shops as she walked to Vincent Gardens. She must get her Mum a bunch of flowers and a bottle of wine for herself. Milk, bread, and a few basics would be sensible too. As her parents had been abroad for a while, Athena doubted the fridge contained much that was still edible. Her list grew as she headed out of the station and set off for home.

Meanwhile, just around the corner from Vincent Gardens, Colin kept watching. Dressed in a chic shirt and sweater combo with dark slacks, he felt like a tailor's dummy, but at least he blended in with the crowd. While sitting in his trendy street café, nursing a cup of hot coffee, Colin was okay. Once he had got his fingers warm and put his fleece jacket back on, he'd brave the elements. It was dry, but boy, it was a chilly morning.

Colin had chosen this spot because it gave him the best view of Athena's home and the adjoining main street without standing on her front doorstep. There was no chance of her slipping by without him spotting her. Just as he thought he should ask for a refill, she appeared.

Seeing Athena stride along the street with her shopping bags reminded Colin of that first day at Larcombe. A ship in full sail, no mistake. Erebus had been right. Other pedestrians scattered before her. Nothing or nobody got in her way. She marched into the side road, skipped up the steps to the bright red door, and, although she fumbled with her keys, she was safe inside in seconds.

"Nine points five from the Swiss judge," said Colin. He finished his coffee, picked up his fleece and made his way to the door of the café. A moving target was the order of the day. He walked further up the street and bought a paper in the newsagents.

He didn't fancy reading it, but the Financial Times provided a helpful screen if Athena reappeared and took a second look at the man wandering along the opposite pavement.

Time drags on a stakeout, Colin discovered. One plus point of being in London was there was always traffic and pedestrians by the hundred, so he never felt exposed. The odds of someone looking out of a window and thinking, 'who *is* that man lurking outside?' were a million to one.

The seventeenth taxi to turn into Vincent Gardens delivered Athena's parents back home. Within seconds of the cab stopping, Athena appeared in the doorway; she hugged her father and helped her mother indoors. Father persuaded the cabbie to lug their heavy suitcases from the taxi to the hallway and then paid him. So Colin thought, judging by the cheery wave the taxi driver gave him as he left, he must have given him a huge tip. Big enough, maybe, to go a long way towards paying for his hernia operation.

After the door had closed on the family Athena, Colin

hoped for a free hour or two. He fancied a bite to eat, and getting inside in the warm again would be a bonus too. Plenty of places existed for people to lunch in the vicinity. It didn't take long to get sorted.

Athena paid close attention to her parents as they told her everything they'd been up to over the past few months. They asked her how she had been and did she still enjoy her job working for the charity. However, Athena was more interested in discovering what was wrong with her mother's health.

"Mummy," she said, "the charity work keeps me very busy, but it's rewarding. We help so many people; I can't tell you. Tell me about the wonderful people you've met this summer. What's up with you? Daddy tells me you've not been well."

Her father sat on the chair's arm by her mother and laid a hand on her shoulder.

"We'll find out more tomorrow when we see Dr Ramanayake. He's a consultant cardiologist, and he's the best. Your mother has coronary artery disease. She had been getting chest pains. She suffered shortness of breath now and then too."

Her mother squeezed her husband's hand and took up the story.

"I had a few dizzy spells and nearly slipped and fell in the shower several mornings. Daddy said it was the champagne cocktails. There was nothing for it; we had to see a doctor in Monte Carlo. The silly man told me to stop smoking, change my diet, and exercise. Darling, if I have to take Zumba or Pilates classes, you might as well kill me now."

Athena asked what they thought Dr Ramanayake would suggest was needed.

"If making '*minor*' lifestyle changes," her mother said,

throwing her hands up in mock horror, "isn't enough to manage my heart disease, I'll need medication to help my heart work more efficiently. Then, in due course, I'll have bypass surgery. The surgery isn't a cure, but it should be manageable if I make the lifestyle adjustments they're referring to."

Athena hugged her mother, and both women shed a tear. However, open displays of affection and emotion were rare occurrences. Athena recalled only a handful of occasions when her mother had held her close. When a grandparent had died or the first time she went away to school, she was hugged, but other than that, they were scarce.

Inside the house, the family continued to talk and bond. Outside, Colin Bailey maintained his vigil, replenished after his lunch break. The evening drew closer, and lights were coming on around him. Yet, he had to stay vigilant. Were Athena and her folks dining at home, or were they going to a restaurant?

Colin tried to imagine Athena in the kitchen. He attempted to conjure up a scene of domestic bliss behind that bright red door but failed. They had to be coming out later. Colin was sure of that. He could not go off duty until they arrived home again and tucked up in bed for the night.

Sure enough, a taxi arrived just before eight. The three Foxes would soon disappear somewhere expensive; Colin decided to set off towards Knightsbridge. Okay, he didn't have a clue where they might go. But he knew it wasn't a drive-through McDonald's. His research had pinpointed the general areas they could get the quality of cuisine they preferred. There was nothing else for it. He picked one of his shortcuts and prayed they were heading towards Brompton Road. It was a quick trip to the Danish Embassy and up Hans Road. He jogged most of the way, arriving less than twelve minutes later.

Colin allowed the time it took for the three of them to exit the house, get into the cab, and then negotiate the evening traffic. He would miss them by minutes, and they could be half a mile away in either direction. Colin was breathing hard and looking left and right at the old A4. A taxi was coming from a road across the street from where he stood.

"Got you," he exclaimed, checking the number against the one he'd scribbled on the top of the FT.

They had chosen to dine at Montpeliano's, one of the best restaurants in London. This was typical Athena; Colin remembered the quality of those first meals at Larcombe Manor before he'd moved to his actual quarters in the stable block. She and her family were a class act.

He couldn't risk getting too close, but there were dozens of places of interest to occupy him for an hour or two. He enjoyed a quiet drink, a snack, and a read of the newspaper, and then he strolled to a spot opposite the restaurant on Montpelier Street. It was half-past ten before he knew it.

The door opened under the blue canopy, and a group emerged from the busy restaurant. A taxi pulled forward from twenty yards further along the street and stopped to collect them. Colin started towards the main road. As he turned the corner and pressed himself against the building in the shadows, the taxi passed him. He recognised Athena's father sitting facing the back of the cab.

"Time for me to clock off and have a good night's sleep," said Colin as he trotted back to their family home, retracing his earlier steps. The taxi had dropped them off and disappeared when he got to Vincent Gardens. Lights shone both upstairs and downstairs. The people in his care were safe until the morning.

After a healthy, rather than a hearty breakfast in the morning, Colin packed and got ready to leave the hotel by seven-thirty. As Athena and her parents were due at Harley Street for an eleven o'clock appointment, he left for Paddington. He needed to drop his kit in Left Luggage and return to babysitting duties. There was no guarantee when Athena would return to Larcombe, but Erebus had been adamant she should return today. Unless she elected to travel on the last train, Colin had to be on the next one. The risk of being on the same train was too high.

After the cold snap yesterday, Thursday morning heralded a warmer day, and the sun shone brightly. Colin took up his post at a quarter past eight; the street was quiet, and the red door remained shut.

Colin looked up the street. He saw an electric milk float making its way from delivery to delivery; other than that, nothing. It was odd that such a busy city should experience these occasional moments of calm. Curious and a trifle worrying, Colin thought. He wondered whether it was the calm before the storm.

In Milton Keynes, one of the disposable cell phones buzzed. A text message had arrived.

'Meet me at Oxford Circus. Today 1.30 pm.'

"It is time," said Karim as he read the message.

"Let us read from the Quran," Irfan said, "that we may become worthy martyrs and kill many infidels.

The three young men gathered together and embraced. In just over six hours, their work on earth was over. As Irfan and Karim read, Arshad referred to the train and tube times to have the details to hand for their journey.

At Larcombe Manor, the surveillance team was alerted

by an unusual piece of traffic. They intercepted a direct message from Pakistan to the maisonette in Milton Keynes. There was no intermediary in Birmingham or Leicester on this occasion. They had received the order.

Erebus and the three remaining senior members met briefly to decide what action to take. Erebus ordered an immediate strike on the Milton Keynes address. The agents watching the property were unarmed in case they attracted the police's attention. Several Olympus staff lived within an hour's drive from the maisonette to supply the firepower this sortie needed.

Five armed men, dressed from head to foot in black, burst through the door of the Milton Keynes property. Their role was to take out the three would-be bombers before they left for London. They found the maisonette deserted.

"The birds have flown," the squad's leader reported to Larcombe. "Repeat: the birds have flown."

Erebus had planned his next moves ahead of this possibility. He instructed Brad, the squad leader, to leave the items he had said for Brad to take with him on the raid. Brad was to leave contact numbers and names for the cell members in Birmingham and Leicester. The items were to appear casually left by the bombers, perhaps tucked into a copy of the Quran to highlight a favourite text or in a bedside drawer.

The names and numbers were for the security services to discover to give them the pleasure of cleaning up the remnants of the cell. The squad needed to be careful not to make it look like they had planted the information. MI5 would receive an anonymous tip-off later today, regardless of the outcome in London. Erebus hoped the squad still had time to stop the bombing before someone had to clean up the remnants of the bombers and heaven knows how many innocent people in Oxford Circus.

The squad needed to move on to the next stage once they had completed their task at the maisonette. The men were to change into civilian clothes, carry concealed weapons, and travel to London. Erebus calculated that they should be at the tube station by noon. The squad then had ninety minutes to trace the bombers and neutralise them - without alerting the public, the police, and the security services, not to mention the attackers themselves.

To reinforce the attack squad from Milton Keynes, Erebus ordered Rusty to take two men with him and drive to London.

"I know I can rely on you, Rusty," he said. "It's all-hands-on-deck for this one. Ring Phoenix on this number and add him to your crew. The more eyes and ears we have at Oxford Circus, the better. It will be tough finding three needles in a haystack which has eighty-five million people bustling through it every year."

Rusty and his men headed for the M4 in an unmarked car within thirty minutes. A team of paramedics followed behind at a more sedate pace in the ambulance. Erebus wanted a means of bringing the bombers back to Larcombe alive, if possible. He had to consider a different scenario. If Olympus suffered casualties, he wanted them returned to Larcombe for treatment or burial. No one would be left behind on this mission.

In Belgravia, Colin watched as another taxi arrived to collect Athena and her parents. They had a fifteen-minute journey to make to Harley Street. He could make it there on foot in thirty-five minutes if he pushed it. His mobile phone vibrated in his pocket.

"Who the heck is that?" he wondered. There was no ID on the caller.

"Yes?" he asked.

"Morning, Phoenix. It's me, Rusty. The shit hit the fan, mate. Get over to Oxford Circus tube station at noon. No funny cracks, mate. We'll meet you outside Top Shop on Oxford Street. I'll fill you in then.

"Okay, Rusty," replied Colin. "Athena and her parents will be on their way home to Belgravia by then. So it'll take me less than ten minutes to get to you from Harley Street. See you later, mate."

Irfan, Arshad, and Karim were already on Oxford Street.

The students had left Milton Keynes at just after eight o'clock. First, there was a thirty-five-minute journey to Euston. When they arrived there, they mingled with others at the station who didn't seem to be in a rush to get somewhere. Time was on their side — no one would question three young men dressed in casual western clothes comprising blue jeans, trainers, and the ubiquitous hoodie. Even the rucksacks slung on their backs didn't attract that much attention. They drifted towards the tube line for their next stop, which was Victoria.

The same pattern followed. A casual stroll to visit several shops, just browsing. When Irfan showed up, they went from Warren Street to Oxford Circus. There was plenty to see there, too and hundreds of people with whom to share the experience.

When Colin ended his phone call with Rusty, the three young men left the station and wandered along Oxford Street West. Colin continued to make his way to Harley Street to keep watch. He couldn't help being distracted by thoughts of what lay ahead of him this afternoon.

Chapter Nine

Erebus was pacing up and down in the drawing-room, impatient and nervous. He had nine well-trained men on their way to Oxford Circus station. His paramedics were travelling there too as a backup; what else could he do? Could they prevent a tragedy, or was it possible his people might get caught up in the suicide attack? His mind was in turmoil. Had he made the right decision?

Thanatos watched his boss and reflected on the past couple of hours. Suddenly he thumped the table with his fist. Erebus stopped pacing and turned towards him.

"What is it, Thanatos?" he asked.

"I think we've missed something," Thanatos replied. "The message from Pakistan threw us off the scent."

"Go on," said Erebus, sitting back at the table.

"Well, look at it; it reads 'Meet at Oxford Circus. Today at 1.30 pm.' The bombers are travelling together, so they won't 'meet' each other, will they? That message arrived early this morning from Pakistan, so if a fourth person was meeting them, they couldn't get there in time for lunchtime today. The logical answer is that the fourth person arrived earlier. The Olympus surveillance section needs to track traffic details between the UK and the Pakistani link over the past twenty-four hours. We have to find the original message. It may be coded or in a cryptic form."

Erebus nodded towards Alastor. He left the room straight away to start the hunt.

"When they were watching the maisonette in Milton Keynes, several youngsters were seen coming and going," said Erebus. "We need their details and any photographs we have of them. We must get this information to Rusty's team and the guys travelling in from MK as soon as possible. Time is short."

Thanatos continued to outline his idea.

"The next thing we need to consider is what role additional players fulfil on this mission. We know the young men contacted at the property were the bomb carriers. It's logical to assume the fourth man will detonate the bombs from a remote location. The bombers carry improvised explosive devices with nuts and bolts in rucksacks on their backs. They will have used a cheap cell phone, electrical wire, a fuse, batteries, electrical tape, and a solid-state semiconductor device. This last piece lets you wire into the cell phone speaker. The speakerphone has more power and is a favoured option when assembling an IED such as this. When dialling the phone, it activates the ringer, connecting those two components and kicks off the signal to detonate the explosive. If I'm right, this fourth person could be a short distance away, but they plan to be at Oxford Circus station. It is such a busy thoroughfare and has loads of potential exits. They mean to wait until the bomb carriers are at the ideal points to cause the maximum damage spread across the site. The bombs will trigger at the same time. It will be carnage."

The others listened in silence to Thanatos as he gave his grim predictions of the scenario unfolding one hundred miles away in London. Alastor had returned to the meeting and heard his colleague's gloomy forecast.

"Are we able to shut down the cell service in the vicinity?" he asked.

Erebus shook his head. "Not practical, old chap."

"Why can't we use those jamming devices you used in the military? They might, at least, disrupt the signal to one or two of the phones and lessen the effects," posed Minos.

"We haven't got time to mobilise them," said Thanatos. "If we had rumbled the true meaning of the message earlier, we could have maybe used the lightweight signal jammers we have in stores. But they only have a maximum range of fifteen metres. That's fine for our guys masking mobile traffic out in the field back to us here at HQ, but in this scenario, the agents must be too up close and personal for their safety."

"Hindsight is a wonderful thing," said Erebus. "We must concentrate on finding the bombers and the other possible players. Then, we need to isolate them and neutralise their effectiveness *before* we reach zero hours. Get me photos and identities of the group of people who used the maisonette in MK now. Get the surveillance boys to hack into the CCTV cameras on Oxford Street. I need to find out where these people are so we can inform the on-site teams."

There was a knock on the door. It was one of the surveillance teams.

"Perfect timing," said Erebus. "What have you got for us?"

"We've found the outgoing message, sir; it was too bland

The Olympus Project

to get picked up at first. Then, on Wednesday, it was sent from Leicester and read, 'Tell them we are fine for a late lunch tomorrow as planned'."

Erebus told Alastor to go back to the ice-house with the operator and hunt for the data he required. He turned to Thanatos and Minos.

"I wish Athena were here. As we speak, she's in Harley Street, but I'd be happier knowing Phoenix was watching over her. Instead, he'll abandon that duty and move across to help Rusty and the team."

Thanatos had expected as much; the boss had always been protective of his second in command. He had thought in depth about the outgoing message and its implications.

"That message confirms my suspicions," he said with a sigh. "The other members of the cell will be in the station too. The sooner we learn what they look like and find them, the better. The odds are against us, but while we still have a chance, then we must stay hopeful."

Minos asked whether they should tip off the TFL authorities so they could evacuate the station. Erebus wasn't happy about that course of action as it risked showing their hand, and keeping the Olympus Project under the radar had to be paramount. They discussed the pros and cons of the situation and anguished over them while they waited for news.

Alastor returned to the drawing-room with a folder and a brief smile.

"The people we had watching the maisonette were thorough. We have excellent photos of five young people. They are as follows:

- Irfan Baqri, 20, student; born and raised in Birmingham

- Karim Rivzi, 20, student; born and raised in Nottingham
- Arshad Usman, 19, student; born and raised in Leicester
- Habeeb Rehman, 20, student; born and raised in London
- Zunairah Jaffri, 18, student; born and raised in London

These five students have visited Pakistan in the past eighteen months. The first three stick to Western clothes and attend a college in MK doing various foundation courses. The last two travel into MK from London on a Monday morning and return to the city on Friday afternoon. They, too, go to college, wear traditional costumes, and appear to lodge with family members during the week."

"Excellent. Get these photos and details to Rusty and Brad, the squad leaders in London, now. Are the surveillance team any further forward with the CCTV yet? We have five young terrorists to find, gentlemen, and one of them is a girl."

Colin was no longer outside the consulting rooms of Dr Ramanayake. He was on Oxford Street heading for Top Shop. He didn't see Athena and her parents emerge from the building. The cardiologist had informed them that Mrs Fox urgently needed a bypass operation. Tinkering with her diet and prescribing medicines was futile. Two of her arteries were so damaged that she risks suffering an ischemic stroke at any time.

The family was stunned, but Athena's father didn't blink. He asked Dr Ramanayake, "How much?"

The consultant made a call, and by just after midday, an ambulance car arrived to take Mrs Fox to a private hospital in the West End. Her husband accompanied her.

Athena agreed to go home to fetch her mother's things for a stay in the hospital. She wanted to add personal touches of her own. She left the consulting rooms at around ten past twelve.

Colin spotted Rusty on the pavement outside Top Shop. The guy stuck out a mile. Anyone less likely to shop there, Colin couldn't imagine. Colin recognised two other familiar faces from Larcombe standing ten yards away as the two men greeted one another. He nodded at them.

"Fill me in, Rusty. What have we got, mate?"

"Suicide bombers. It's a group of three blokes, at least. They're hitting the station at half-past one."

"What's the plan?"

"A squad raided their place in Milton Keynes this morning, but they missed them. They've followed the bombers into the city and should be here any time now."

"How many of them are there?"

"Five, giving us nine altogether."

"How are we going to take them out of the frame?"

"I reckon we can Taser them if we can catch them unawares; one man in front to ask for the time or directions and one behind to nullify any threat. Then we use the cars we travelled in to get them well away from these crowds. Erebus has sent the paramedics up as a backup. So, once we discover where they parked, we can deliver any of these lads that cause us extra trouble to them. They will remove them to Larcombe afterwards."

"The pet cemetery will be busy."

"Let's get somewhere quiet for a minute. I need to give you your kit. I know you weren't carrying when you came up for this babysitting job. Have they got a toilet in this shop?"

Colin and Rusty stood in the gents' toilet on the basement floor within two minutes. Rusty passed Colin a Taser and then handed him the PSS pistol.

"I brought this along, mate. I know you liked it."

"Thanks. It's quiet, but if I have to use it, we might have a job explaining to the transport police why we're carrying a lad with a big hole in his head."

The two guys from Rusty's team joined them when they got out onto the street.

"The MK squad are here. Three agents on this side of the street and two outside, Next on the opposite side of the road. The squad leader is on this side; he wants to talk to you."

Rusty wandered up the street. Despite the civilian clothes, it wasn't too difficult for the two ex-SAS men to work out who each other was. They shook hands and worked out their plan of attack. A minute later, Rusty and Brad received a call from Larcombe.

It was Erebus.

"I'm sending you details of the five terrorists."

Rusty didn't react, a slight tensing of his jawline perhaps, but nothing more.

"There are three bombers. They are wearing Western clothing and carrying backpacks. The other two, a man and a girl, will likely arrive at the station by Tube. They will be in traditional clothes:- a thobe for him and an abaya for her. She will have her head covered with a niqab. One of these two will detonate the bombs using a mobile phone. Our best intelligence suggests the three bombers will enter the station over the next hour. They plan to reach one of the many busy intersections at one-thirty. The other two will want to have sight of their fellow cell members. They will then call the numbers at the precise time to cause the greatest loss of life."

"Okay, boss," said Rusty. "Do you have eyes on the three bombers above ground?"

"Still waiting for news. Sadly, we have plenty of cameras from which to choose."

"I'll pass the details of the three bombers to our teams, and they can take them out of the picture."

"Good hunting," said Erebus and ended the call.

Rusty and Brad changed their plans, as they now had the new information. Brad split his team into two groups of two and briefed them on their roles. Rusty gave his two men their instructions too. Rusty, Colin, and Brad made up the team responsible for tackling the threat underground.

Athena had collected a bag with her mother's things from home. She was now setting off to hunt for those personal items she wanted to gather before heading to the West End to visit her Mum in the hospital. She was walking to Sloane Square tube station for a District line train that got her to Oxford Circus after a brief change over at Victoria.

Rusty, Colin, and Brad were preparing to go to the station. Brad checked with Team 1, who watched for Irfan Baqri. There was no sighting.

Brad got the same report from Team 2, who had been searching for Karim Rivzi. At the same time, Rusty contacted Team 3. No sign of Arshad Usman.

Rusty's mobile rang again. It was Larcombe.

"The three bombers are on the move. We have them on CCTV; they have just come out of Primark near Marble Arch. They'll be with you in fifteen to twenty minutes.

Rusty rang the paramedics who sat in the ambulance in 24 7 Parking around five minutes away. The ambulance crew was primed and ready to move at a second's notice.

Irfan, Karim, and Arshad had separated. Irfan had

crossed the street, and the other two followed ten to fifteen yards behind him. As they approached Oxford Circus itself, Karim moved ahead of Arshad. They were well-schooled to enter their kill zone with little or no attention. As far as any staff or transport police at the station were concerned, they looked like your typical student: casually dressed, not in any hurry to get where they were going — looking moody. No different to millions of other teenagers around the world.

The ambulance containing the paramedics eased into position. Two men sat in the front and two in the back. The busy streets of London are so used to seeing emergency vehicles that no one takes any notice. If there had been a young policeman patrolling his beat, he would have passed by without a look. As usual, there were no policemen in sight.

Team 1 struck first. Irfan saw the entrance to the station and steeled himself to walk towards his destiny with his head held high. A man appeared before him, and Irfan almost collided with him.

"Watch where you're going, mate," said the ex-SAS agent. Irfan tried to sidestep him, but suddenly he felt something pressed against his neck. The Taser delivered an electrical current that interfered with Irfan's neuromuscular system. It incapacitated him. Or, to put it the way Rusty had described it when he had trained his men at Larcombe, 'they collapse like a sack of shit, but they're fine again in no time.'

The ambulance's back doors opened, and the paramedics helped Irfan into the vehicle. Then, the doors closed, and the ambulance moved further up the street. They secured Irfan's arms and legs in the ambulance, taped his mouth, and removed the backpack.

Karim and Arshad should have made up the distance between themselves and Irfan and seen what was happening even with them crossing the busy street. But Teams 2 and 3 had neutralised them in much the same manner, and they both lay stunned on the pavement. The driver and his mate left the ambulance and helped the agents get the two terrorists into the back. Karim and Arshad were dealt with like Irfan, trussed up like a turkey for Christmas dinner. Three bombers were now out of the game.

The teams reported their progress to Rusty and Brad, and the ambulance headed as far away from the crowds in Oxford Street as possible. Those bombs needed to be made safe before half-past one. One advantage of having so many skills at your disposal when working for an outfit such as Olympus was that ingenious solutions for tricky problems were commonplace.

The ambulance carried the usual medical paraphernalia you would expect. On one wall, though, there was now a microwave oven sealed with metres of metal tape on the edges to create a Faraday cage as near as made no difference. The cell phones had been removed from the backpack bombs and wrapped in aluminium foil, cutting off communication. When the terrorists called their target phones and expected to detonate the explosives, their call would not be received if the science bit worked.

The three men underground had spread out and covered the station's upper levels as much as possible. They were on the alert for the remaining two terrorists — three pairs of eyes scanned the passageway where incoming passengers emerged.

Rusty could see Colin on the far side of the busy concourse. He gave him the thumbs up to confirm that the first part of the mission had been a success. The time was now twenty past one.

Colin breathed a sigh of relief. Those three young men wouldn't be bringing their version of 'Death in the Afternoon' to Oxford Circus today. What of the other two, though?

Habeeb and Zunairah had arrived from Victoria a few minutes earlier. Everything was going as planned, and they headed towards the surface. Irfan, Karim, and Arshad were about to appear. Together, the five would cause mayhem and fear in the centre of the capital city.

For the two students who had been steadfast in their refusal to become westernised, despite being born and brought up in the UK, politics ranked ahead of any religious fanaticism driving them.

These two had recruited the other three at college. They persuaded the three students they were discriminated against by the society they thought had nurtured them. Although they grew up in Britain, they were not considered British by many. Habeeb and Zunairah exploited their Muslim identity crisis and helped them develop a more radical interpretation of Jihad. They encouraged others to embrace activism to combat their alienation and seek revenge for the injustices young Muslims suffered in Britain. The students had been vulnerable subjects and followed their mentors like sheep.

Habeeb and Zunairah emerged from the underground and positioned themselves in their appointed places. They looked across the concourse for their colleagues; there was no sign of them. What was keeping them? It was twenty-eight minutes past one.

Colin saw Habeeb first. He searched the same side of

the building for the girl. As soon as he spotted her, he called Rusty.

"I've got eyes on them both, Rusty. There's a problem, mate; both are carrying backpacks. There were five bombers, *not* three."

Rusty signalled to Brad to move closer to where Colin was standing. The three men were poised, ready to react as soon as they saw any movement from either terrorist to use a mobile phone. But because he couldn't see Irfan and the others, Habeeb hesitated. Should he make his call or wait a while longer?

Brad called his men from Teams 1 and 2. They were on standby in the entrance hall of the station. The ambulance crew didn't need everyone in the vehicle to transfer their prisoners to a safe place. Six ex-SAS men were ample for three lads. Brad learned that the ambulance was on the return journey and that two paramedics plus Team 3 stood guard over the three would-be bombers.

The concourse teemed with people rushing to and fro. Rusty decided to take out Habeeb Rehman first. He ordered Team 1 to create a disturbance to distract the terrorist. The sound of someone shouting that they had lost a wallet lifted over the general din, and a scuffle broke out a few yards away from the male terrorist. Rusty had used the ploy to quickly cover the ground between them and was on top of Habeeb in seconds. He took him to the floor before he had time to blink.

Zunairah looked frantically left and right; she couldn't see Habeeb. Where were the others? It was time. She got her mobile phone out of her purse.

Colin watched someone cross his eye-line; he recognised Athena's familiar walk. She had shopping bags and a large bunch of flowers and was heading for the entrance to the trains.

"Athena!" he shouted. "Hit the ground, now."

Athena spun around and saw Colin. She couldn't work out why he was there in London, but the urgency in his voice convinced her she was in danger. Athena darted around the nearest corner and crouched by the wall with her hands overhead.

Zunairah dialled. She looked straight at Colin, who was now moving towards her. Dozens of people pushed and shoved at him as panic took hold. Women screamed. Children were in danger of being trampled underfoot. A small crowd showed an unhealthy interest in Rusty as he frog-marched the disorientated Habeeb out of the station with one of his team.

Colin drew his pistol as he got nearer to Zunairah. Her phone was ringing out, but nothing was happening. The eyes that stared at him from the narrow slit of the niqab were full of hatred. She dialled again. Colin was a foot from her; he raised the gun and shot her between the eyes. As she slumped to the floor, Colin saw Brad with a paramedic running towards them with a stretcher.

Colin let them scoop up the dead girl and rush her away. He followed them after he had grabbed Athena by the arm. She crouched close to the wall, clearly frightened and traumatised after her experiences. Colin thought she looked as if she was trying to say something to him, but she was struck dumb with shock.

One minute later, the ambulance pulled away from the station into the heavy traffic. Colin was on board. Zunairah's body was on one side, and Habeeb was tied up securely on the other. Rusty guarded him.

"Where are the others?" asked Colin.

"Brad and the rest of the team members are making their way to where we have stashed the terrorists. They are using the transport they came in from Milton Keynes," replied Rusty. "Olympus, think of everything. You know that, mate. We dropped the other three off at a safe house near St George's Fields. It's a ten-minute drive."

"Go on, Rusty, say it."

"What the heck were you thinking?"

"Until you called me in on this caper, my total concentration for the past couple of days has been on keeping Athena safe. Erebus wants her around to carry on Olympus after he's gone. I didn't think; I yelled out."

Athena stared at him, realisation dawning.

"Have you been stalking me?"

"Only following orders," he replied.

Rusty looked at the two of them and wondered if he might have missed something. Phoenix had a thing for her. Who'd have thought? He changed the subject. They had better get back to what was vital and discuss the terrorist cell.

"I think I've worked out what happened back there," he said. "When we get to the safe house, I bet you a dollar to a doughnut that those three lads had a mobile phone too. If they had each reached the prime position, each of them would have dialled out at half-past one. Whoever constructed the bombs wired cheap mobiles in place, then did a quick shuffle of the backpacks. He gave one of the phone numbers to each bomber and got them to play 'pick your backpack' before they left Milton Keynes. It was a version of 'Russian Roulette'. They didn't know which of their colleagues they would blow up or whether they were sending themselves to kingdom come. Zunairah realised things had gone wrong and kept dialling, praying she had her number or Habeeb's."

"Just as well she didn't," said Athena, regaining her usual composure.

"We were lucky," said Colin.

"Almost at the safe house," said Rusty. "Where had you been heading before this started?"

Athena told them that her mother was in the hospital awaiting an operation in the morning. Rusty wanted to avoid driving around London in the ambulance more than necessary. He suggested Phoenix accompany Athena to the West End so she could visit her mother as planned.

"After you've done that, Phoenix, here are my keys. You can pick up the firm's car from the NCP car park on Bayswater Road. Sorry that we left it some distance away. Then you'd better travel back to Larcombe together. Do you need to go home for a few things first, Athena?"

Athena nodded and added, "Phoenix and I can sort something out."

"What will you be doing, Rusty?" asked Colin.

"Cleaning up," Rusty replied. "We'll let Brad and his team take their transport back to Milton Keynes. My lads and the paramedics will squeeze into the ambo with our guests. It'll be cosy, but it's only for a few hours."

"What are we going to do with her?" asked Athena, nodding towards Zunairah.

"This one comes with us. There are a few places we could get rid of a body in London that I know. However, we don't want to hang around until the early hours. Events at the station will have alerted the police and MI5. Fortunately, we didn't leave too many clues for them."

"Apart from the CCTV," said Athena.

"Not even that," smiled Rusty. "Larcombe hacked into

the cameras to get eyes on the bombers. Then, when they checked out of the system, they switched off some problematic ones. So we won't appear on any screens the police might check."

"So we're home and hosed then," said Colin.

"Don't count your chickens," said Rusty. "The boss might want a word with you yet."

Chapter Ten

The ambulance pulled into the underground parking space of a three-bedroom maisonette in Park Steps. Rusty rang his crew and arranged to transfer the two terrorists upstairs once the coast was clear.

It surprised Colin that Olympus used the property at the luxury end of the market as a safe house. Athena saw his confusion.

"Where would you least expect to find people who work outside the law? Only an idiot rents a two-up, two-down in Hackney."

"You two better be on your way," suggested Rusty.

Colin and Athena got out of the ambulance and climbed the ramp towards the street. Rusty watched them go, wondering if they would hold hands before disappearing. They didn't.

"I suppose you *were* trying to save my life Phoenix," said Athena once they got far from the car park, "so I'd better thank you."

"My pleasure," said Colin.

"I had no idea you were stalking me. I didn't realise that Erebus thought I needed a wet nurse."

"From my conversations with him when we meet in the orangery, he's fond of you. So I had orders to ensure nothing happened to you in London and get you back to Larcombe unharmed."

"How could I get into trouble? I was spending time with my parents, for heaven's sake."

"Erebus feared that you might try a 'lone wolf' revenge attack on the terrorist cell because of your partner."

Athena sat quietly for a time as they continued towards Beaumont Street.

"I'm sorry," Colin said. "It must still be tough coming to terms with what happened. When my wife Sue died, I suppressed my emotions and threw myself into my work."

"Erebus must think highly of you," said Athena, changing the subject. "Cosy meetings in the orangery. I bet you even get the best porcelain?"

They reached the hospital where Mrs Fox was tucked up, with all mod cons, waiting to go for her operation on Friday morning.

Colin told Athena he would retrieve the car from the NCP place and return it whenever she was ready to leave. He watched as Athena made her way up the steps. She stopped at the doorway and checked her watch. It was just before two o'clock.

"Pick me up at three, please, Phoenix. I won't stay too long with Mummy; my father is here too, and we don't want to tire her."

"Three o'clock it is, ma'am," Colin replied.

Athena came back down the steps and touched his arm.

"Erebus was right. If I had been armed and stumbled upon the scene you encountered at Oxford Circus, I would have killed all five of them in a heartbeat, regardless of the danger to myself and the integrity of the Olympus Project. I suppressed my emotions, too, when Simon died. I don't know whether I'm ready yet to trust myself to feel something again. How do you know it's time?"

"I'm the last person to ask," said Colin and turned away to head off to Bayswater Road.

Colin reached the car park and found the firm's car; he drove to Paddington to pick up his luggage. By the time he'd made the round trip, there was only a short time left to while away waiting for Athena. At three o'clock on the dot, he pulled alongside the private hospital entrance. Athena came out, followed by her father.

"Vincent Gardens, please, driver," Athena said calmly.

"I thought we'd grab a taxi, darling," her father said. "One can't be too careful with these minicab people."

"Don't worry, sir," said Colin. "A free trip, isn't it, miss?"

He loved winding up Athena; she looked daggers at him when he checked the rear view mirror.

"Do you know this man?"

"A little," said Athena through gritted teeth.

"I'm sure we'll know more after the drive back west later," Colin said brightly. "It's good to meet you, sir. I hope your wife makes a full recovery after tomorrow's operation."

"Thank you," said Mr Fox. "Sorry, I didn't catch your name?"

"Call me Pat, sir."

Colin glanced in the rearview mirror. Athena was staring out of the window.

"That one went right over her head," thought Colin as he drove back to Belgravia.

Meanwhile, the ambulance left the safe house and chugged down the M4 towards Bath. The driver was aware

The Olympus Project

of the extra weight on board. But, out of habit, he didn't want to attract unwanted attention by speeding or using his lights and siren.

There was no rush to get anyone on board to a hospital. One passenger was beyond help. Others, no doubt, realised their prospects for the future didn't look great, and Rusty and his team took advantage of the chance to relax.

On the M1, Brad and his team headed home too. Once dropped off in Milton Keynes, they disappeared to their hometown or city. As Olympus agents, they were on standby twenty-four-seven, waiting for the call to dispose of the bad guys. Brad's last place to check was the maisonette.

He parked farther up the road and took a pair of binoculars out of the glove compartment. He saw no sign of anyone in or around the building.

"Neighbourhood Watch my arse," he said. "It looks as if I'd better do it then."

Brad rang the local police and reported a possible break-in. He supplied the details, and when asked for his name, he ended the call. He sat in the car for twenty minutes before a police car arrived. Twenty minutes after that first responder, the place swarmed with people in highviz jackets and paper suits.

Brad drove back to his house on the outskirts of MK. A decent result today, he thought. We took the bombers out and lined up the rest of the cell for the authorities to arrest. It was completed without a scratch; sleep would come easy tonight.

While Brad sat in front of his TV checking whether the news carried a report on the Oxford Circus furore, Colin sat outside the Fox residence waiting for Athena.

The sound of the red door slamming shut warned him of her arrival. He leapt out of the car and opened the boot.

He stood by the rear driver's side door handle if she was still mad at him and wanted to ride in the back. Instead, Athena glowered at him and left her case on the floor by his feet. She walked around to the front and got into the passenger seat.

"Hurry," she shouted, and Colin put her case in the boot alongside his kit and did as he ordered.

"Pat?" she asked.

"Yes, ma'am?" asked Colin, just keeping a straight face.

"No, you stupid man, why Pat, for heaven's sake?" she insisted.

"They're never as funny when you have to explain them, Athena," he said with a laugh. "Let's leave it at that." He whistled a few bars of the 'Coronation Street' theme tune as he negotiated the A4 traffic.

The further they travelled away from London, the easier the conversation flowed. Both were in tune with the topics that were off the agenda. They did not mention terrorists, her mother's state of health, her late partner, or Colin's past life before Pulteney Weir. Colin found Athena excellent company. When he turned the nose of the car into the driveway of Larcombe Manor, he sighed.

"I imagine you must be tired, Phoenix," said Athena.

"A bit," replied Colin. "But truth be told, I'm just sorry we've arrived back so soon. It's been fun chatting with you."

"We don't have to stop talking if you don't want to," said Athena.

Colin stopped the car outside the main building. He turned towards her.

"If you're not too tired, how about I slip into something more comfortable?" she whispered.

"If you're sure," Colin said.

"Great,' said Athena. "I'll see you in the pool in fifteen minutes."

With that, she got out of the car, retrieved her case from the boot and left. Colin sat in the driver's seat, feeling hot and bothered.

"Bloody hell," he said as he drove to his quarters. "She will be worth it when she stops messing me around. Still, I mustn't grumble too much. At least she'll be in that costume again, and that's something, I suppose."

Colin should have remembered the well-known phrase, the best-laid plans because he found the dreaded post-it note from Erebus when he got to his room.

'Need to speak. Urgent.'

Colin groaned. He changed his clothes and looked at his swimming trunks in the drawer — not tonight.

He found Erebus alone in the drawing-room.

"Ah, Phoenix, there you are. Take a seat. I'm unfamiliar with this, but what is it they say? Do you want the good news or the bad news?"

"I'm sorry..." said Colin, but Erebus held up a hand.

"The good news first. The Devon police view Sir Godfrey Penrose's demise as an 'accidental death'. Our view is that the items you left at the scene provided a glimpse into his murky past that several people preferred didn't surface. The coroner will find it hard to come to any other conclusion under the circumstances. On Sunday, you will travel north to finish the Dunfermline mission. You will have the items you need ready for you by tomorrow evening."

Colin shuffled his feet. He was glad to hear the good news, but what came next?

"No doubt you recall your first few days here at Larcombe Manor. I made it clear that the authorities should suspect not one scintilla of suspicion of our activities. We sent you to London to prevent Athena from exacting revenge on Al Qaeda, the umbrella organisation controlling both the bombers who killed her partner and those you met today. By drawing attention to yourself at the station, you risked exposing your true self, Colin Bailey, a killer everyone believed dead. Moreover, you shouted a warning to Athena, using the code name she is known by here at Larcombe and not in the outside world. I'm very disappointed, Phoenix."

"The outcome at the station might have been very different," said Colin. "We were fortunate. The first three bombers were removed from the game in textbook fashion. However, Rusty had to take a risk to take Rehman out of the picture. The Jaffri girl could have had her own or his phone number on her mobile. If so, Rusty and I would be in body bags, plus a few hundred innocent bystanders. More important than that, Athena might have been blown to pieces too. Our second in command walked right into the middle of the kill zone. I needed to protect her if the Olympus Project is to continue after you've gone."

"I see your point, Phoenix, and well-argued. The surveillance section will review their procedures to see if we could have prevented these gaps in our knowledge. It was a risk sending the teams into the station and its surroundings without knowing each of the five cell members was carrying bombs. That cannot happen again. Remember the lessons learned today, Phoenix, and be on your guard. Because we knocked out most of the CCTV equipment in the area and the teams kept most things under the radar, the authorities have little evidence. There were no bodies left for them to examine. We have a cleaning crew based in London for such eventualities. They arrived at the scene minutes after you dashed out of the concourse with the girl on the stretcher. Fragments of her hair, skull, brain, etcetera are in the sewers and heading out to sea by now. When you and Rusty performed your heroics, the crowd's panic meant that few of the witnesses the police *had* tracked down could give credible statements. We're doing what we can to keep fogging the mirror, so they never see the full picture. There's been no sign of the police using crime scene people to comb the concourse for forensic detail. It will need a close eye for another couple of days, but we should be able to breathe easily by Monday."

"Once again, sir, I'm sorry to have been so careless; it won't happen again. Do we have any news from Brad in Milton Keynes?"

"Of course, there *was* one more piece of good news, old chap. The police were tipped off about a possible burglary, and, bless the locals, they called in the security guys once they found the data we left. Brad's people are standing by to inform us of any further arrests in the chain. A series of dawn raids will take place in the Midlands. It feels good to throw a bun to the official arm of the law now and then."

"A pity they drop the bloody thing, though, as often as not," said Colin.

Erebus managed a thin smile.

"Off you go then, Phoenix; good hunting next week. At our group meeting this morning, we discussed you, by the way. After you've completed this job, you deserve a holiday. It will give you time to recharge your batteries. So far, we have kept you here at Larcombe instead of sending you into the field, as we have with Brad, for example. No doubt you have guessed why."

"I never thought it through, sir. I guess it was for my good."

"First, having head-hunted you, we needed to assess whether we made the right choice. Second, we wanted to give you a haven where nobody could discover your real identity. If we *had* made an error of judgement, then it was easier to rectify if you were on our doorstep."

"The pet cemetery again," said Colin.

"That won't be necessary, old chap. You have proved beyond doubt the useful acquisition I convinced Athena and the others you would be."

"Will I return to Larcombe after my short vacation?" asked Colin.

"I'm duty-bound to ask Athena for her opinion, Phoenix; with her up in London until this evening, we couldn't make a firm decision."

"OK, I understand. If that's it for tonight, sir, I'll be off to bed."

"Goodnight, Phoenix. Sweet dreams."

Colin walked back to his quarters, wondering where he might go for a few days after going to Bonny Scotland. On their tour, he'd avoid Aberdeen and the other cities that Maiden's Hair visited. There was no point in risking anyone recognising his alter ego, Owen Collins, the roadie. Surely, there was somewhere he could go where there was 'live' music, a bar, and a comfortable bed? He decided he needed to search on his laptop as soon as he got in and make plans.

It was late, and the stable block was quiet when he slipped into his room.

"I thought you'd never come back," whispered Athena sleepily.

Colin jumped but recovered his composure and turned on his bedside light.

"Erebus called urgently. I'm sorry I missed our swim."

Athena pulled back the sheet that covered her. She wore her costume.

"I didn't want to swim alone. When you didn't arrive, I

came here to find you. I saw the note from Erebus, and I felt tired. I stretched out on your bed, rested my eyes for a second, and then, before I knew it, here you are."

"Here I am," Colin said. "Was there something in particular you wanted?

Athena was so close her perfume invaded his nostrils. He felt his body respond straight away; that earlier indifference and frostiness had gone. She raised herself onto her knees and rested her arms on his shoulders.

"I don't want to be alone tonight," she said, "with my mother facing that operation tomorrow. Just hold me, Phoenix. Please?

Colin's erection did the sensible thing and retired for the night.

"Of course, Athena," Colin replied.

He lay beside her and she soon fell asleep with her head on his chest. As he lay there, listening to her steady, relaxed breathing, he thought it was a funny old world.

Colin Bailey, the vigilante killer, had been transformed into a perfect gentleman by a goddess. Well, at least for one night.

Chapter Eleven

Colin felt Athena stir and move away from him. It was dark, and she wanted to leave the stable block before anyone discovered she had spent the night there. Innocent though it may have been. Before she left, she kissed him softly on his forehead.

It was time for him to get up and head for the shower. A cold one today, despite the chill of the late October morning. His next port of call was the swimming pool, and while he ploughed his way up and down his lane, Rusty appeared for his daily workout. Rusty called out to him.

"A good night last night, Phoenix?"

Colin ignored him at first, but Rusty wouldn't let it go.

"A cosy drive back with her ladyship, eh? Did you come straight back, or did you take the scenic route?"

Colin realised Rusty was referring to earlier last evening. He was unaware of his overnight guest — what a relief.

"We came straight home. I got a summons and a mild bollocking from Erebus about, you know what. So then I had an early night. Athena planned to go swimming, as I recall. So how did our visitors spend the night?"

"It was uncomfortable," said Rusty. "It ain't the Hilton that they're running at the bottom of the ice-house, and the visitors had an early call this morning. They're in discussions for the next few hours. The sooner they co-operate, the longer it will be before they join Zunairah. She's got a nice spot under the shade of a beech tree, as I understand it. A crew took her to the pet cemetery at half-past seven."

Colin still remembered the look on Zunairah's face as he pressed the gun against her head. He saw no fear of death in those eyes, just hatred. Colin wondered whether he should regret pulling the trigger, knowing what he knew now. That she couldn't have exploded any of the bombs with the phone she picked, but he cast the thought aside. She made her choice to die yesterday, and he couldn't risk her taking anyone else with her if he could help it. He resumed his swim, content that he had done the right thing.

"Fancy a brekkie later, mate?" called Rusty as he caught him up in the next lane.

"Sounds good," called Colin as he sprinted away from his colleague.

The morning passed uneventfully after that. Colin and Rusty had a full English and several rounds of toast washed down with mugs of coffee. The items Colin needed for the trip to Scotland on Sunday arrived at his quarters as promised. There was even a well-stuffed envelope with 'Holiday Money' scribbled on the front, hand-delivered by a steward in the early afternoon. Colin felt like a kept man. He wished he could get his finances sorted out, but Colin had to face facts; he had years ahead of him before he could legally be declared dead.

Colin spent the afternoon preparing for his next

mission. He went over his plan for Donald MacDonald for the umpteenth time. Colin wandered to the canteen for a light meal in the early evening. He wasn't that hungry and planned to work out where to spend his time off as soon as he got back. When he had eaten and left the canteen, he saw Athena making her way across the lawns towards him.

There was an awkward moment when they stopped and spoke simultaneously.

"Sorry," said Colin, "you first. Tell me, how is your mother?"

Athena brushed his cheek with the tips of her fingers.

"Daddy says the procedure went fine. But unfortunately, she's currently attached to various tubes, drips, and drains, making things look far worse. She's still drowsy and in discomfort this evening, but they'll have her up and out of bed sitting in a chair tomorrow. Daddy says she should be home in a week, and then it's three months allowing the body to heal."

"Will he be on his own with her during that time, or will Erebus let you take leave to help out?"

"Daddy is arranging for a nurse to live in, at least for the first couple of months. He can't sit around the house for too long; he'd go nuts. I'll ask Erebus for time off on the occasional weekend. With Olympus's global operational scale, I can't visit her too often. When she has recovered from her procedure, she has to adopt a healthy lifestyle to reduce the risk of developing further heart problems. We need to get her to stop smoking, eat healthy food, drink less, and hopefully, exercise a little bit."

"I'm glad she's through the first part, at least," said Colin, and Athena squeezed his arm.

"Thank you for last night," she whispered. "It was sweet of you not to take advantage of me."

"That's funny," replied Colin. "That's what I was going to say."

Athena smiled. "You've eaten, I take it?" she asked.

Colin nodded. "I'm going back to my room to decide where I might spend my few days' holiday. I assume Erebus told you I wasn't coming straight back after Dunfermline?"

"He did, and he asked if I objected to you being sent out into the field to live somewhere handy for any future direct actions you might carry out. I told him I wanted you to stay here at Larcombe for good."

"Really?" said Colin. "Do you still need to keep a close watch on me?"

"No, Phoenix," she said as she walked away from him towards the canteen. "I can't bear you being hundreds of miles away when I might need you to hold me as you did last night."

Athena stopped. She walked back and held his hands in hers.

"It's been a long time," she said. "Be patient with me."

Colin kissed her on her lips.

"I'll see you when I get back from my holiday Athena; take care until then."

Athena walked towards the canteen, and Colin headed to the stable block. He turned to glance back as he neared his quarters, and Athena stood by the door to the building, waiting for him to look her way. Instead, she gave a brief wave and went indoors.

Colin started planning his holiday and couldn't concentrate. He only thought about how great it had been to kiss Athena. He imagined kissing her body from tip to toe.

"Another cold shower before bed," he groaned, "and up early in the morning to see if I can't finally plan this bloody holiday."

Colin was at Bath Spa station again on Monday, the first leg of his journey about to begin. Everything he needed for his mission and a short break was in his trusty rucksack. He also carried a sizeable wedge of notes to buy any required items.

Colin hadn't seen Athena since that Friday evening.

The train left the station on the short hop to Bristol. Colin peered out of the window and was glad he'd return to the Roman city once his holiday was over. He hadn't fancied pitching up in a strange town and starting anew. Colin had the potential promise of a relationship with Athena on his return. He couldn't tell how significant that relationship would be in his life yet, but it looked good for now.

Colin understood the next six or seven hours would be a drag. He would be trekking across the country to Birmingham New Street, then up the west coast further and further north until he arrived in Edinburgh. Colin soon found his eyes dropping, and he slept while the train chugged through to Gloucester and Cheltenham. He changed trains again before he knew it. While in Birmingham New Street, he had a few minutes to spare, so he bought a magazine and a hot sausage roll. When Colin looked at the change he'd got from a tenner, he wondered how long his money might last him. Things had gotten dearer even since he'd returned from The Gambia.

The sausage roll tasted great, and the magazine kept his interest for a few moments, but he needed something to occupy his mind. Staring out of the window as the train made its way through the Midlands wasn't much of a treat. Colin watched the changing scenery on the other side of the glass and counted off the stations as he travelled further up the country. As the train threaded its way through the busy traffic hub of Crewe. Colin thought that although the price of a sausage roll had changed dramatically, many more things changed very little.

At last, Colin stood on the Edinburgh platform, waiting for his final connecting train. Half an hour later, Colin walked out of the station at Dunfermline. It was approaching nine o'clock and bloody freezing. Well, what did he expect in late October in Scotland?

His research found a reasonable bed-and-breakfast within a short walk of the station. It wasn't long before he unpacked his overnight things from his rucksack. He slept, knowing if everything went to plan, he'd be off on his holiday within twenty-four hours.

Donald MacDonald was in his customary position; he sat in his car watching the children as they arrived to start the school day. He slumped in his seat, so it was impossible to see anyone sitting in the car from the other side of the green.

The policeman had left the house at a quarter to eight. He had his staple breakfast diet — a bowl of porridge and a tumbler of whisky. Donald MacDonald was on a slippery slope.

His career had gone down the toilet. Despite the damning evidence against him, Donald believed the two sisters had stitched him up. He even complained to the few friends he had left that the pathetic sentence he received was punitive.

The crafty copper conveniently forgot the other young girls he sweet-talked into giving him favours to stop him from telling their parents tales about what they'd been doing.

"If I turn up at your house, in my police car, and say you were smoking and drinking lager in the park, who do you think your mammy's going to believe, eh? Right then, darling, there's a way we can make this problem go away."

That slippery slope led to him downloading more and more material from the internet and even more so after his father had gone into the home. Somehow Donald kept that fact quiet. A factor behind his sentence's leniency was his invalid father's care. Donald's brief painted a sad and sorry picture of the effects on his father's life if Donald, his sole support, was given a custodial sentence.

With his father out of the way, and Donald's 'sole carer' role discarded without a backwards look, there was no one to see what he did. Donald was free to watch what he liked when he liked. The more he watched, the more he wanted to act out his fantasies. Deep inside was a 'good angel' telling him it was wrong and that he should get help. The whisky helped to drown out that voice.

He needed more substantial amounts to keep the angel quiet these days. Donald couldn't function without a drink inside him as soon as he awoke. On his other shoulder, the devil angel won the battle, and Donald's visits to the school became a daily occurrence during term time. To begin with, he had just been looking. He had been taking photographs of the prettiest girls in the last couple of weeks. The surveillance section at Larcombe Manor identified most of them from Donald's computer.

Donald was a day or two from selecting his target. He had driven around this town often over the last twenty years and knew the streets well. The nights were drawing in now too. A few children he watched attended after-school clubs, and some of his favourites walked home alone after four o'clock in the afternoon. He planned to follow them and choose his spot. Then, his fantasies could become a reality once they were in his car.

The final late arrivals ran through the school gates before they were locked, and Donald drove his car back home. He planned to spend the next few hours looking at his picture collection. Then, maybe today, he would decide on which girl to abduct.

Colin checked out of his room and walked around the town. He knew where his target lived, but he didn't plan to go there. The dossier he studied in such detail at Larcombe suggested where Donald would be later that afternoon. Colin pulled his coat closer to him and leant into the bitter wind. The rucksack on his shoulder contained the few necessities he had selected for this mission. The inclement weather kept most of the town's folk indoors, so only a few saw a stranger wandering past the shops and heading out towards one of the town's more prominent schools.

Colin was in position. He could watch for Donald's arrival without attracting attention to himself. He had a picture of the policeman's car and its registration number. The school turned out in less than half an hour; Donald never missed that. Colin eased the rucksack from his shoulder and removed a few items, putting them into his coat pockets for a speedy retrieval.

It was fast approaching three o'clock when Colin spotted him. Donald MacDonald's car turned into the tree-lined road and headed for the next junction. He executed a sharp right turn across a line of cars arriving on the school run and avoided colliding with one lady in a people carrier. She sounded her horn, and if Colin's lip-reading was accurate at that distance with a small pair of field glasses, she questioned his parentage.

Donald's progress was unsteady as he stuttered and weaved his way into a parking space on the far side of the green in front of the school gates. Colin studied the man. Donald was already drinking from a hip flask.

Colin moved quickly and quietly, approaching the car from the rear. Donald was preoccupied with what was happening by the school gates as children came spilling out. He was drunk as usual, and this made him careless. His doors were unlocked.

"That makes my job even easier," thought Colin, who was inside the car in a second. He wrapped his hand around the nose and mouth of the former policeman and let the chloroform-soaked cloth do its work. Donald was in no condition to struggle. The whisky incapacitated him *before* Colin arrived, and being slumped in the seat to avoid people seeing him was asking for trouble.

Donald's vision and hearing began to fail; he was unconscious within seconds. Colin knew that he needed to keep the cloth in place so that Donald didn't wake up for a while. It was a delicate balance. If Donald stayed under for too long, he might die from heart or respiratory failure. On the other hand, Colin wanted the coroner to be in no doubt that this death was self-inflicted.

The clock moved ever forwards as children, picked up by their loving parents, scampered to their homes. Others lingered on the nearby roads chatting with friends.

Meanwhile, Colin patiently waited for the comforting safety of the night in the car. He checked that Donald was still under and got out of the vehicle. Colin started the final stages of his plan and took two envelopes from his rucksack. These he placed on the dashboard. His last task was to switch on the car's engine. Donald was still away with the fairies when Colin removed the cloth from his face.

Colin closed the car door, slipped his rucksack back over his shoulder, and returned to the spot he had chosen to watch from at the outset. He listened and waited. Deep in the Honda Jazz, nothing stirred.

At six o'clock, he decided enough was enough; time to leave Dunfermline. As pleasant as his stay had been, he was now on holiday. The sooner he got hundreds of miles south, where it might be warmer, the better. So he began the walk back to the station.

The parked car was unattended, but something looked amiss to the police, who arrived at eight o'clock. They were alerted by a dog walker who heard a car engine as they passed by and strolled over to take a peek. A dryer vent hose wedged in the rear passenger door connected to the car's exhaust pipe. Inside the vehicle, they found a middle-aged man. He was dishevelled, smelled of drink, and almost lay in the driver's seat. They discovered two letters. One addressed to John MacDonald of Braeside Home for the Elderly and one to 'Whoever finds me.'

The police read this letter and the driver's intentions were explicit: -

To whoever finds this note, I hope I have committed suicide. I take complete and sole responsibility for my present situation. I have done things of which I am ashamed. If I continue to live, I will again offend and commit more serious crimes.

Colin had congratulated the Larcombe team before travelling north on the note's excellent handwriting and overall tenor.

The team had to thank the quick-thinking agent who scanned examples of Donald MacDonald's handwriting. It gave him something to do while he waited for the downloaded files to transfer to his memory stick.

In time, the police delivered Donald's unopened letter to his father, and later a verdict of suicide was duly recorded.

As Erebus and the others back at Larcombe Manor suspected, the police uncovered the same incriminating files on Donald's computer as the Olympus crew had. The evidence could get neatly brushed under the carpet.

As the police removed the mortal remains of Donald MacDonald from his Honda, Colin Bailey headed south towards England and a well-earned rest. Everything changed when they pulled into Manchester Piccadilly. He was wide awake now. Someone on the platform straight in front of his carriage window stared at him. The look on her face was one of disbelief. It was Therese Slater.

It was plain she had returned from Europe. Colin wondered how long she waited before she gave up on him and returned to her northern roots. He could tell she was still confused and uncertain about who she had seen.

The minor facial modifications he underwent at Larcombe Manor, plus the blue contact lenses and frames, fooled the vast majority. However, Therese had been up close and personal with Colin Bailey, and he saw she now convinced herself it was him. She found it hard to accept he was alive when the world thought him dead.

Therese didn't appear to be catching this train, but Colin still had to decide what she might do with the knowledge she now possessed. Was it possible she'd go to the police? He didn't believe Therese would do that to him. It was more likely she'd sell her story to the newspapers to set herself up for a comfortable life. Colin needed to find out, even if it meant he had to get off the train in Manchester and catch a later train south. But, first, he *had* to talk to Therese.

Colin gathered up his things and rushed to the door. Just in time, he got it open and jumped onto the platform. Therese walked tentatively towards him.

"Is it you?" she asked. "I thought you died."

"That's what everyone is supposed to believe," said Colin.

"You look different; that's what threw me. When your carriage stopped by me, I saw you and couldn't believe my eyes. For two whole months, I waited for news. I kept waiting to hear they had found your body at last. I wanted to move on with my life. I never expected to see you alive again. When the bar work dried up and my money ran out, I returned to my sister's. I'm still looking for work, but I found a place of my own to rent a few weeks back. It's at Runcorn near my sister. It's not in a great neighbourhood, but you must do the best you can when you're on benefits."

Colin only half-listened to Therese's wittering. Instead, he tried to work out what to do next.

"Look," Colin said, "I've got a few days off; why don't we spend it together?"

"Do you mean it this time?" said Therese.

"It wasn't my fault we didn't get away to the Netherlands in July," said Colin. "Blame that copper, Hounsell."

"My number is still the same, Owen or Colin, whatever you call yourself. Why didn't you call before? You know I'd drop everything to be with you?"

"That's my girl,' smiled Colin. "I've never forgotten what you looked like when you dropped everything last time."

"I've never forgotten how you made me feel, either. Are you sure we can't just do it here in the station?"

Colin knew his priority was to get off this platform and away from the crowds. So he drew Therese to him and kissed her hard.

"When is your train?" he asked Therese.

"No more than five minutes," she replied.

"Okay, if I return to Runcorn with you?" asked Colin. Therese nodded. Colin dashed to get a ticket, and they soon sat in a compartment on their way to Runcorn. It was midnight when they arrived by taxi at Therese's first-floor flat. They crept in and made it upstairs to her room without disturbing anyone.

Colin woke up at five o'clock. With Therese snoring beside him, he spent the next three hours wrestling with his conscience. Colin's conscience didn't trouble him in the past. He had no problem crossing people off his list in the most decisive way. They deserved it. He was rectifying other people's mistakes.

As soon as they closed the door behind them last night and rid themselves of their clothes, Therese reminded him how passionate and exciting the sex had been between them. He was exhausted.

A few days in bed with Therese wouldn't help recharge the batteries as Erebus intended, but it remained an enticing prospect.

Then there was Athena. Was he guilty of having cheated on her? They hadn't shared more than a few kisses. Who was he kidding? She was way out of his league.

Athena was a beautiful, intelligent woman with a great body who would, in time, be his boss when Erebus took his place in the celestial navy. Her partner, Simon, dying in the London bombings must have wrecked her emotionally for a while, but Athena was no shrinking violet despite what Erebus thought.

Colin asked himself whether Athena needed him for one night of passion for getting back in the saddle again. After that, he might be yesterday's newspapers.

"Bloody hell," he thought. "This relationship lark is complicated, isn't it?"

What the hell? Just this once, why couldn't he have his cake and eat it?

One thing he understood now; Therese wouldn't hand him over to the police. This knowledge was based on the energy she'd put into their lovemaking earlier and the fact she couldn't wait for them to get off on holiday together somewhere. It was after those few days' holiday that concerned Colin. What did she expect from him then?

Things could get messy. If he ended it after the holiday, Therese might turn nasty and threaten to expose him. Perhaps if he kept her sweet by promising to be a frequent visitor to Runcorn? But, on the other hand, if he avoided her discovering where he was based and wanting to follow him south, he *might* get two helpings for a while.

As morning broke over the shabby street that Therese called home, Colin realised their brief encounter at Manchester Piccadilly could lead to Therese putting too much significance on their relationship. She might get clingy.

If she asked him for commitment, he might have to find a permanent solution to the problem.

Although he had only been with Olympus for a few months, Colin 'The Phoenix' Bailey knew the importance of the organisation's integrity. Nothing must jeopardise that.

Chapter Twelve

At Larcombe Manor, Erebus prepared to bring the morning meeting to order. Athena sat on his right-hand side, reading the overnight reports. Thanatos and Minos sat on his left, deep in conversation over the terrorists still in the ice-house.

Alastor was a late arrival. The door burst open, and he stood, out of breath, with a copy of the Daily Record under his arm.

"Sorry for the delay, Erebus, but I had to pop into the city to get a copy of this regional newspaper. Phoenix has played a blinder on the Dunfermline job, judging by the report here."

"He hasn't been in touch yet, has he?" asked Athena as casually as she could.

"Phoenix is on holiday, my dear," scolded Erebus. "I'm sure you'll get a postcard in due course, saying 'Wish you were here' or something along those lines."

Erebus winked at her. Athena looked flustered for a change as their banter passed straight over the heads of the other three men around the table.

"Phoenix is a good addition to our organisation," said Thanatos, "efficient and single-minded."

"He chose well on this mission," said Alastor. "There doesn't appear to be any doubt they will rule it as suicide. 'The body of Donald MacDonald was found in his car yesterday evening. It's thought he died from carbon monoxide poisoning.' The press reported the charges brought against him earlier. They've mentioned 'additional evidence discovered at his home supporting the note left in his car for the police.' The Fife regional police chief stated to the Record, 'Donald MacDonald was a troubled soul, whose actions had destroyed his long and conspicuous career. We pass on our condolences to his family and hope that Donald is now at peace.' A neat package presented to the authorities, leaving them to tick the boxes on their interminable paperwork and move on to pastures new."

"Excellent," said Erebus, "and he'll be here at Larcombe Manor with us for the foreseeable future, as Athena informed us on Saturday morning," he added cheerily.

As Athena picked an overnight report and changed the subject, she sensed several pairs of eyes turn her way. Erebus must suspect a growing connection between her and Phoenix. She didn't want the others to have time to think about what might lie behind her mentor's comment.

"This report from Level Three of the ice-house is disturbing," she said. "We don't want to keep these men here for too long, do we? It's been a while since our last snap inspection from the charity commissioners. Although they've suspected nothing amiss with our set-up, having four people under interrogation simultaneously could be a problem. I hope we can clear things up soon."

Erebus nodded.

"I share your concern, Athena, but we must tread carefully. Although we carry out our operations secretly, we have always tried to maintain the highest standards. Our interrogation techniques get the information we wish. Any method forbidden by international law is out of the question. We must trust Henry Case and his team to persuade our guests to give us the answers we need to hear."

Athena appreciated Henry Case had a formidable reputation; he was undoubtedly good at his job. Athena couldn't think of anyone better suited for the job they performed than Henry. She was the only person around this table aware that the chief interrogator's nickname was 'Head' Case among staff in the ice-house.

"If we don't make significant progress today, then we might invite Henry to report to us here at our morning meeting," she suggested.

"That sounds reasonable, Athena; so be it," replied Erebus. "Let's move on to the next item on our official agenda."

Up north in Runcorn, Therese stirred beside him. Colin slid out from under the covers and headed for the bathroom. He needed a pee and a shower, in that order. He wanted to leave Runcorn this morning to find a more exciting place to spend the next few days relaxing.

After easing the load on his bladder, Colin touched the shower door and tested the water. The steam rolled out of the stall, creeping over the mirror. That's what he needed - a refreshing hot shower. He stepped into the cubicle. Just as he leant his head back and was soaking his hair, it occurred to him. He hadn't got a towel. Colin slid the door open to get one from the towel rack.

Therese's smiling face appeared next to the open shower door with a towel wrapped around her.

"Looking for this?" she asked.

Therese dropped the towel, and Colin groaned as seeing her incredible, dark, athletic body made him react immediately. But, unfortunately, his body failed him again.

Therese leant into him and kissed him beneath his ear. Colin reached for her lips, giving up any ideas of non-cooperation and kissed her, trapping her tongue with his. He reached one hand under her thigh and lifted it higher, opening her up and pressing his swollen member against her. He continued to kiss her and slipped inside her.

They continued to pleasure one another as the hot water pummelled their bodies. Therese slid up and down, grinding against him and using her legs as leverage. She worked him hard. She gripped his back with her fingernails, her legs quivered, and her sighs escaped in one massive wave of ecstasy.

They paused to catch their breath, and then Colin began to thrust into her once more. They both panted and gasped as her hips pressed back to meet him. He continued to push until wholly drained, and then he grabbed the soft towel she had brought with her and wrapped it around them.

"I'm hungry. What's for breakfast?" Colin asked.

"Wasn't I enough?" said Therese, pouting.

"More than enough," said Colin, "but sex always gives me an appetite."

"I can see I'll have to keep making you hungry then," said Therese.

The rest of the morning drifted away as the couple found something to eat and decided where to go for a short break.

"Blackpool's a great place to visit," enthused Therese, "any time of the year."

Colin was unconvinced. He remembered the looks on the guys' faces from Maiden's Hair when they turned up at the venue after being given a few days off from the grind of their tour. Blackpool is the most deprived of England's larger seaside towns and suffers far more poverty and crime than the national average.

Life is a struggle with high unemployment and the worst death rate in Britain; alcoholism is rife, and drug-taking is common. On the Grange Park estate, one of the largest in Lancashire, residents talk of dealers operating in full view on the streets. Colin had listened to Vincent Gagnon and the rest comparing the seaside resort with many of the worst parts of the cities back in their native Canada.

"Man," Vincent had said, "you can keep your stick of rock and kiss me quick hats. And what the hell is it with you Brits with donkeys on the beach?"

Colin listened to Therese wax lyrically over the miles of beach, promenade, and its attractions. While she chatted away, he thought he ought to ask Erebus if there were any direct actions in Blackpool that justified a visit for business rather than 'pleasure'.

At long last, he got Therese to pack a bag and phone for a taxi so they could set off to the station. But, unfortunately, it was early afternoon, and no matter how efficient Virgin Trains were, it took three hours via Liverpool Lime Street to get to the seaside.

"Half a day of my holiday wasted," thought Colin, "apart from that memorable time in the shower."

Therese knew Blackpool well, so she soon found a decent hotel. Colin wasn't slumming it in the back streets. Not when Erebus was paying. They had a second-floor room that might have overlooked the Central Pier if the other buildings hadn't been in the way. However, it was central, and near the front, so it fitted the bill.

They spent the rest of Tuesday checking out the double bed, finding a restaurant that served something other than fish and chips, having a few drinks, and then running back to the hotel for an early night.

"This sea air is so bloody tiring," said Colin.

"Just once more, sweetheart, please?" purred Therese.

They fell asleep just after three o'clock.

The weather proved more like winter on Wednesday and Thursday, so most of the daylight hours found them dashing between Madame Tussaud's, where Colin half expected to see himself, the sea life centre, and Ripley's Believe it or Not.

Therese wanted to see everything associated with the Tower. So, they visited the Ballroom, the Dungeon, and Jungle Jim's. Colin drew the line at the Eye, no matter how good the view might have been if it hadn't been raining across the sea to Ireland. He didn't wish to go four hundred feet up in the air to stand on a sheet of glass. No, thank you.

He paid for Therese to go up on her own. Half the reason for that had been to get a few minutes of peace. The other was to cast a wary eye over the scene he saw around him if he looked past the glitzy façade of the Pleasure Beach and the Golden Mile.

In the bars they visited, Colin overheard the locals talking of a worrying visitor to the town, the dole tourist. Thousands claiming housing and incapacity benefits had moved to the town for a year-round holiday but had forgotten to pack their bucket and spade. So many people were unemployed. Yet when you go to the bars and clubs, they're filled with people. It made no sense to Colin.

He remembered those early days with him and Karen

when they used to nurse their drinks to last through an evening in the pub. They listened to the live band, with only enough money for one night out at the end of the week. He worked hard to provide for his wife and daughter. Karen did her bit, too, once Sharron was a few years older. So why weren't other people prepared to do what they did back in the day?

Sat with Therese in a café at lunchtime on Thursday, he looked at the people sitting around them. Everyone else in the place seemed on drugs. You could tell the ones with a few quid. They showed the telltale signs of being on cocaine or heroin. Heaven knows what the rest of them had taken.

Therese was sympathetic to a degree. Her life in Manchester had given her a rough grounding in how hard things could be for many people.

"You've no idea what it's like living up here, coming from the soft South. Although, of course, there is work out there if you put in the effort to find it. But many people here enjoy sitting on their backsides doing nothing, and the government makes it worthwhile for them not to do otherwise."

Colin shook his head. It didn't make sense.

When they had finished their meal, they made their way outside. The rain had stopped, and the sun made a valiant attempt at breaking through the fast-scudding dark clouds. Colin stumbled over two women sitting on the edge of the pavement, drinking cans of strong cider. It was just after one o'clock. They could barely talk, so when they slurred a few words at him, he wasn't sure whether they swore or wished him a pleasant day. They looked old before their time, which came as no surprise.

The rest of the afternoon soon passed as they visited the Pleasure Beach, and Therese even persuaded Colin onto the scarier rides. They found a lounge with a female impersonator and a DJ who favoured the seventies and eighties dance tracks in the evening.

"Terrific." thought Colin. "If I had a chance to explore this town alone, I bet I could soon find a place with a live band playing hard rock. But, unfortunately, this stuff doesn't do it for me."

It did it for Therese, of course. She wanted Colin to dance with her the whole bloody night. He joined in as best he could, but his heart wasn't in it. No matter how long she stayed on her feet, her appetite for more exercise in the bedroom when they got back wouldn't be affected.

As she dragged him to his feet for yet another disco track he hated, he imagined himself falling asleep during his first meeting with Erebus when he returned to Larcombe.

"The idea was for you to recharge the batteries, old chap," he heard him saying as Donna Summer let it rip.

When they returned to the hotel after another late night, drifting from bar to bar, they fell into bed. Therese was as insatiable as Colin had forecast. She fell asleep on top of him. When the sun rose, he was too shattered to move her. The best day of their holiday, and he was in no position to enjoy it.

Colin woke Therese up with his laughter. He had realised that the statement was ludicrous, given his current status, and laughed until the tears rolled down his cheeks.

"What's so funny?" asked Therese, annoyed at having her sleep disturbed.

"Sorry, not your fault. I thought of something, and it made me laugh. You get back to sleep Therese. I'll shower and take a walk to breathe fresh air."

"I sometimes wonder if you only want me for the sex,"

she said, throwing a pillow at his back as he walked away from the bed.

"You get as good as you give, sweetheart," chided Colin. "We both came into this with our eyes wide open."

Therese sat on the edge of the bed and looked at the floor.

"Look, I don't even know who you are. I don't understand how you died, but then you didn't. How did that happen? You said you had a few days' holiday owed. Where do you work? Do they realise who you are? Why are you entitled to a holiday when you've only worked with them for a few months? What kind of job is it?"

"That's a lot of questions, Therese," said Colin. "Give me five minutes, and I'll be back. I'll try to explain as much as I can."

As he stood in the shower, Colin knew he had reached the turning point. He could return to the bedroom and tell Therese as little of the truth as he dared so they could move on with their relationship, or he could go back, tell her there was nothing to say, and take her somewhere quiet, kill her, and dispose of her body. By the time he showered, dried himself and dressed, he needed to come to a decision. No pressure, then.

Colin found Therese where he had left her and sat on the bed. She looked up at him with those dark brown eyes looking sad and on the verge of tears. Then, she stood up, and he studied her naked body. Those breasts were still the best he'd seen. What was he thinking? She linked her hands behind his neck and laid her head on his shoulder.

"Talk to me," she said.

"When you look as incredible as this, the last thing I want to do is talk," Colin replied. Instead, their lovemaking was more tender and sensual than ever. Later that morning,

Colin began to tell her a story as they lay in each other's arms.

"Things went wrong in Bath back in July," he said. "I got careless. I'd taken the wife of that copper you met as a hostage. I wanted to keep him off my back long enough to let me finish the jobs I had planned. They found her while I did a job in London that day. On my way back to Bath, I took a quick detour to visit my daughter's grave for the first time in ten years. I'd returned to England earlier in the year after living abroad for that time. That visit to the grave was a mistake. It delayed me. I'd have been at the house when the coppers turned up and may have used his wife as a bargaining tool. They closed in, and I hadn't a clue. My plans fell apart. I had to get out of the city and as far away from the West Country as possible. I was running back to the car park where I'd left my van, and there were police everywhere. The next thing I know is the bloody copper bundles me over a wall and into the river. He's trying to overpower me, and I am not giving up without a fight. We both reckoned without the strength of the waters around the Weir. How either of us escaped, heaven only knows. It was a miracle. As darkness fell, I made my way downstream and escaped. They had given up on me surviving and had gone home for the night. I guess they dragged the Weir and the surrounding river first thing in the morning. Even though they didn't find me, they always believed my body would turn up somewhere along the river. It's been four months, and they'll stop looking soon with luck."

"Where did you hide, though?" asked Therese.

Colin was tap dancing, thinking on his feet.

"There are plenty of empty spaces out there, Therese. I roughed it for a while. It was summer. A few weeks ago, I was in a pub and heard two blokes chatting about this organisation looking for people. I got in touch, and after an interview, they hired me. They wanted people who liked hard work, didn't mind getting their hands dirty, and were prepared to travel around the country chasing up clients. They weren't interested in my life story. I got offered the job, no questions asked. As you can imagine, it suited me. The money's good, and as long as I hit my quotas, it appears they'll keep me in employment."

Colin was pleased with that explanation; it had been close to the truth in many ways. He only omitted to tell Therese what nature of employers he had and where they were based.

It looked to have done the trick. Therese had only one more question.

"This lovely holiday is coming to an end. When will I see you again?"

"I need to get back and find out where my next job is," said Colin. "You said you still have the same mobile number, so I'll put it on my new phone now and I can ring you as soon as I get more free time. I lost my numbers when my old phone ended up at the bottom of the river."

After grabbing a bite to eat, they checked out of the hotel and took a taxi to the station. By mid-afternoon, Colin saw Therese back to her place in Runcorn. She wanted him to spend the night there, but he told her he had to get back. His bosses might need him to travel over the weekend, ready to start a new job on Monday morning.

"It's been great," he said with a smile as he left her. "We must do this again sometime."

"Can't wait," shouted Therese as he got into the waiting taxi and headed back to the station. A slower cross-country train delivered him again to Bath Spa after several changes. He had ample time to get the minicab out from the Manor

The Olympus Project

to pick him up from the station. The company mini-cab dropped him outside his quarters at seven in the evening.

Colin unpacked his things and walked to the canteen for a quick snack. No sooner had he returned to his room and got stuck into a bacon roll than he heard a light knock on his door.

It was Athena.

"Hi. You're back, I see," said Athena and came in and sat on the bed.

Colin kept munching.

"We were pleased with the expert way you handled the outcome in Dunfermline."

Colin nodded and put down his bacon roll.

"How's your mother?" he asked.

"She's recuperating well, thanks, but under protest, as you can imagine."

Colin smiled.

"Did you enjoy your break?" Athena asked.

"Plenty of sea air and exercise," Colin replied. "Glad to get back. I missed the old place."

"Did you miss me too?"

"Maybe," said Colin smiling. "Has there been any excitement since I left?"

"We had a breakthrough in the ice-house."

"Oh, dear. Nothing serious, I hope."

"Don't be daft. Head Case and his team have a couple of the boys we brought back from London to talk. He's reporting to us on their progress tomorrow morning at our meeting."

"Don't call them boys," said Colin. "They were old enough to be prepared to blow themselves up and many others along with them. When the time comes, they will pay the price."

"You're touchy tonight, Phoenix. I expect you're tired. Do you want me to go?" Athena asked.

Colin *was* tired and imagined that if she stayed, it might lead to something. But he knew he couldn't do her justice, not tonight, not after the last few days. But, on the other hand, Colin didn't want her to get the hump. So, he gritted his teeth.

"No, stay as long as you wish."

Athena stood up from the bed, walked to the door and locked it.

She turned around to face Colin and undressed.

"Give me strength," thought Colin to himself.

Athena took off her top. With every passing second, she revealed more of her body. He couldn't wait. Her breasts, covered by a red lacy bra, came into view when she removed her top further. Slowly her cleavage and bust were out, and he felt himself getting harder. And then her top came off, and she stood in front of him in her bra. It was a magnificent sight. She moved her hands back and unhooked her bra. She slipped her bra straps from her shoulder and let her bra drop to the floor. Colin was amazed by her body.

"Athena," he said, "you are stunning."

"Be gentle with me," she whispered as she stepped out of her skirt.

Colin stood up and walked towards her. He cupped her breasts in his hands and kissed her lightly on her lips.

A sharp urgent rap on the door interrupted them.

"Phoenix? There's an emergency meeting in the big house. Your presence is needed. Head Case has got news that won't keep until morning. You'd better get up there sharpish,"

It was Rusty.

Colin and Athena stood face-to-face, their breathing ragged. She sighed as her hips moved against Colin's erection.

"So close, and yet so far," she groaned.

"There's no rush," said Colin. "I'm not going anywhere. You made sure Erebus kept me close by at Larcombe. There'll be other nights."

Athena reluctantly pulled away from him and dressed. Colin waited until both of them had regained their composure and were ready to face Erebus and the others. Erebus suspected something was going on between them. No point advertising the fact by pitching up to a meeting with flushed faces and dishevelled clothing.

Chapter Thirteen

Although of necessity, they had to leave his quarters together, Colin and Athena separated as soon as they emerged from the stable block. When Colin entered the drawing room for the emergency meeting, Erebus was deep in conversation with Henry Case. The older man nodded to acknowledge his arrival.

The others filed into the room soon afterwards. Minos and Thanatos walked in together, followed Athena, and behind her came Alastor. Half a dozen senior ex-SAS operatives attended too, which suggested something big.

Erebus looked around the room to check that everyone was present. Satisfied that everyone had arrived, he asked Henry Case to go through the past week's events. Henry stood up to outline the techniques he and his team had utilised.

Colin hadn't yet met Henry Case. After learning his nickname, he was keen to discover why this guy made people say he was unstable. On the face of it, Henry appeared normal. In his late thirties, he was five feet eight inches tall and had a slim yet athletic build. His accent was that of a highly educated upper-class person.

Colin imagined him having the right connections Erebus and the other ex-military people at Larcombe had been seeking. His interview must have been a breeze. Colin and the others listened intently.

"As you know, we do not dabble in the dark arts here at Olympus, meaning those techniques are unacceptable under the conventions that apply to interrogating terrorists or terrorist suspects. Naturally, that impairs our progress, but we must have standards. Interrogation is a battle of wits with the prisoner, enticing him into talking by building up a relationship, pretending you have learned things that you haven't, to dupe him into giving away information. Over the past eight days, we have been battling with four such prisoners. At first, we deprived them of sleep, which is the most effective way of breaking the will of our detainees. Then, we subjected them to twenty hours of constant interrogation. Within hours, we saw Irfan Baqri, Arshad Usman, and Karim Rivzi showing signs of distress. By the end of their second session, we felt nothing to be gained from having them undergo any further stages."

"Why," asked Athena, "what did they tell you?"

"Everything," replied Henry, "unequivocally. I am sure you have learned of the core leadership group in this version of a terror cell. It is a ring network, and Habeeb Rehman headed this link in the chain. The late Zunairah Jaffri was his second in command. These ring networks overlap, as we know, and an operational cell can often become autonomous. Rehman was the link to the other parts of the network in the Milton Keynes cell. He alone was cognisant of members' identities in subcells, which themselves only had tenuous knowledge of whom or what made up the central core."

"So, the three men knew their leader, but nothing material of the rest of the whole set-up," said Erebus.

"Precisely, sir," replied Henry Case.

"Decision time then," said Erebus. "What do we do with these three little fish?"

"They imagine the people who picked them up in London came from a secret service branch. They have no idea where they are. We could drop them by the side of a road somewhere in the Midlands. We can allow them to resume their studies," Henry Case suggested. "It seems harsh to dispose of them."

"That's a dangerous game Henry," said Erebus. "What if they complained to the media about their treatment by the authorities? The secret services would be alerted to the fact that there's another player in the game."

"Can't we turn them?" asked Athena.

"If they know so little, what value do they represent?" said Colin.

Henry Case shrugged his shoulders, "So be it."

Erebus held up his hand.

"Not so fast, Henry. Let's keep these three for a while longer. I need to confer with my colleagues. First, we must agree on the best course for Olympus. Any other considerations are secondary to that."

Erebus asked Henry to continue.

"As for Habeeb Rehman, he was made of stronger stuff and, following up on Phoenix's point, his value is significant. He required us to move on to another tool in our kit bag: sensory deprivation. We left him in one of our air-conditioned rooms on Level Three with earmuffs, gloves, and goggles. By the end of the second day, we expect the detainee to be on the verge of a breakdown. Instead, Rehman remained only moderately disturbed. As it turned out, our final ploy was to treat him to noise and lots of it. He was stripped, sat on a stool, shackled hand and foot to the floor, and then we blasted him with strobe lights and excruciatingly loud rap music with the air-conditioning maxed out. That was a schoolboy error, as he lapped it up. After twenty-four hours of that, we had to revise our playlist. Someone suggested classical music or country and western might do the trick. Giles from the surveillance techies had the key. He said while Phoenix underwent training, he had mentioned a liking for a band called Judas Priest. We downloaded a few albums and gave them a shot. Rehman broke and spilt his guts within six hours."

"It's not to everyone's taste," said Colin with a smile.

"I've never heard of these people," said Erebus, "but if it worked, then we should be grateful. Well, Henry, what did we learn?"

"We now have Rehman's contacts within the ring with which they interacted. A list of names, addresses, landlines, and mobile numbers is in a file I handed Erebus earlier this evening. The most important information Rehman gave us concerned the suicide bomb attack on Oxford Circus station. That attack was a trial run. Al Qaeda plans to strike the capital during the Olympic Games. They have outlined plans for coordinated attacks on the Olympic Village, which involve hostages, particularly high-profile athletes from around the USA and Great Britain. They plan to target several medal ceremonies on the same day into the bargain, as they have identified these as soft targets. So many flags flying, anthems playing, and people more relaxed, happy, and, as a result, less vigilant. That is not a pleasant thought.

Copies of this intelligence will be handed to you as you leave. Thank you."

The room fell silent as the agents absorbed the news. Erebus stood up to give notice that the meeting was at an end. Colin was the only one to speak. It was his final comment on this chapter of his new life at Larcombe Manor: -

"Gold, Silver, and Bombs,"

Next in The Phoenix series

vinci-books.com/gold-silver-and-bombs

When the world watches, a shadow strikes. Can anyone stop the impending chaos?

As the world converges in London for the 2012 Olympics, an unseen threat lurks in the shadows. With British security forces stretched thin, a lone wolf moves undetected, threatening chaos. Tayler's noir crime thriller unravels the fragile illusion of safety, keeping readers breathless as danger strikes where least expected.

Turn the page for a free preview…

Gold, Silver and Bombs: Chapter One

Jeremy Faversham sat astride his favourite animal. His beloved hunter, Bonus Magnet, was part Irish Draught and part English thoroughbred. Bonus magnet stood at seventeen hands and was eight years old, and Jeremy knew the horse had been a good find. On a brisk January morning, he could think of nowhere he wanted to be than in the saddle, hacking across the glorious Cotswold countryside. He was among friends. The cares and stresses of the working world were far, far away.

No two fox hunts were ever alike. The continuous chaos of the chase appealed to him. Jeremy knew he must be on constant alert, and he rigidly stuck to the centuries-old protocols and accepted the inevitable uncertainty.

Jeremy reflected that Foxhunting was a way of life rather than a mere sport as he negotiated a tricky downhill slope. Over the years, it framed his life. While working in the City at the bank, he often saw himself viewing his financial experiences in a hunting context.

Just like himself, the fox was a predator. Jeremy Faversham might have appeared to be the country gentleman, suitably attired for the occasion, but there were skeletons in the closet. Those skeletons attracted several groups of people. People from those groups now watched the banker ride across open ground towards Downend Farm.

The Phoenix was one man with a pair of field glasses fixed on the edge of the woods. He not only followed the banker's progress; Phoenix kept an eye on the hunt saboteurs too, who lurked in the cover of the trees. From time to time, he switched his attention to the hunt followers. At least having a moving target eased the boredom.

"Is everything going as planned?" whispered Colin.

"Faversham's heading in the right direction," replied Rusty, a few hundred yards ahead. He watched events unfold on the opposite side of the field.

"I'll keep tabs on the great unwashed and the hunt supporters to make sure they don't interfere," Colin replied. "It's good to have them on the scene, though. Unfortunately, it will muddy the waters when they investigate the accident."

"Roger that," replied Rusty. "I'll move ahead and confirm the equipment is in the correct position. I'll double-check too that our clean-up crew are alert and poised to move in as soon as our target is down."

The Olympus agents resumed their duties; communication needed to be minimal on a mission. Many parties were scattered across this small corner of the West Country. Each had its agenda. The days when the hunting crowd rode in these fields and woods by themselves following their sport were long gone.

Donald Chalmers had worked at Downend Farm for over fifty years. He went straight from school to work on the land. Now retired, Donald lived in a cottage half a mile from where he stood. He had been part of the hunting scene in these parts the whole of his life. Donald's wife, Catherine, passed away seven years ago, and they had no children to help fill the cottage with warmth and laughter. Instead, they spent much of their lives outdoors. They enjoyed the companionship of and working with horses and dogs daily — an uncomplicated style of country living fast disappearing.

Donald rose early, just as he did every morning of his working life. Nothing had changed. He saw no reason to stay in bed now that he was retired. He walked across from his cottage to this spot, which was his usual vantage point. It was a place he had occupied on dozens of occasions. This was a spot that gave him a glimpse of his old life. He might not be in the midst of the action anymore, but he could tell anyone who listened to him what was what.

The trees thinned out as he made his way up the path to the step over the fence. Donald spotted a small gathering of watchers huddled against each other by the fencing. They had dressed for sitting in their cars rather than standing on a chilly stretch of Cotswold countryside in the early morning. Donald smiled to himself, not because of their discomfort but because he knew he had an audience.

Donald nodded a greeting as heads turned to acknowledge his arrival.

"Hello there," he said. "Shall we see good sport today, do you think?"

Few intelligent comments came in response to his question. Donald knew his educational commentary would fall on virgin territory. These townsfolk were trying to experience a slice of authentic country life without getting their brand-new boots dirty or snags from thorns or branches in their fashionable jackets. Thank goodness he had not stumbled upon a group of bloody saboteurs. If they found his favourite spot, he would have to walk another mile to get as good a viewing point.

Donald enlightened his unwitting students about the fox and his many attributes. "A fox can sense changes in temperature or a subtle change in the speed of the wind; he knows the lie of the land and the distances between strategic points accurately. Mr Fox knows who you are and who I am. He can tell the difference between a human being wearing a hunting kit and when they are not."

Donald pointed to the far left-hand side of the field. "Can you see the way the land drops away over yonder? If they have picked him up, the fox will head there. We will watch him dart over the brow of the hill. When he reaches the bottom level, he will have earned himself time. The hunters will be slow negotiating the steep descent, and the hounds will fall back a touch. Mr Fox will dash into a covert in the woods and emerge later to descend to the stream. He might choose to lie low for an hour or two. By the time the hounds re-discover his scent, Mr Fox will be miles away. He will stroll back to his den at his leisure. If they are lucky and keep on him, the fox will take them further into the woods. Mr Fox understands that the hunter is disadvantaged on rough terrain. Not every pack of hounds can negotiate the thick, clinging undergrowth they will find there. You mark my words. The fox decides when the chase has ended, not the hunter or the hounds."

Donald took his hip flask from his inside pocket and took a swig. The fire of the brandy warmed him as it made its way down his throat. He basked in the glow of admiration from his students, who had soon recognised they were in the company of a real countryman. They resumed their vigil in silence.

A little further on, closer to the sounds of the approaching hunt, Wayne Saunders had his binoculars. He checked his other saboteurs, ensuring they stood in the ideal spot to disrupt proceedings. Wayne had been at this game for a decade. Wayne got involved at Bristol University, although he hadn't needed much persuading. When the ban came into force, they thought they had won. Seven years later, they were more active than ever.

Wayne knew most hunts understood the exact woods which harboured fox-cubs. Patches of forest or brush, owned and protected by hunt supporters, were where the fox might have their litter. Many foxes stayed in the same coverts from generation to generation. Wayne and his cronies had learned this and kept records of which woods to police and which to ignore.

A lot of the saboteurs' work went on before the meeting started. One of the best methods was to pre-spray. Wayne delegated that job. He had done it when a rookie, but it meant getting up early. Wayne was no fool. As this was one of the first meets of the season, he had several saboteurs out in the fields, ready to blow their horns and call. This blowing and calling confused any new hounds and tried to wrest control of the huntsman's pack.

This morning he asked his rookies to lay a few false trails too. Then, if the dogs became interested in the incorrect path, the saboteurs could increase the blowing and shouting. Wayne had often seen this tactic work, and soon he would know whether their preparation paid dividends.

Jeremy Faversham still galloped in pursuit of the bulk of the mounted field. He was not a fit and healthy young man any longer. There had been too many executive lunches and fine dining for that. His horse was sound and keen as mustard, but the extra weight he carried meant that Jeremy was way off the pace these days.

Many of the field, who paid their subs money on the day for a good ride across the countryside, rarely saw a kill or the hounds at work. The majority cared little for the technicalities of hunting, and the Field Master kept them in the background until the hounds were well on the fox's scent. Only at the death were they encouraged to follow on at close quarters.

The overweight banker and Bonus Magnet were nearing the woods. Each rider had their particular route through familiar parts of the ground they were hunting. Jeremy had used the same approach many times. This path led to the five-barred gate and access to the scrubby bushes and trees lining the wooden fencing that marked the boundary to Downend Farm.

The Phoenix and his Olympus colleagues had discovered this route too. They had studied Jeremy Faversham for months. Jeremy would take the simple course and thread his way through the trees and bushes until he reached the far side of the woods. Then, as he lost the momentum his gallop provided, he dismounted, opened the gate, and led his horse into the next field. Finally, he would close the gate behind him and set off again.

This less dangerous shortcut often brought Jeremy closer to the action while many of his companions risked life and limb trying to jump fences and fallen trees. On other occasions, if the fox led the pack in a different direction, then Jeremy was one of the last to arrive at The Old Bell Inn, which was the place where riders and followers gathered.

Bonus Magnet gamely galloped onwards. The gate was now clearly visible. Jeremy and his horse were alone; they were isolated from the leading riders by physique and design in equal parts. Bonus Magnet weighed up the obstacle. He recognised its construction and its size. To clear this gate would not be a test for him. Landing on the other side with his rider thumping back into the saddle after the exhilarating leap was another matter.

There were two strides to the gate as Jeremy heard a sudden noise and sensed something on the other side. No, not something, someone. In those final seconds, Jeremy Faversham saw a figure spring from the bushes. His brain tried to process what it was as he catapulted forward out of the saddle.

Bonus Magnet had cleared the gate but crumpled on landing. The poor horse had spotted something that appeared to be materialising out of the ground, just where he intended his front hooves to land. The horse's brain could not compute what he saw. Jeremy realised it was a commando in camouflaged combat gear pointing a rifle straight at him.

Both Jeremy Faversham and Bonus Magnet died in the fall. The Olympus clean-up crew rose from their hiding places in the nearby bushes without a sound. First, they removed the cardboard commando, so familiar on the firing range back at Larcombe Manor, and the spring mechanism which had released him when Bonus Magnet prepared for take-off. Next, the crew eliminated any evidence of anyone else in this part of the woods apart from the stricken banker and his horse. Once the team completed their task, they disappeared as quickly and quietly as they had arrived.

The news of the infamous banker's death covered the front page of every newspaper. There were features on every television news bulletin. However, nobody openly celebrated

Jeremy Faversham's end, as his shady financial dealings had blackened his character. The public shed more tears over the death of Bonus Magnet than over the demise of the wealthy banker.

There were pictures of his four-hundred-acre estate in Gloucestershire. The weekend supplements contained details of his ski chalet in Chamonix and his *pied a terre* in South Kensington. The red tops concentrated on the complete chapter and verse of his salary scale, share options, and latest bonuses. Every part of Jeremy Faversham's life was exposed to the world.

The media circus moved out of town within days and on to the next big news item. In time, the picture became more apparent for those who watched more intently.

A few newspapers carried a report of the autopsy for Bonus Magnet. The eight-year-old thoroughbred died from head and neck trauma because of a sharp fall. No medical evidence emerged that might have caused the animal to collapse suddenly. The saddle and tack appeared to be in position and firmly secured. The coroner determined that the horse lost foot control during a fast gallop and Bonus Magnet's death was accidental.

In due course, the inquest into Jeremy Faversham's demise occurred at the Gloucester Coroner's Court. The Medical Examiner's report showed that the banker broke his right collarbone and suffered multiple skull fractures. The Master of the Hunt told the court Jeremy had been an experienced and enthusiastic rider for many years. The coroner looked around the sparsely populated room. He recognised the banker's family and friends; he spotted a few local reporters. The other people in the room might have been from the national press. He could not tell. Considering what a swine this Faversham had been, it was a surprise not to see more faces.

After all, Jeremy Faversham committed a fraud that almost led to the collapse of a City of London bank. That fraud costs investors millions of pounds — investors such as Mr Michael Kent, the Gloucester coroner. Much of the forty million pounds Faversham raised from two hundred-odd clients at his private investment firm vanished. Rumours spread that he had misspent and embezzled twelve million. Michael Kent wanted to dance on this man's grave. Kent wished he had a bigger audience to watch him do it. Individuals need to be held responsible for their actions, he thought. They needed to know the actual consequences of their behaviour. It was no good for the Government to bail out these banks; that would not give sufficient incentive for them to mend their ways. They needed banging up in jail, locked up for a bloody long time, and the key should be thrown away.

As Michael Kent listened to an old codger called Chalmers rambling on about what he saw that morning, he mused on the prospects for his old age. He had been looking forward to retirement, looking through the glossy brochures for the cruise ships. Michael Kent was a confirmed bachelor. He had a close circle of friends who bored him to tears. So he toyed with the idea of selling up and spending his time on a series of ships. What could be better? Travel broadens the mind, and he would have new companions at the dinner table every couple weeks. That seemed attractive until Jeremy Faversham got his sticky fingers on Michael's expanding pension pot, and it disappeared without a trace.

The Gloucestershire coroner dragged himself away from his fading vision of the Captain's table and caught the last few words of Donald Chambers's diatribe.

"Hunting takes place in all weathers unless there is a risk of injury to the horses, such as hard or slippery ground. The hunt will always pack up as dusk falls. That morning the conditions underfoot were perfect. When I saw Mr Faversham riding by me on the far side of the field, he was going at a full sprint."

At the back of the court, a well-dressed observer with a military bearing sat listening. Major Michael Purvis had not suffered at the hands of Jeremy Faversham. Instead, he was enjoying a day away from Larcombe Manor. Alastor noted every tick in every box of the due process that a coroner's inquest took. In time, he would deliver a detailed report to Erebus and his colleagues in the Olympus Project. It would show that after the coroner's deliberation, Jeremy Faversham's death was an accident, no more and no less.

Once again, the meticulous planning and first-class execution that typified the work of Phoenix and his fellow Olympus agents turned up trumps. Those two hundred clients might only retrieve a small proportion of their lost money. Even so, Jeremy Faversham would never again have his hand in the till.

After the banker met his maker in the copse overlooking Downend Farm, the people out on such a lovely morning carried on their business. The Master of the Hunt arrived at The Old Bell Inn with his Field Master. They were not the first to arrive.

Several dozen riders, both men and women, milled around in the car park and on the approach road to the seventeenth-century watering hole. Some walked their mounts towards horse-boxes, while others engaged in warm equestrian conversation.

The scene greeting the Master was one his predecessors had met over the centuries. This idyllic moment was soon spoiled as the riders mingled with hordes of so-called supporters and the noisy arrival of a rag-tag army of saboteurs.

The Master knew a hundred riders rode with him today. Many now made their way home and were scattered abroad in the lanes and tracks across the shire. The social side of hunting had been so much more agreeable when he rode as a boy. So many oiks followed the field in their flat caps and wax jackets these days. These oiks drove like idiots, squeezed into their people carriers, had no affiliation to country pursuits significantly, and had no respect for the countryside. They worked in towns and cities from Monday to Friday and played country folk on the weekends.

The saboteurs pestering his hunt were mild by comparison with those that followed the horses in the neighbouring county. Last year, a hooded thug attacked a fellow Master during a hunt trying to drag him from his horse. Later in the day, as the Master prepared for the drive home with his horse and hounds in the lorry, a group of masked men set upon him with baseball bats leaving him on the ground unconscious.

So far, the local saboteurs were only guilty of the more run-of-the-mill crime of trespassing. Those still involved in hunting across the country knew the police were reluctant to get involved. It was fair to say that seven years after the hunting ban came into force, the cruel sport of the hunt saboteurs was as popular as ever. The hunts don't get much help from the police when they are attacked by hunt saboteurs, whether they blow a hunting horn to get hounds to run onto main roads or launch vicious attacks on humans.

The Master dismounted and joined a group of familiar friends. A stiff drink would be welcome over the coming hour. The food on offer in this beautiful old country inn would take away the bad taste of the unsavoury elements they attracted these days left in the mouth.

"Hello there," he called to the small crowd of riders. "Has everyone returned safe and sound?"

"There's no sign of Faversham as yet."

A few sniggers and negative comments were whispered among the banker's fellow hunters. He was not as popular as he had imagined. Jeremy Faversham had lived locally on his vast country estate for many years, but he was not entirely accepted. He splashed his money around, or more correctly, other people's money. Several of the hunt supporters having a go at him had been happy to be in his company when his generosity extended to buying rounds for everyone in the bar.

"I expect that poor horse of his protested at the extra weight Faversham expected him to carry," someone shouted.

An hour later, the hunt's staff left the Old Bell Inn car park, and the grass verges by the side of the road. Meanwhile, back in the woods overlooking Downend Farm, the emergency services had arrived, summoned by a woman walking her dogs.

Wayne Saunders had seen Jeremy Faversham riding by. Wayne was supposed to concentrate on the leading pack of riders well in front of the banker. However, Faversham's face had been in the media so much that Wayne immediately recognised him.

"Arrogant bastard," he thought as the banker galloped towards the woods.

With his mind back on the hunt, he reflected on how things had gone so far that morning. The rest of his fellow saboteurs did everything he asked of them. There was no sign of the local press providing much of a presence, so they shelved a banner demo on this occasion. His instructions had been to mingle and chat with the supporters, acting the part of followers, to find out which way the hunt was heading. Several of them were to spray their hand with Intimate and pat the hounds if they could get close enough to rub it well into their coats.

As the hunt progressed, Wayne kept an eye out for the police. He spotted a couple of cars, but they were well away from the action. They waited for the saboteurs to regroup by their vans and vehicles to move out after the hunt finished. Wayne was happy about that. It meant they would not be blocked in by hunt supporters trying to score a cheap point after having the saboteurs sniping at them throughout their so-called sport.

Wayne had headed towards Downend Farm on foot after the few riders not now cooling off after their workout. As usual, he kept his eyes peeled. Wayne did not want to get too close to the riders; they knew him too well. He also steered clear of confrontation with the followers, the beaters, and the rest, just in case a few turned nasty. Wayne wondered where Jeremy Faversham could be as his eyes darted from side to side for danger. He looked over his shoulder towards the copse. Wayne could see no sign of any horse and rider. Surely, Faversham must be through the spinney by now, he thought, but looking ahead towards Downend Farm, he could not pick out the portly banker among the handful of riders he saw.

Wayne Saunders had met up with his colleagues, and they carried on making themselves unpopular with the hunting fraternity. They sounded their horns, shouted, and protested about the continued existence of the hunt, even in its much-altered state since the ban. The whereabouts of Jeremy Faversham soon became the last thing on his mind.

The Olympus Project

Wayne remembered one odd thing that morning when the news of the banker's death reached him via a local radio broadcast. He spotted a few walkers as he glanced over his shoulder towards the woods. On reflection, it was a strange place to view the hunt. Wayne was unsure whether they had been regular supporters or the casual brigade from town. They wore dark clothing, hooded jackets, and balaclavas. They cast their eyes down or to the side when he looked towards them, so Wayne did not see their faces. The man at the back carried something in a canvas cover, around two metres long. In that few seconds, he surveyed the scene behind him. The image of a surfboard had leapt into Wayne's mind. He discounted that straight away as being just plain daft.

When he read the inquest verdict in the local press later, Wayne remembered that group of strangers and the item one of them had been carrying. He could not fathom what it meant. There were other fox hunts to follow and saboteurs to recruit. Wayne Saunders forgot all about Jeremy Faversham, the woods near Downend Farm, and the surfboard.

Gold, Silver and Bombs: Chapter Two

Colin and Rusty had met the clean-up crew in a lane leading to the Old Bell Inn. But unfortunately, they could not partake of the sumptuous spread the Master and his friends would soon be tucking into after their morning exercise.

Colin knew that before the food and drink had time to settle in their digestive systems, they would hear the news about Jeremy Faversham. He knew their mission had been one hundred per cent successful. The whispers and the rumours would creep around the walls and low ceilings of the old coaching inn, bouncing off the brasses and the pictures of hunting scenes.

Long before the horses, dogs, and 4x4s returned to their various paddocks, kennels, and garages, their owners would have learned of the death of the crooked financier — a man who robbed around two hundred unsuspecting, innocent investors of their hard-earned cash. Colin Bailey would lose no sleep over his passing; he did not imagine many others would either.

The Olympus agents climbed into plain vans with tinted windows that they had parked on the quiet stretch of countryside. They moved off without fanfare and merged with the lunchtime traffic. The trip back to Larcombe was uneventful, and just over an hour later, they drove between the stone pillars and negotiated the winding driveway that led to the Olympus headquarters.

"Home Sweet Home," muttered Rusty.

"Another day, another dollar," chipped in one of the clean-up crew from the back of the leading van.

"Another day, another dead villain," said Colin quietly.

"Amen to that," said Rusty.

The agents left the vans with the transport section and walked across to the old stable block, where the staff had their quarters. After a brief conversation and removing their communication devices, several went to the ice-house. They returned the kit to the store and handed the camouflaged commando to the lads in the indoor firing range. The subject of the conversation had been food. Thinking of the Old Bell Inn and its excellent food had made everyone hungry.

Colin and Rusty were out of luck. The rest of the crew headed for the canteen in the terraced cottages where the estate workers lived many years ago; however, Colin and Rusty made for the orangery. Colin phoned Erebus and told him they were back from the Cotswolds mission and ready for their debrief. The elderly gentleman awaited them. He saw the vans coming up the drive and had already walked over from the manor house to their usual meeting place.

The three men met in the orangery. Erebus had anticipated his two agents' needs. A large pot of coffee and three cups stood on a tray between them, and another plate was piled high with bacon rolls.

"Dig in, chaps," said Erebus enthusiastically. "I've eaten my lunch, but after a fresh morning's exercise in the country, I expect you both need something appetising."

Rusty and Colin tried to express their gratitude without losing any of the roll, butter, and bacon they were devouring.

"While you two are catching your breath, I'll just recap today's events, and you nod in the right places."

Erebus went through the agreed itinerary for that morning's direct action. Colin and Rusty nodded when he looked over the top of his glasses to confirm the successful completion of a specific objective. Eventually, Colin could reassure his leader that the morning had gone without a hitch, thanks to their fieldwork beforehand.

Erebus sat drinking his cup of coffee, deep in thought. Colin and Rusty sensed the meeting was not over yet; Erebus wanted to share something with them. They had learned to read him well over the time they worked for the Olympus Project. Erebus was deciding how much he should reveal.

After a few minutes, which the two agents filled by further demolishing the food on their plate and washing it down with a second cup of coffee, Erebus began to speak.

"It is common knowledge among our country's intelligence chiefs that it will be impossible to prevent a well-planned terrorist attack on mainland Britain. As we learned earlier this year, the Olympic Games in London is the most likely target for suicide bombers. Our section here at Larcombe Manor supports this view without reservation. A secret government report on possible threats from Al-Qaeda and other Islamic terrorist organisations indicates a conservative estimate of the deployment of two hundred terrorists. The threat is likely to be much greater. The influence of homegrown terrorists is of even greater concern. Despite the deaths last year of Bin Laden and Al Awlaki, their organisation is still strong. The terrorists are developing new measures for the new countermeasures that MI5 and MI6 have devised. They are more security-aware. They will avoid wearing certain types of clothing and overtly praying before carrying out a suicide attack because they know the police will watch for those types of signs. The London Games will be subject to the biggest security operation in our nation's history. The highly patrolled sporting venues and stadia are unlikely targets. Public transport will be an option, as will the more isolated venues. We must be watchful and not underestimate the internal threat. We know recruitment and radicalisation are rife within our prison system. The internal threat is growing more dangerous. Extremists are conducting non-lethal training without ever leaving the country. We can no longer expect to track potential terrorists by monitoring passenger manifests between this country and Pakistan. Should these people evolve into suicide bombers, our umbrella of intelligence resources would struggle to find them on any radar screen."

Erebus had sat forward in his chair as he addressed the two agents. He now sat back and looked closely at them.

"This could prove to be the toughest nut we've had to crack so far, gentlemen."

Colin sighed.

"What are you thinking, Phoenix?" Erebus asked.

"I dislike nuts, Sir."

Rusty nearly choked on the last bacon roll. Erebus placed his cup back on the tray and rose from his chair.

"Well done this morning, gentlemen. We will have to wait until the inevitable 'accidental death' verdict from the Gloucestershire coroner. Then, if no complications arise, we can draw a line under the Jeremy Faversham case. So rest up this afternoon, chaps; I'll see you both later at the meeting."

"A meeting, sir?" said Colin.

"Ah, you haven't seen the message I sent you this morning. You can catch up with things after you return to your quarters. Time is ticking ever onwards. August will be upon us before we know it, and we must devise our plans post-haste. This evening will see the start of that process."

Erebus left them in the orangery. As Colin and Rusty finished the last pot of coffee, they chatted over the likely themes of any plans that Olympus might conjure up to combat the terrorist threat. Erebus had been right. It was a difficult nut to crack. London was going to be teeming with people of all nationalities. Identifying potential dangers could be extremely difficult. The Olympus Project agents were familiar with the task. Security around the Olympics would involve many other agencies and possibly even the armed forces. It could become a case of too many cooks.

"We'll be bumping into one another at every turn," said Rusty. "This will be a nightmare, mate."

A steward from the manor house came into the orangery to remove the tray and the crockery. Colin and Rusty took that as a signal to return to their quarters. Erebus wanted them rested for the meeting this evening.

Colin checked his emails. Sure enough, Erebus's invite to the meeting was there. So were various updates on intelligence surrounding cases Colin would be involved in over the weeks before the Games. First, a mother had reported her daughter missing in Oxford, but the authorities were slow in responding. There was a note about the potential transfer of prisoners from one high-security prison to another. Colin was interested in that one in particular.

Finally, who was likely to be on the passenger list? He filed both items away and then opened a series of messages from Athena.

"Are you free?"

"Do you want company?"

"Why aren't you answering? Is there something wrong?"

Colin delayed replying to these until after he had been to the pool. A few dozen lengths of exercise were what he needed. Colin had spent too much time standing around on the damp ground in the countryside for his liking. When he got back, he was dog-tired and lay on his bunk, intending to take a nap. Colin forgot Athena and her messages. He slept until Rusty knocked and stuck his head around his door.

"Come on, mate. We need to be somewhere."

When they entered the drawing-room for the meeting, Erebus was deep in conversation with Henry Case. Finally, Erebus nodded to acknowledge the agents' arrival.

The others filed into the room soon afterwards. Minos and Thanatos walked in together as usual; Athena followed them, and Alastor came behind her. Several of the more senior ex-SAS operatives attended too.

Erebus looked around the room to check everyone was ready. Then, satisfied that they were, he asked Henry Case to go through the past few weeks' events.

"As we agreed at our last summit meeting, the radicalised students involved in the Euston Station caper were dropped off at the service station near Spaghetti Junction. We have monitored their movements since that time, and no direct action is currently necessary."

"Did we have any luck in converting them," asked Athena, "and bringing them around to a less radical way of thinking?"

"We deemed it in the best interests of Olympus to

nurture the other contact we identified in the local Muslim community. He has had to work with caution. However, his information will prove to be most valuable to us. As for Habeeb Rehman, he was of no further use after he told us everything. He is now at rest, alongside the body of his colleague, Zunairah Jaffri, in the pet cemetery. We have identified the contacts Rehman interacted with in the ring and are keeping a close eye on their movements. We have used the list of names, addresses, landlines, and mobile numbers that Rehman provided in the end. The majority are of only a minor concern. We removed those deemed to be a real threat to national security."

"Did this create any response from the cell?" asked Minos.

Henry Case allowed himself a brief smile.

"We used subtle methods to remove these people, Minos. Have no fear. It is normal for people to return home to Pakistan to deal with family affairs, such as bereavement or a wedding. Accidents happen over there, too, you know. Older people succumb to sudden heart attacks. We placed notices in the local press in the Midlands to explain why these links in the chain had not returned and were no longer active. So far, the remaining cell members and any recruits are happy in their ignorance. As you will recall, the most important information Rehman gave us was regarding the trial run at Oxford Circus. Al Qaeda's plan is for the main strike to occur during the London Games. They planned coordinated attacks on the Olympic Village, the taking of high-profile hostages from both Britain and the USA. More terrifyingly, they plan to target several medal ceremonies on the penultimate day of the Games. The fallout from these attacks would be catastrophic, as you can imagine. Any prospect of going ahead with the final day's action, the pageant of the Closing Ceremony, and joie de vivre associated with such an event are lost forever."

The room fell silent as the Olympus agents and their masters absorbed these images. Then, finally, everyone realised the importance of Henry Case's comments. The next few days and weeks spent preparing to counter such a threat would take every ounce of their intelligence, resourcefulness, and courage.

Henry 'Head' Case had completed his initial report. Erebus stood up and took his time rearranging the folders and other items on the table in front of him before he finally addressed his audience.

"Thank you, Henry. I am sure we can agree we have a significant problem. Before I put forward my suggestions, does anyone wish to comment on what we've heard so far?"

Athena was the first to speak.

"Habeeb Rehman and Zunairah Jaffri have been eliminated. We have removed the most dangerous personnel from the cell operating in the Midlands and closely monitor everyone else involved. What possible threat can this group represent? They can't mount a credible attack on the Games with the scrutiny they are receiving. We may not be alone in watching these people; our lacklustre national security services might have stumbled across them by now. So why are we not concentrating our attention on potential terrorists arriving in the country from Pakistan, Afghanistan, and similar locations?"

"If we have a mole inside the cell," said Colin, "we should analyse the information Henry has gathered before we dismiss their threat. As for arrivals, good luck with that. Terrorists come in all shapes and sizes. The world will descend on Heathrow this summer to participate in or watch the Games. So let's concentrate on plans that counter any hopes of kidnapping and bombing within the environs of the Olympic venues that our intelligence section earmarks as confirmed targets. Whether Leicester, Lagos, or Lahore, where these beggars come from, does not matter a jot. Stopping them is what matters."

Athena was miffed. As one of the five leaders of the Olympus Project, she was not used to an agent questioning her views. Moreover, her relationship with Erebus over the years was stable. Her mentor had told her that when he felt it was time for him to stand aside, Athena was his natural successor.

Erebus paced around the room for a moment or two; then, he returned to stand by the head of the table. He looked at the assembled gathering of his most trusted and valued people.

"We have to make a decision. We have divided opinions on how we should best go ahead. I suggest we take a vote. But first, considering how important the matter is, I want you to go away and think carefully. We will reconvene at nine o'clock tomorrow morning. We will vote then, and, whatever the outcome, the Olympus organisation must receive your total support."

The meeting ended. The silence as the agents and their leaders left the room was deafening. Colin and Rusty made their way to the stable block. Colin saw Athena turn and look in his direction as she strode out of the room with Erebus. What was Athena thinking? Was she angry at his blatant opposition to her proposal? Or was she hurt because he had ignored her since his trip to the Cotswolds?

Colin and Rusty chatted amicably on the walk back to their quarters. Rusty had been thinking along the same lines as

Colin as far as their next moves were concerned. He favoured being proactive wherever possible; he would probably have taken direct pre-emptive action by now.

"How many terrorist organisations do we have operating in the UK, Phoenix?"

"Fifty of all creeds and colours, maybe a few more."

"Yes, but how many are interested in or have the capacity to attack the Olympic Games?"

"Just a couple, I reckon. The intelligence gatherers in the command centre will have a better handle on it."

Rusty slowed his walk and glanced over his shoulder to ensure they were alone.

"Exactly my point. There are just a couple of outfits and a dozen, perhaps twenty, faces to identify and take out of the game. Twenty bodies, unlike something far, far worse if an IED makes it into the Olympic Stadium when it's packed with athletes, officials, and spectators. Munich was bad. Atlanta was bad. The last thing we need is London's legacy being a major tragedy. If we did things my way, there might well be a bonus. Once word got out that we had removed several of the main players from the picture, it would deter any fringe extremists who might have been contemplating a solo effort."

"We must see which way the vote goes in the morning. Erebus was right when he said this was a tough one to tackle. Neither choice guarantees success. A single bomber working alone would be hard to stop. There will be too many people and venues, and the Games security will never cover everything."

The two men stopped outside the door to Colin's room.

"It sounds daft," Rusty grumbled, "but we'd better pray that any threat comes from an organisation with a load of people on the ground, working together. At least we will have a chance of picking up their communications or spot their activity en route to a venue."

Rusty strolled off towards his quarters with things on his mind.

Colin entered his room and flopped onto the bed. He intended to spend the rest of the evening relaxing. Colin thought through both his preferred scenario and that of Athena. Although both plans had merit, he had to admit that he felt hers potentially too conservative. If the vote went against him tomorrow, he would throw his weight one hundred per cent behind Athena's suggestion and then cross his fingers that the proverbial did not hit the fan.

The knock on the door was quiet but insistent. Colin was surprised to ascribe so much meaning to a few simple taps of the knuckle on wood. Despite being dog-tired after the busy day in the country, he knew there would be no rest until he found out who was calling at this late hour. He dragged himself off his bed and opened the door; it was Athena.

"I'm sorry, but I had to see you," she said, gently pushing Colin back into the room. She closed the door and locked it. Colin flopped back on the bed, his hopes of a good night's sleep forgotten for now. It must be important if Athena needed to speak to him urgently. He patted the foot of the bed and asked her to make herself comfortable.

Athena perched on the end of the bed. Her hair was loose and falling across her face. Colin was unsure what she came to say, but she seemed to struggle to find the words. She moved closer, tucking her long legs up under herself. Her right arm rested on his knee, casually enough, but it was a closeness that Colin found disturbing. It was unexpected but far from unpleasant, and, despite his tiredness, he felt deep in his body that something stirred.

Cancel that previous notion, he thought. If she stays much longer, a good night's sleep could be forgotten, full stop, let alone for the time being.

While Colin revised his overnight schedule, Athena moved closer still. She leaned her face in, kissed his forehead and eyelids, and then eagerly found his mouth. Colin fought the temptation at first, but then, as he realised resistance was futile, he responded, kissing Athena enthusiastically in return.

Colin realised he had been way off the mark, thinking Athena was mad at him for suggesting a different approach to the Olympic security problem. But, if she was, this was a strange way to show it. I should ignore her text messages more often, he thought, as Athena grew more amorous.

His hands slid across her back as she was now virtually on top of him. He broke the kiss temporarily, despite her groan of protest. Colin pulled her blouse and dragged it over that mane of hair, which fell over her bare shoulders and hid her face from his searching eyes.

Seconds later, they kissed again, and his hands moved to her breasts. She sighed, and her fingers trailed across his chest. "Wait," cried Athena and rose from the bed. She removed her bra. Colin clawed at her jeans, and they somehow removed the rest of their clothes. They collapsed onto the bed, and time stood still. Athena kissed his chest, his neck, and his mouth. Gently, she caressed his hips, thighs, and buttocks; she neglected the obvious. His erection was massive.

"How on earth could she have missed it?" thought Colin.

He kneaded her breasts and lowered his head to suck on them. Athena fell back, and Colin kissed her stomach and thighs. In turn, he pleasured her with his mouth and fingers, and she responded by taking the length of his shaft in her hand and stroking it. Colin knew he had to stop her before he lost control, and he parted her thighs and entered her. Athena cried out. It had been so long since she had been with her late partner, and Colin was much bigger.

Colin felt more confident now and moved inside her again, slowly at first. Athena moaned and arched her back as he made love to her gently, increasing the dance rhythm until both of them climaxed, leaving their bodies vibrating with intense pleasure. Colin lowered his face to her lips once more.

"I've wanted to do this since the first day I saw you at Larcombe Manor."

Athena kissed him and moved her hips. She encouraged him to stay where they were, locked together as one.

"Perhaps you should finish what you started then?" she whispered.

Colin's first thoughts of what Athena's late-night arrival meant were correct. It was over two hours before they finally fell asleep in each other's arms. Nevertheless, Athena was content; she finally set free the ghost of her lover from seven years earlier. She would never forget Simon, cherishing his memory and their time together. Now with Phoenix, she hoped she could look forward to a future filled with promise, a promise of loving and being loved.

Before he dropped off to sleep, Colin wondered what the last few hours would count for in the morning. He had always wanted to make love to Athena. She intrigued him from that first lunchtime here at Larcombe Manor. He realised she was a strong, forceful, and independent woman. That she was gorgeous was plain to see; what concerned him most was her breeding and intellect. Colin was unquestionably a clever man whose education had been cut short by his mother. Although he was always confident he could have made it to a redbrick university and made a fair fist of studying a degree course, Athena seemed way out of his league.

"Blokes like me don't pull a bird that attractive." he thought as they sized one another up at the dining table under the watchful eye of Erebus.

The older man had marked his card, too, in the months since his arrival at Larcombe. Erebus was aware of the potential for his successor at the helm of the Olympus Project and one of his most accomplished agents to become involved.

Colin was not sure whether Erebus approved of such a liaison or not. He told him to be cautious because Athena was still vulnerable. She lost her partner in the London bombings in 2005. Nevertheless, Athena had shown him affection before and after the Oxford Circus affair. Indeed she spent an innocent night in his room on one occasion. Tonight had been inevitable, but whether their relationship would continue to develop or whether Erebus and the organisation's demands would quash it was unclear.

Colin had other problems. There was Therese for a start. What was he supposed to do about her? Why was life so bloody complicated?

For most men with this dilemma, the answer would be simple enough; to be fair, most men would not get themselves into this situation. However, Colin Bailey had always been a different kettle of fish. His parents had neither wanted nor loved him. Karen Smith had been a good-time girl who trapped him into marriage, falling pregnant after one night of passion. Colin had not known *how* to love her.

Colin discovered that he could truly love their daughter, Sharon, and he did so without reservation, but a father and daughter's love is unique and very different. Sue Owens taught him about sexual desire, and their affair had been passionate to the extreme. Over their decade as lovers and, eventually, as man and wife, that passion had never diminished. Over time, it had matured into a loving relationship that both partners contributed to and savoured in equal measure.

Colin loved Sue Owens; his grief at losing her to cancer turned his heart to stone. It was this lack of feeling that had allowed him to hunt the targets he identified. Eight of the names he had added to his list while in The Gambia. More names had been on that list, but the close attention of DCI Phil Hounsell diverted him from his mission.

He should never have kidnapped the police officer's wife; that had been a mistake. It was a mistake that almost cost him his life, let alone his freedom.

As for Therese, Slater had bumped into her as part of his preparation for the Manchester job. There could have been anyone working behind the bar that afternoon. Therese was an attractive woman with a fantastic body. Colin had an itch that needed to be scratched. He was not proud of himself. Sex with Therese had been exciting and physical. She left him wanting more.

Events in Bath had led to his plans unravelling in an instant. He had been ambivalent; the coin was in the air. He could meet up with Therese and disappear into mainland Europe for a few months, or he could go in another direction, perhaps to Ireland and rest alone until the coast cleared for him to return. Phil Hounsell took the decision out of his hands. Therese had travelled to Holland alone.

At Larcombe Manor, Colin had met Athena, and that itch resurfaced. Was that all it was? Was he capable of feeling something deep and meaningful towards her? The

Scottish trip to eliminate Donald MacDonald changed everything. Who could have predicted that Therese would be on a station platform slap bang in front of his carriage window?

She had recognised Colin, even after his minor facial surgeries in West Africa and at Larcombe. The few days in Blackpool satisfied that blessed itch for Colin, but he wondered just where Therese thought it might lead. That train trip back to Bath after he left her soon passed. As the scenery flashed by, Colin saw little of it as he weighed up whether it was time to dispose of the sexy barmaid.

Not because she had become a threat, as she had not done so yet; Colin had not tired of her. It was Athena. He had to admit that Athena was in his head every hour he spent in Blackpool. She was a constant presence in his thoughts these days. As his eyelids grew heavier and heavier, Colin wondered why relationships were so bloody complicated. He dropped off to sleep without finding the answer.

Gold, Silver and Bombs: Chapter Three

Mornings at Larcombe Manor followed a regular pattern. Agents were either leaving for a mission at the crack of dawn or returning from a job well done. Erebus and his closest cohorts breakfasted early and arrived promptly for their morning meeting at nine o'clock. Permanent staff in the stable block had been out of bed, ready for work in the ice-house by eight.

When Colin awoke, Athena had left.

He looked at his watch — a quarter past eight- and needed to move fast.

As he headed for the shower, he spotted a post-it note stuck to the screen of his computer. It contained a heart, a kiss, and 'A.' Colin sighed. The conversation he knew they needed to have would not happen immediately, but it had to occur sooner rather than later.

Almost as soon as he re-emerged, showered, shaved, and was ready to face the day, his phone rang.

It was Erebus.

"Good morning, Phoenix. I trust you slept well?"

Colin wondered if the boss knew about last night. Did he spot Athena creeping back to the main house? Erebus was a crafty old bugger; he did not miss a trick.

"Like a log, sir. A clear conscience helps," said Colin, with his fingers crossed.

"Touché, Phoenix. I need to see you after the morning meeting. We have this damned vote to get out of the way first, plus other items on today's agenda. It should be over in an hour, though. So let's say we'll meet up in the orangery at half-past ten, alright old chap?"

"That's fine with me, sir," replied Colin.

Erebus ended the call.

Colin finished dressing and walked across the manicured lawns towards the manor house. You could not help but be impressed by the magnificence of the old building, especially on a bright morning such as this. The Georgian edifice towered over him as he climbed the slope towards the patio. The secrets of the outbuildings had to stay hidden away from prying eyes, but the manor house deserved to be open to the public. What a shame they could never wander unaccompanied in the grounds or go on tours to see the exquisite furniture and paintings graced the interior.

"A penny for your thoughts, mate," called Rusty, running to catch him.

"I was thinking how beautiful this place is," said Colin.

"Whoa. Something's perked you up, and no mistake."

"Yeah, well," said Colin, a little flustered.

Rusty gave him a light tap on the shoulder.

"Only kidding, Phoenix. Whatever has made you believe this world's a beautiful place, long may it last. I reckon things will get worse before they get better, but I was always a miserable bleeder."

The two agents covered the last few yards into the

meeting room in companionable silence. Colin respected Rusty; he was a tremendous ally. You would not want to be on the wrong side of him. That was a certainty.

Rusty respected Phoenix too. When Phoenix arrived at Larcombe Manor, he had been wary of what Erebus saw in him. Rusty had questioned why Erebus had brought him into the fold. Everyone else who worked for Olympus was ex-service personnel. Most field agents were ex-SAS with a proven track record. Even Giles and the intelligence people wore a uniform for part of their careers.

Phoenix had a dark and troubled past. Rusty knew little or nothing of much of it. Erebus and the others at the top table kept secret what exactly he did before he arrived. Rusty knew he was a killer.

As the months passed, he had grown to appreciate just how good Phoenix was at his job. Phoenix did not take pleasure in killing or glorifying what he did. He believed when the system failed the victims, it was only proper that an agency such as Olympus should exact the punishment.

He's a perfect fit for the organisation, thought Rusty. Erebus had found the final piece of the jigsaw. The Olympus Project may have considerable adversaries ahead to face, but they were well equipped to conquer them with Phoenix on board.

The two men entered the room. Stewards moved back and forth with cups of tea or coffee. A folder for each attendee waited for them on the table in front of their chairs. On the side table, Colin saw a black tin box.

Colin wondered who was looking after the 'swingometer' this morning. It was akin to election night on TV. He and Rusty bid good morning to their colleagues. The clock on the wall showed one minute to nine.

Erebus and the rest of his inner sanctum swept through

The Olympus Project

the furthest door, and the morning's business could get underway.

"Good morning. I hope you have given the matters we discussed yesterday much thought. When you open your folders, you will find a ballot sheet. Please indicate which of the two options you wish Olympus to pursue. Fold your sheet in two and place it in the box provided. Minos will not vote. He will be responsible for the count."

A rustle of papers and a scramble of feet followed as the people around the table followed Erebus's instructions. Everyone voted in little more than a minute, and Sir Julian Langford QC unlocked the black box and tipped its contents onto the table.

Colin quickly checked the table to see how many Olympus people there were at the meeting today. He counted twenty. Bloody typical. No sign of 'Head' Case and the rest of the intelligence section people.

Minos handed Erebus the result; he read it out.

"Votes cast in favour of Option A; supported by Athena, ten. As proposed by Phoenix, the number of votes cast for Option B is also ten."

Colin had feared that this might happen. He did not know whether Henry or the others would have gone with his idea or not. But Erebus was now in a spot. He held the casting vote; surely, he would go with his future successor Athena?

Erebus sat at the head of the table, his thin, elegant hands steepled in front of his lips. His elbows rested on the arms of his chair. Eventually, he spoke.

"After consideration, I have determined that I shall vote for Option B."

Colin was stunned. There were several gasps around the table as people realised Erebus had gone against the wishes of his second in command. He had done so to follow a course of action proposed by the newcomer.

"Let us move on to the next item on our agenda," said Erebus.

Colin looked across to Athena at the right-hand side of Erebus. She gave a brief smile and a slight shrug of her shoulders. The woman was a class act, Colin mused. It must hurt, but she will never show it.

They dealt with the remaining agenda items in their usual efficient manner. There was updated terrorist cell activity and the latest report from the mole.

Further details have emerged about the proposed movement of high-security prisoners. A report covering the preparations for London 2012 by the authorities was in the folder for future reading and analysis.

Colin tried hard to concentrate, but he was fighting a losing battle. Erebus wrapped everything up before a quarter to ten. Everyone then left the room except Athena and the Three Stooges. They stayed behind with Erebus.

Colin had hoped to talk to Athena to clear the air, but not about what happened last night. That could wait a while longer. He was more concerned with the vote result, with Erebus siding with him instead of maintaining a united front.

Colin and Rusty walked back to the stable block together.

"Never saw that coming, Phoenix," Rusty said. "I mean, your idea was superior, but when the votes were level at ten apiece, I thought the old man would go for Athena, for sure."

"So did I," replied Colin.

"What are you going to do now, mate? I'm going for a swim."

"I'm going to take a rain check, Rusty. Erebus has summoned me. He wants another get-together in the orangery in thirty minutes."

"You are fast becoming his blue-eyed boy, Phoenix. Athena will be miffed."

Colin let Rusty have that one. He didn't want a long conversation about his relationship with Erebus and Athena. That was dangerous ground. Rusty was not daft. It would only take one ill-advised comment, and he could add two and two to make a 'relationship'.

"See you later," said Rusty and strolled to his quarters.

Meanwhile, Erebus and his colleagues finished discussing Option B's itinerary in the manor house.

"I have another meeting now. I know I can rely on your support for our chosen strategy. So I suggest we meet this evening, after dinner, to finalise our detailed plans."

Alastor, Athena, and Thanatos stood up and left the room.

Minos lingered behind on the pretext of tidying up the ballot box and sheets until he and Erebus were alone.

"Why did you give your casting vote in favour of Phoenix? Your ballot sheet in the box carried a vote for Athena. The way you fold a piece of paper is so distinctive. It could not have belonged to anyone else."

Erebus smiled.

"Caught out by one of my trusted colleagues," he said. "You are right. Based on people's comments and body language yesterday, I weighed up the likely number of votes for each option. I felt sure that Phoenix would have won the day convincingly if Henry Case and the others had been here. I hoped I could allow her to save face by voting for Athena, losing by a narrow margin. In the end, I had to use my casting vote, and given that scenario, I hoped she could reconcile her loss as a 'toss of the coin'. I needed her to believe it could have gone either way. I am a sentimental old fool, Minos. She will still succeed me as leader of Olympus in time. But it will do her no harm if, now and then, she doesn't get her way. She will be a better leader if she learns from the experience."

Minos nodded sagely. He wanted Erebus to think he understood completely, but in all honesty, it baffled him. Exciting times lay ahead.

At half-past ten, Colin left the stable block to meet his boss. Colin found Erebus in the orangery awaiting his arrival. He sat in a chair holding a sheaf of papers. He gave a deep sigh as Colin approached.

"Take a pew, dear boy," he said without looking up from the material he had been studying.

"Am I needed for something, Erebus?"

"I have a job for you, Phoenix, that requires your particular talents. Despite other pressing matters that need our attention, this nest of vipers is too much of a menace for us to ignore any longer."

"May I?" asked Colin, leaning forward and offering to take the papers from his boss.

"Certainly, Phoenix," sighed the old man. "Just holding these sheets of paper makes me feel unclean. I despair of the depths to which a few depraved members of our so-called society can descend."

"I'll study this and plan our response as soon as I finish," said Colin.

Erebus stood; he rested a bony, liver-spotted hand on Colin's shoulder.

"Plan, by all means, dear boy; it's what you do best. But make sure the bastards suffer, please."

Colin nodded, "Understood, sir."

When he returned to his quarters, he started reading. Over two years ago, Tanya Norris ran away from her family home in Oxford. Tanya was fifteen. She stayed with a school friend and then drifted from town to town, seeking temporary work. Instead, she ended up homeless on the streets in Swindon.

Tanya was vulnerable. A sadistic gang who manipulated and controlled a crop of underage girls in the sprawling Wiltshire town had groomed her and sold her for sex in a few weeks.

The Olympus Project investigation team uncovered a staggering amount of background detail. It impressed Colin. It did not make for pleasant reading, but he couldn't deny its thoroughness. Tanya's mother had reported her missing, but the police had few resources available to find a delinquent teenager. They were too busy filling in forms and persecuting motorists to hit their traffic offence quotas.

There were four men involved in the grooming and abuse. They were two sets of brothers who had preyed on pre-teen and underage teenage girls for the past five years at least. Six weeks ago, Tanya Norris became pregnant. The gang attempted to make her miscarry. Her condition went into a rapid decline. One gang member drove her to a local hospital, not out of concern for her safety but to dump her on someone else's doorstep. They had no further use for her, so she got shoved through the passenger door onto the pavement outside without slowing down. Tanya was very sick; without quick action, she may have died.

Fortunately, the staff spotted Tanya and hurried her into the emergency room, where they treated her immediate injuries. The doctor looking after her noticed other scars and bruising, plus the usual demeanour and pallor associated with a habitual drug user. She interpreted this as indicative of her young patient suffering abuse over a long period, whether self-administered or by a third party. She became concerned for Tanya's welfare, but Tanya shut down. Months of abuse, the frequent misuse of alcohol and drugs and the Svengali-like control the gang members exerted over her left her afraid of her own shadow. She trusted no one.

As Tanya recovered in the hospital, the doctor spent as long as she could, often in her own time, building up the young girl's trust. There was no mention of police or social services. The doctor did not interrogate her about her family or friends. She gently probed, trying to get the youngster to open up to her more on each visit. In time, the dam broke. Tanya cried, and the entire sad story tumbled out between the sobs and the tears.

Once the full horror of Tanya's treatment at the hands of the gang became apparent, the young doctor made a phone call. That first call was to a national newspaper. Giles and his team at Larcombe intercepted that call and opened a case file. A male and female field agent drove to Swindon and took steps to relieve the young doctor of any further responsibility in Tanya's case.

Tanya Norris had gone when the doctor reported for her next shift. She discovered that Tanya's parents so-called had arrived from Newbury. The friendly reporter meeting the young doctor for a scoop on what happened to these vulnerable girls was working on another political scandal. He had been notified by a concerned senior colleague at the hospital that his informant was a stressed-out young NHS doctor. She was a doctor who worked incredibly long hours and was prone to flights of fancy.

Tanya was in a safe house in Devizes where a nurse looked after her, ensuring her physical wounds healed.

Someone else would need to be with Tanya over the coming months to help her back to something approaching normality because her mental state would take far longer to heal. Over the next couple of days, the male and female agents who posed as her parents interviewed her and the sheets of paper that Phoenix now read contained Tanya's tale.

Colin read what was becoming a familiar pattern across the country. The four men came from Muslim backgrounds, in their early to mid-thirties. Their victims were almost exclusively white. Over the past five years, people with suspicions about what was happening contacted the police and social services. Unfortunately, no one had followed up on those suspicions. Colin shook his head.

"I can hear the conversation. 'We will be racists if we accuse them of something'. Either that or because of their backgrounds, they wouldn't have believed the girls might be telling the truth. The authorities discounted any rumours or complaints as unreliable."

He continued reading.

These girls were between twelve and fifteen years of age. Most of them came from broken homes; some had run away from home, like Tanya Norris. Others were already in the care system and were frequent absconders. In a matter of weeks after meeting the men, they received presents, and then alcohol was followed by coke and heroin.

They were ferried to the town in expensive cars and lulled into believing the men cared for them. It was easy to see why they fell for these tactics. They never had much love at home. For a few, it was the first time in their life that anyone had shown them affection.

In time, the drugs made Tanya and the others dependent on the gang, and it soon became impossible for them to leave. That was when Tanya's nightmare began. She described her ordeal to the Olympus agents. Page after page detailed where, when and how the rapes and torture occurred. If she showed any sign of resistance, her punishment was severe.

Colin had only read a few pages, and he understood why Erebus reacted as he did. He felt the same disgust — the same wish to punish these men without mercy.

After the four men had used and abused her for days, they set her to work for them. Tanya travelled in the same expensive cars she enjoyed in those first innocent days. Now she went to various addresses around the town where dozens of men paid hundreds of pounds to her captors to have sex with her.

Inevitably, Tanya became pregnant. Her treatment at the hands of the brothers was horrendous. The gang blamed her for being stupid and not taking precautions. The beatings and verbal abuse continued until the bodged attempt at a miscarriage and that final car ride to the hospital. After that, they continued to exploit the remaining girls under their control without a single thought for Tanya.

Colin closed the file. He took it back to his quarters and locked it in a drawer. He took a shower because he felt unclean. Colin then dressed in casual clothes and visited the gym. He knew he needed to keep active. Colin always found that punishing his body allowed him to forget his pathetic minor problems. He used the time he lifted weights and rained blows on the punchbag to plan his response to what he had read. It was time for the four brothers to answer for their crimes.

Grab your copy...
vinci-books.com/gold-silver-and-bombs

About the Author

Ted Tayler is the international best-selling indie author of the Freeman Files and Phoenix series. Ted lives in the English West country, where his stories are based. He was born in 1945 and has been married to Lynne since 1971. They have three children and four grandchildren.

His thought-provoking mysteries appeal to readers of Sally Rigby, Joy Ellis, Pauline Rowson, and Faith Martin. His action-packed thrillers are a must for fans of Mark Dawson and J C Ryan.

Gus Freeman's cold case investigations are carried out with reasoned deduction rather than bursts of frantic action. In each of the 24 books, unsolved murders are accompanied by romance, humour, and country life. The core message in the 12 Phoenix novels is that criminals should pay for their crimes. Unfortunately, the current system fails to deliver the correct punishment, so Phoenix helps redress the balance.

Acknowledgments

The love and support of my family; without them, this would have been impossible.